T0265826

THE PIEROGI PERIL

THE PIEROGI PERIL

Geri Krotow

**SEVERN
HOUSE**

First world edition published in Great Britain and the USA in 2024
by Severn House, an imprint of Canongate Books Ltd,
14 High Street, Edinburgh EH1 1TE.

severnhouse.com

British Library Cataloguing-in-Publication Data
A CIP catalogue record for this title is available from the British Library.

ISBN-13: 978-1-4483-1142-2 (cased)
ISBN-13: 978-1-4483-1143-9 (e-book)

All Severn House titles are printed on acid-free paper.

MIX
Paper from
responsible sources
FSC® C013056

Typeset by Palimpsest Book Production Ltd.,
Falkirk, Stirlingshire, Scotland.
Printed and bound in Great Britain by
TJ Books, Padstow, Cornwall.

ACKNOWLEDGEMENTS

Set in the real places of Buffalo and Western New York, this is a work of fiction and all places and names refer to fictional characters and places. While there is a real Saint Stanislaus parish in Buffalo, the St. Stanislaus parish where Lydia participates in the pierogi contest is completely fictional and written from my imagination.

ONE

June 1982
Buffalo, New York

'One more batch,' Lydia Wienewski muttered to herself in the large commercial kitchen of Lydia's Lakeside Café and Bakery as the utilitarian clock above the griddle and next to the dining room swinging door struck one minute past midnight. No longer Sunday night, her precious time when she prepped for the upcoming week, it was officially Monday morning. Her feet screamed from standing next to the butcher block work surface where she deftly scraped bits of pierogi dough up with a stainless-steel pastry cutter.

A tall work stool stood next to her, but she'd never gotten the hang of baking or cooking while sitting. Foggy memories of her great-grandmother sitting at a farm table in the more rural area of Western New York while she filled and sealed dozens of the beloved Polish dish came back to her, as did holiday times spent with her mother. This was the magic Lydia found in her vocation: she was creating a meal for a patron to enjoy today, but she also relished keeping family memories alive, if only in her heart. Vocation wasn't a word used nowadays, not unless you were planning on becoming a priest or nun, but she remembered reading that it meant a calling. More than a career. That's what food was to her. She'd been called to it since she could remember. And pierogi was her favorite savory food to prepare.

You should have entered the pierogi contest.

Guilt mingled with disappointment in herself for missing out on such a wonderful opportunity for Lydia's Lakeside Bakery and Café. For the first time ever, the city of Buffalo was hosting an international cooking competition this summer. There would be various cook-offs focusing on different dishes in Italian, German, Polish and French categories during the Buffalo International Food Festival. The French cuisine competition seemed out of place in a region known more for its Eastern European foods, but recent news articles had hinted at a 'surprise guest judge.' Grandma thought it might be Julia Child, which Lydia found exciting but improbable. Lydia had read about the culinary competition in the *Courier Express*, one of two daily papers. The festival was hoping to attract cooks from far beyond Western New York. Key public affairs personal in both the Buffalo Mayor and Erie County Executive's offices were keen on rebuilding Buffalo's reputation. The Blizzard of '77 five years ago had made Buffalo the butt of many late-night TV comedians, which Lydia had watched first-hand. The recent Bethlehem Steel Mill layoffs only added to the impression of the once Queen City being cut off at the knees. Kaput. Done. Not only would participants vie for the chance of a ten-thousand-dollar prize pot for each cook-off, the winners would get a year's free advertising in both local papers and on two of three local television stations. One of the stations was received far into Canada, their near neighbor, which was especially exciting for any restauranteur looking to attract international patrons. It was a no-brainer to at least enter the contest for exposure if nothing else.

She'd clipped the article out and folded it neatly, placing it in the vinyl-covered calendar she kept in her purse.

And then missed the cut-off date.

Not that she hadn't had good reason to. Working nonstop at her newly opened business while still helping Pop at Wienewski's Wieners & Meats, the family butcher shop, made it easy to forget about anything else.

'*Meow.*' Pacha curled around her ankles, bemoaning her late hours. Even a once-feral cat appreciated his rest. Pacha was one of the litter that Luna, the family's butcher shop cat, had produced last winter. When Lydia had taken ownership of the café and bakery property, she'd noticed evidence of mice in one of the outer buildings and immediately decided she needed feline protection. Now that the litter was grown, it made perfect sense to find homes for all but Luna, who remained in charge of rodent duty outside of the butcher shop. Pacha and Lydia shared a special bond that had been forged when Lydia cared for Luna and the kittens through the very harsh winter. Pacha would climb up and into her parka and curl up under her arm whenever she fed the litter. Hence his name, which was Polish for armpit.

'"Pacha" is much more dignified than "armpit," right my big boy?' She spoke to her furry companion as if he was human.

'*Meow.*'

'Shh. It's OK, I'm almost done.' Lydia was totally cognizant of health regulations that forbade domestic animals, etcetera, in a commercial kitchen, but she wasn't worried about the health inspector popping in at this hour. Besides, Pacha proved invaluable when it came to what Lydia considered more credible threats to human health. The cat she'd adopted for her business proved his rodent hunting prowess time and time again.

She wiped her hands on the front of her apron as she walked to the commercial refrigerator and pulled out the remaining filling for this last few dozen pierogi. When patrons unfamiliar with Polish American fare asked for a description of a pierogi, Lydia explained that they were not unlike ravioli, only with a thinner dough pocket and different fillings. Her fillings included sauerkraut, cabbage, potatoes, and her most popular, farmer's cheese. Lydia's comparison to Italian dishes stopped at saying farmer's cheese was akin to ricotta, though. Farmer's cheese was nothing like the creamy Italian cheese she loved in her family's lasagna. The pierogi cheese was squeakier and had more of a bite to it.

'This should be just enough.' The dough ball rested as she stirred a beaten egg into the farmer's cheese and threw in a dash of salt. Lydia was garnering favor with locals and tourists alike for the simple, delicious dish.

Rolling out the dough was her favorite part – no surprise as she considered herself a baker more than a cook. Once the dough was at the exact thickness she demanded, she took her favorite pierogi glass and dipped it in the small pile of flour she kept on the rolling surface. In less than a minute she cut thirty-six perfect circles. Five minutes later she'd placed a scoop of the cheese filling in the middle of each circle, and began folding the dough over the filling.

'Gently, gently.' She whispered the usually unnecessary instructions to herself as she worked. When it got this late and weariness threatened to weigh her enthusiasm down it always helped to use the same words she'd heard her great-grandma and her mother say to her as a tiny girl. Pressing into the dough too quickly was death to a pierogi. The dough needed to be shaped over and around the filling, the edges sealed with tiny light-touch pinches.

She slipped the finished pierogi into the simmering pot of water and waited for the plump concoctions to float to the surface, a sign of being done. Using a slotted spoon, she moved each to a shallow baking pan with expert ease . . . until the last pierogi did what she never wanted them to do.

It burst, its contents swirling atop the bubbling water. *Please don't let this be an omen for today's sales.* The wasted pierogi was more likely an admonishment from her guilty conscience for blowing off the pierogi cook-off opportunity.

'Would you look at that, Pacha. I make twelve dozen pierogi, and the last one is dead on arrival.' She let out a long sigh and acknowledged she could no longer escape the weariness that running two full-time businesses was costing her. She had to plan better, but until then, maybe more nights camping out here at Lydia's Lakeside Café and Bakery were in order. The drive home to Cheektowaga was quickest at this time of night, but was also an extra twenty minutes she really couldn't afford.

'Tomorrow night it'll be you and me, Pacha. Slumber party.' Maybe she'd be able to convince Stanley to join them.

That thought kept her mind off the transgression of losing out on such a great opportunity with the contest as she stored away the pierogi that would hopefully sell out at lunchtime, just a few hours away now. After she did the last bit of clean-up, she turned off the lights and locked the door behind her. She strode to her purple Gremlin, parked willy-nilly in the graveled lot adjacent to the café. The night's air held the humidity of the day, and she told herself that there would be another pierogi contest. Hopefully. Maybe.

Exasperated, Lydia got into the driver's seat and slammed the door shut, cutting off the comforting sound of water lapping against the seawall. Lydia's Lakeside Café and Bakery was her dream come true, and no way was she going to let one mistake on her part ruin the excitement that swirled in her belly each and every day since the café's first patrons sat at their tables and picked one of her meals from her meticulously curated Polish American menu.

It was one contest, one cook-off. She'd gotten this far without one, hadn't she?

Lydia cranked up the radio for the drive home and shifted into gear.

'Here, take this with you.' Pop emerged from the family butcher shop's walk-in freezer later that morning holding a good-sized box in his brawny arms. Lydia noted that his right arm was still a bit thinner than his left, but both hands gripped the corrugated container with apparent equal strength.

The box was filled to the brim with the family's infamous kielbasa. Wienewski's Wieners & Meats sold everything from Polish sausage to homemade horseradish, but its most requested item was fresh and smoked kielbasa. Pop had continued the legacy left to him by his parents and grandparents. Lydia had never intended to do more than help out at the shop, but when she'd returned from Ottawa and her failed attempt at pastry school last Christmas, Pop had unfortunately suffered a massive stroke. She'd garnered her wits and used everything she'd ever learned growing up with a butcher father, including getting the family business back on solid financial ground. Some might say she'd saved the business, but she preferred to think of it as nothing more than what a Wienewski did for family. Whatever it took.

'Did you write up a receipt for this, Pop?' She took the heavy load from him. Pop was steady on his feet again but her mother had drilled it into the entire family – Lydia's older brother Ted, her younger sister Teri, and Grandma – that Pop's weakened body could not afford a tumble, no matter how seemingly minor.

'No, and I'm not going to,' Pop grumbled as he closed the wide stainless-steel door behind him. 'You helped me out since you've come back home, now let me do the same for you.'

'But you've been supplying the café with kielbasa since it opened, Pop. It's too much.'

'You worry about making the pierogi and *placek*.' He referred to the yeast coffee cake with golden raisins and tender crumb topping. 'I'm taking care of your kielbasa for this first summer.' He stopped, a familiar glint to his eyes. Bright blue like hers and

Grandma Mary's, his mother. Lydia's nape prickled. *Oh no*. Pop was about to—

'You know they're doing a pierogi contest as part of that big Buffalo food festival, right? Did you know it's at St Stanislaus this weekend?' He spoke casually, as if she'd fall for his manipulation attempt to make sure she'd entered. To oversee her life without making her think he didn't trust her. Which he shouldn't.

'I think I saw it in the paper, yes.' She replied with the white lie while trying to quiet her quaking insides. Of course Pop hadn't missed the pierogi contest. He read both the *Courier Express* and *The Buffalo Evening News* daily, line by line, even the stock market figures when Pop Wienewski had never owned a stock in his life.

'I'm telling you, dear daughter of mine, you're going to win the pierogi contest.' Pop assumed she'd sent the application in.

Lydia quickly changed the subject. 'Did you think about entering, Pop? You and Mom know so many people in that part of town.' The East Side was where Polish immigrants had originally settled in Buffalo in the late nineteenth and early twentieth centuries, decades before moving out to Cheektowaga and other Western New York suburbs.

Pop swiped the air with a dismissive wave. 'I don't have time for that fiddle-faddle. My specialty is kielbasa, not pierogi. I'm busy enough here. My business is already established. Yours . . .' He shrugged as if he had nothing to worry about, as if Wienewski's Wieners & Meats was booming.

But Lydia saw the frown that flickered across his mouth, thought about the extra trays of pork chops and T-bone steaks that hadn't sold yet. They still had a few days before they'd have to remove the pricey cuts from their inventory, but she liked to see their meats move more quickly. Business had been up and down this year, with her discovery of their former meat supplier's body in their backyard sausage smoker adding to their woes last Easter.

Had it only been a couple of months ago that she and Grandma had been considered murder suspects?

'I hear you, Pop.' *So please hear me.* 'I'm swamped myself, trying to get the café and bakery off to a good start. You've helped me so much.' She nodded with her chin at the sausages, the weight of which were making her arms numb. 'I'm not ready to do the competition yet. I'm too busy. Maybe next year.'

'Lydia, are you saying you didn't enter the pierogi contest? What have I been telling you about networking and greasing palms? In a legal way, of course.'

'Like I said, I'm in over my head right now, Pop. It's all I can do to make enough pierogi for the café.'

'Right.' Pop let go an extended sigh, his only outward sign of frustration. Whether with Lydia's failure to overextend herself or the butcher shop's revenue slowdown, she wasn't certain. 'See you later, Lyd.'

''Bye, Pop.' Lydia knew it was pure chicken on her part, but she wasn't about to tell Pop she had no intention of coming back tonight. Especially after disappointing him over the pierogi contest. She planned to stay at the café overnight. And not alone.

'I think your father's right. You should have signed up for the pierogi contest. No one can beat yours, and you know it.' Stanley Gorski, her number one fan and on-again, off-again – and now very much on again for what they both hoped was the long term – boyfriend popped one of Lydia's raspberry jelly sandwich cookies into his mouth. He washed it down with the hot coffee he'd made for them atop his parents' kitchen stove. 'Thanks for bringing me these. I can't believe you consider them throwaways.'

'It's more appealing to my customers if the edges aren't as brown.' But she knew Stanley preferred slightly overdone cookies. 'I didn't admit it to Pop but I did see the contest in the paper last week. I meant to enter, honest, but then we had the rush at the café for three days in a row, and I forgot. I feel like such a loser about it. It would have been great for my business.' Guilt tugged on her determination to be a successful business owner and independent woman like Grandma Mary encouraged her to be. Once the café and bakery was more established, she needed to up her game.

'One of my classmates is a member of St Stanislaus parish, where the pierogi cook-off for the Polish part of the festival is taking place. All they're talking about is the contest. How often does a regular Buffalo church get to be part of an international cooking competition? I'm sure she'd be able to get you in, no problem.' Stanley's mouth broke into a slow, sexy grin. 'It'd be a kick saying my girlfriend is the Pierogi Princess.'

'Please.' She rolled her eyes but her stomach felt the gentle brush of butterfly wings nonetheless. Stanley's compliments always did this to her. 'I'd love to, but the truth is I've got enough on my plate. And doesn't your class have more to do than worry about a pierogi cook-off at St Stanislaus?'

'We're all busy with our internships this summer, yes, but the Food Fest is a big deal, Lyd.' Stanley was heading into his last year of law school and 'internship' really meant 'work round the clock for a reputable law firm and pray they'll hire you after you pass the BAR exam.'

Compassion jerked Lydia from her pierogi woes. 'I'm sorry, I haven't even asked you how you're doing. How's the internship going?'

'I didn't give you much of a chance to say anything, did I?' Stanley leaned over his family's Formica table, not unlike the one in Lydia's garage loft apartment, and kissed her fully on the lips. When she'd arrived for a quick 'hello' Stanley had pulled her into his arms and they'd engaged in a preferable method of communication until his mother's steps had sounded on the stairs. 'I'm fine. The law firm is . . . demanding.'

'You're too modest. I'll bet they've already decided to offer you a position.'

'That'd be great, but it's downtown. The commute wouldn't be fun in the winter.' Stanley was the ultimate planner, unlike Lydia who tended to throw herself into a task and ask questions later. Learning to plan a business and menu had come with hard effort.

'Your father drives his truck all over Buffalo no matter the weather,' Stanley's Mom, Annette Gorski, chimed in as she came through with a basket of laundry, this one wet, and stopped halfway through the screen door. 'Lydia, George has some eggs for you. He left them in the basement refrigerator.'

'Thank you, and please thank him.' Lydia looked from Annette to Stanley and back again. 'One of you has to tell him to stop. I'm never going to be able to pay him back.'

'No paybacks allowed. Trust me, Gorski Dairy will start billing you soon enough. You're family, Lydia. Gorskis help each other get our businesses going.'

Lydia blushed. She and Stanley weren't engaged, yet. But it had crossed her mind lately that it would be the next logical step in their relationship. Except . . . life. He was holding down two jobs between the law firm internship and helping out his father's dairy business, and she was working at both the family butcher shop and her café and bakery. When was there any time to discuss their future, much less make it happen?

The screen door banged behind Mrs Gorski and Lydia stood up. 'I've got to get going. Please tell me you can come to the café later? I'm planning on camping out there tonight.'

Stanley's deep brown eyes lit with interest. 'I can't let you sleep alone, not by yourself, can I? You need my protection.'

They both laughed, but Lydia kept her private thoughts to herself. It did get kind of creepy at the lake by herself at night. She wasn't one to scare easily, but finding a murdered body in their family smoker this past Easter had changed her. She didn't take anything for granted these days, especially time with Stanley.

TWO

L ydia waved at Stanley as she drove off, the free eggs packed next to the box of kielbasa in her hatchback. She noticed white smudges she'd left on the steering wheel last night and chuckled. No matter how well she washed up after baking or making pierogi she managed to leave flour prints everywhere.

She raced her beloved purple Ford Gremlin toward Lake Erie along the route she'd driven ad infinitum over the past two months while balancing her double career. It was the reality of being responsible for two separate family businesses that were located the better part of twenty miles apart; there was never enough time in the day or night to get it all done.

Half of her heart remained in Cheektowaga, the Buffalo, New York suburb where she'd grown up. It was still where she officially lived in her parents' garage loft with Grandma Mary, Pop's mother. The butcher shop was only a few blocks away, on Cheektowaga's main thoroughfare, yet ever since she'd found Louie's body her view of the area had become a bit darker.

The memory of how awful Pop's meat supplier had been to her family had faded, but not the image of his murdered corpse that she'd discovered in the family backyard sausage smoker on Good Friday. That would take more time, she figured. It'd only been two months since Easter, after all.

Lydia rolled down the car window and let the morning lake breeze wash away the ugly memory that still hung over that time. She and her Grandma Mary Romano Wienewski had made a good team and solved Louie's murder, after which Lydia had dived into getting her dream café and bakery up and running in time for Memorial Day weekend at the end of May.

Lydia's Lakeside Café and Bakery claimed the other half of her work heart. The property she'd bought on the shore of Lake Erie in Acorn Bay would be her full-time gig once Pop was managing the butcher shop fine on his own again. Her business had had a decent grand opening two weeks ago, and was enjoying a slow but steady increase in patrons. Locals and tourists alike enjoyed the Polish American fare she served at lunchtime. Both savory and fruit crepes with a nice dollop of sour cream were popular, as were her platters of fresh and smoked kielbasa. But hands down the lunchtime winner was her pierogi, served piping hot, golden brown with a sheen of the butter they were pan-fried in. Her bakery was becoming a favorite with the early morning crowd, too. Few could resist her baked goods, a decent mix of traditionally Polish cakes, breads and cookies alongside more familiar American fare like cinnamon rolls and raspberry jam filled yeast doughnuts. Open for breakfast, followed by lunch was a good start and she hoped to add a dinner service to Lydia's Lakeside offerings before the end of the summer. The popularity of her pierogi on the lunch menu filled her with hope that her planned dinner service would be successful, too.

The beginning guitar chords of 'Waiting for a Girl Like You' came on her favorite rock station and she turned the Gremlin's volume dial up. She and Stanley had tickets to see Foreigner at Rich stadium next month in a blow-out, four-band concert. It seemed silly to be thinking about something so fun when her work life, and her family's coffers, demanded every ounce of her brainpower.

Stanley. It'd only been fifteen minutes and she missed him as if they'd been apart for years. Yes, he was a much more pleasant distraction from her career angst. The love she'd lost and found again never failed to remind her that there was more to life than fresh or smoked kielbasa and placek, Polish sausage and coffee cake.

The earlier clouds had cleared, and as she crested the last rise in the highway the view opened up to a panorama revealing a deep blue sky and aquamarine lake that stretched to its darker horizon. Lydia soaked in the beauty, tears of gratitude leaking out of her eyes. The wind gusting through her rolled down windows probably added to her eyeball discomfort, too.

Before she got too sappy the highway ended. She belted out the last refrain of the number one Billboard Rock Tracks ballad with Foreigner's lead singer Lou Gramm as she merged into local traffic.

Perfect timing.

. Within minutes she turned onto the café's driveway. Two vehicles in the paved customer parking lot caught her attention. One
car was a large, wide-bodied Buick Electra station wagon with
room for several passengers. The second auto was quite compact,
and reminded her of the small cars she'd seen on the road when
she lived in Ottawa.

Ottawa. Lydia gulped, then pushed the thought aside. She'd left
her disastrous time at the French pastry school behind her
when she'd returned to Buffalo last Christmas, but unexpected
reminders had a nasty habit of popping up, like the tiny car in her
café parking lot.

A quick glance at the dash clock revealed it was twenty minutes
until the café's lunch opening at eleven-thirty. Maybe a large family
had shown up early, but she didn't see anyone waiting on the wide,
covered porch at the front entrance.

Hmm.

It could be a group of bicycle enthusiasts. Her location was
convenient to a scenic road that ran south along the lake, and she'd
seen a few different groups take advantage of the parking lot.

Grandma hadn't phoned her at the butcher shop, and she'd
only been away from a phone for twenty minutes, so she assumed
all was well. Grandma, Freddy the cook, and her younger sister
Teri had arrived on time for the breakfast service, and she'd
left them before it was halfway over to make her run back to
Cheektowaga.

She drove along the graveled drive for the remaining one hundred
yards or so, past the good-sized lawn that fronted the sprawling
café and bakery building and separated it from the main road.
Reaching the graveled parking lot at the back of the building, she
pulled in next to Grandma's gold Ford LTD wagon. The oversized
station wagon was a ridiculous car for a widow who lived in a
garage loft as far as Lydia was concerned, but Grandma insisted
it allowed her to keep her independence. She'd bought the car to
travel to Florida with, when she was engaged to the man she
now only referred to as the 'rat-scum bastard who jilted me, that
son-of-a-bitch-no-good-jerk.'

Lydia grinned to herself. She was sorry that Grandma had gone
through that awful breakup, but grateful that they ended up rooming
together over her parents' garage. It was still their domicile, at

least until Lydia was able to move out to Acorn Bay, to be close to the café and bakery.

She opened the car door and stepped out, the wind whipping her hair into oblivion. Lydia marveled at how different the weather often was less than a half-hour drive from home. Slamming the door shut, she picked up the box of kielbasa and allowed herself a quick glance around the property. *Her* property.

The bulk of the main building, along with a grove of tall pine trees, kept the additional structures hidden from the main road. A tiny cottage, a storage shed typical of most Buffalo suburban backyards, and a former barn that had been converted into a commercial storage garage of sorts, added to the property's appeal.

The café itself gave the overall impression of a house by the sea thanks to the nautical themed sea green paint job and trimmings left by the previous owners. They'd operated a seafood establishment and employed a definite captain-y, pirate-y ambience. She'd spent hours standing here, envisioning the building painted white with red trim in tribute to her Polish American menu. And the cottage, now mostly empty save for the odd bit of broken furniture, was where she planned to settle down and make her first home. With Stanley, of course, even though they hadn't talked about when they'd actually settle down together in detail yet. The weather-worn bungalow was almost livable, except for the lack of heating. She mentally added 'cottage furnace' to her wish list of repairs.

Normally she'd take her time walking to the kitchen, stroll around the property and soak in her good fortune. There was no time for dawdling, though, not with lunch service beginning soon. As she walked past Grandma's LTD, Lydia saw that Grandma had left her purse on the front seat, probably distracted by last night's date with Detective Harry Nowicki.

An unbidden image of Grandma and Nowicki together flashed before her eyes and she groaned. This had to be from lack of time with her own lover.

Great. Now she was thinking of Stanley as her 'lover,' as if she was sixty-five like Grandma and not twenty-nine.

Pushing the uninvited thoughts away she put down the box of kielbasa, quickly opened the driver's door and retrieved Grandma's forgotten bag.

'Lydia!' Grandma's voice boomed across the lot and reached into the car, forcing Lydia to look up, too quickly.

Pain radiated from the side of her head to her nose thanks to bonking her head on the car frame. Like when she'd knocked her head back on the icy slopes in Glenwood, New York during her illustrious attempt at downhill skiing a few winters ago.

'Oof.' She kept the groan to herself and straightened as if nothing had happened. No sense getting Grandma all wigged out that she'd hurt herself.

'What's going on?' Lydia asked over her shoulder, buying herself a second to focus. But there was no reply, and when she straightened the kitchen entrance was vacant. Grandma had gone back inside.

The enormity of her double responsibilities with two family businesses sagged her shoulders more than the items she carried.

'Tonight. I'll take a break tonight,' she grumbled to herself as she walked the final steps to the back door, two purses on one shoulder, the box of kielbasa in her arms. She placed them all on the concrete stoop and hustled back to her car to get Mr Gorski's eggs.

She carefully balanced the eggs atop the box of sausage and used her foot and hip to open the screen door. Careful to not drop her cargo, she entered the kitchen. And froze at the frenzied scene before her. It wasn't the usual energy she associated with lunch-time preparation. Her staff buzzed about as if it were the middle of lunch service, an hour from now.

'I need three more pierogi orders, Freddy. One each sauerkraut, potato, and cheese.' Teri, Lydia's younger sister, spoke to the cook with authority that belied her nineteen years on the planet. Dressed in a white button-down shirt and black slacks with a red serving apron at her waist, she was Lydia's vision of the perfect server. 'That pair at table five is demanding, let me tell you. They want more sour cream to dip the pierogi in, too.' Teri rolled her eyes.

'They'll get their pierogi when I finish the blinis for table nine.' Freddy suffered no fools, patrons or not.

Grandma burst through the service door, her cheeks flushed and her sapphire eyes blazing. 'I told Lydia she needed to think about a liquor license. Table five wants a "wine pairing" with their pierogi! Have you ever heard of such a thing?'

No one noticed Lydia. They were too busy.

Lydia's mind shifted into overdrive. The staff had agreed to arrive two hours early each day, per her wishes, so that they were always prepared. No matter that, until today, there had never been a need to be ready so early for lunch. It usually took at least a half hour after opening for the mid-day meal for customers to show up.

'Why are we already serving lunch? What's going on?' she asked.

Three pairs of eyes pinned her to the spot.

Teri screamed.

'Ay yi yi!' Freddy dropped his spatula onto the hot griddle.

Grandma stared at her for several heartbeats before she calmly walked over to stand in front of her.

'Here, honey, give me those eggs. Take my towel,' she pushed the thick, white terrycloth rectangle into Lydia's hand as she gently removed the box from Lydia's arms, 'and hold it to your temple.'

'What? Why? Teri, what's your problem?' Lydia turned to her sister as she held the towel. She didn't have time for one of Teri's all too frequent emotional outbursts. 'Here, hand me my apron, will you? What's with the screaming? You've got Freddy all upset.'

Freddy shot her a furtive glance over his shoulder. He'd turned back to the griddle, as if afraid of her. She had to admit, her tone was off-putting. But what was with Teri's scream?

Teri ran up to her, holding the red apron with Lydia's Lakeside Café and Bakery embroidered in white across the bib. 'You're bleeding all over the place is what my problem is. Wait a sec to put that apron on. You don't want to stain it. Give me that towel.' Teri quickly wet the towel at the sink, grabbed Lydia's hand, then helped her put it to her temple.

'What the hey?' Lydia pulled her hand from her sister's and looked at the towel, now boasting a bright red stain. 'Oh, crap!'

'Keep the towel on your head!' Teri ordered.

'It's just a small bump, no big deal. I hit my head on Grandma's car. I'm fine, everyone, relax!' She'd made them all take the Red Cross First Aid course in the days up to the grand opening. The focus had been on grease burns and knife wounds, but really, did they have to get so dramatic over a bump on the head?

'No, you relax, Lydia. You look like you're trying out for the lead role in *Halloween*. You've got to get cleaned up, fast.

The most important customer you have ever served is out there. Right now. That's why we opened early, without waiting for you. They were already standing on the front porch while we were setting up.'

'Why didn't you call me? You knew I was at the butcher shop.' She aimed her query at Grandma, who shrugged and went back through the swinging door with a plate of eggs.

'There wasn't time to call anyone, Lydia. We had to act, pronto,' Teri answered as she filled glasses with ice, then carried them to the adjacent soda dispenser.

Lydia let her imagination run wild. 'Wait, let me guess. Reggie McKenzie? Chuck Knox? Or, maybe, is it André Savard?' She mentioned the names of a Buffalo Bills football player and his coach, and a Buffalo Sabres hockey player. Local pro athletes were beloved for their embrace of the Buffalo, which included patronizing family-owned taverns and restaurants. Excitement swirled in her belly. 'No, wait, don't tell me. Is it a rock star?' Maybe Foreigner was in town early, to check out the stadium ahead of their gig?

Grandma burst back into the kitchen and shook her head when she spotted Lydia in the same spot she'd left her fifteen seconds ago.

'Lydia! We need you. Now.'

'No. The customers aren't from Buffalo,' Teri continued as if Grandma wasn't there, intent on imparting crucial information. 'It's a woman we've never met, but she says she's very important to you. That you know her.'

'They came down from Ottawa,' Grandma added. 'As in Canada.'

Her sudden lightheadedness wasn't from her head wound. '"They?" How many are out there?' Lydia asked. Her stomach's happy reaction turned sour. Her instinct had been spot-on, as far as the small auto in the parking lot went. *No. It couldn't be . . .*

'It's some woman dressed up way too much for lunch, if you ask me, and she brought seven customers with her, though one's just leaving. That's a lot of hungry mouths in one group, Lydia,' Teri grumbled. Acting cranky was her way of expressing her anxiety.

'Less explaining and more serving, folks.' Freddy didn't bother to glance up from where he plated up a perfectly browned pork chop and drizzled gravy over it, finishing with a sprig of curly parsley. Without a single pause he turned back to the stove and slid pierogi from a large pot of simmering water and onto the griddle, next to a pile of caramelized onions. Not for the first time, Lydia was grateful for the middle-aged man who'd shown up in response to her classified ad. His years of tavern cooking experience on Buffalo's East Side proved invaluable.

'You're right, Freddy,' Lydia confirmed, ignoring her quaking insides. If her instincts were right about who was out in the dining room, it was time to face down her biggest nemesis of all time.

You've got this.

Wasn't she the one who ran into the lake or cannonballed into a pool, with no advanced pinkie-toe temperature testing? She shrugged off the tote bag and purses, aided by Grandma and Teri, who was still dabbing at her forehead. With zero preamble, Lydia pushed Grandma's and Teri's ministrations aside and stalked to the swinging door. She dropped the blood-soaked towel into the laundry bin along the way.

'Don't, Lydia! You need a bandage first,' Teri yelled.

'You can't serve people looking like that!' Freddy boomed.

'Let her go. She's on a mission from the Blessed Mother.' Grandma had a unique way of blending her personal version of Catholicism and pop culture.

The lively conversation that greeted Lydia in the dining room reassured her that despite Teri and Grandma's complaints, the patrons were enjoying their time, which usually meant they were also happy with their food.

A cloud of smoke hung over the tables closest to the kitchen, making it difficult to see the diners, and Lydia fought to keep her reaction from showing in her expression. The no-smoking area of the café she'd insisted upon making remained unoccupied. It wasn't that patrons were smoking that made her want to screw up her face in disgust; some people did smoke, especially with their after-meal coffee.

No, it was the distinct aroma of foreign cigarettes. Myriad images flooded her mind's eye: laughing in smoke-filled cafés and bars in Ottawa, walking through the frozen streets with her pastry school classmates, driving away from Ottawa feeling at

once liberated and a total failure. It also brought back memories
of someone she'd hoped to forget . . . Lydia tamped down a sudden
desire to flee from the café, from a part of her life she had
no desire to revisit.

Keep going. With no more hesitation, she aimed her focus on
table five.

There, at the six-seater set with white and red linens and a
matching red poppy and white chrysanthemum silk flower centerpiece, sat the two people she hoped she'd never, ever, see again,
be it in this lifetime or the next. A third place setting looked like
it had been used, but the chair was empty.

Not as overtly religious as Mom or Grandma, Lydia preferred
to leave prayers to the Blessed Virgin to her matriarchs – the power
of the rosary being perhaps the single subject the two women
agreed on. But even she, a part-time Catholic at best, had prayed
a lap around the rosary beads for extra good measure that this
very scene would never play out. Yet here she stood, and there
they sat.

She bit her lip and placed fisted hands on her hips.

Why couldn't the people who sat in her café have stayed put
in her nightmare memories of Madame Delphine's French pastry
school, along with the shame of being caught in the midst of her
most awkward extracurricular sex-ploit?

But no. For at table five sat her old French pastry tutor from
L'ecole du Cuisine in Ottawa, Madame Delphine Chenault, and
her son – Madame's wannabe teaching assistant – Pierre. Madame
Delphine's cheeks puffed out as she chewed a bite of pierogi
cheese from the remains on her plate, while Pierre delicately dipped
a slice of Pop's smoked kielbasa into Grandma's fluffy white,
homegrown, homemade horseradish. Unlike the other patrons,
some of whom she now realized must be students of L'ecole du
Cuisine, neither had noticed her yet. Lydia did the most intelligent
thing she could, given the futility of the situation.

She spun on her heels and made a break for the kitchen.

'Mademoiselle Wienewski!' Madame's cry sliced through
Lydia's chaotic thoughts and pulled her up short.

'Lydia!'

Lydia spied one of her old roommates from pastry school,
Elodie, through the smoke at one of the tables.

'Hey, girl!' Chloe, her other ex-roommate, waved. The three of them had formed a fast friendship, bonding over Madame's strict tutelage. And nights filled with too much Canadian beer and not a lot of common sense.

'Oof.' Lydia stopped so fast that her sneakers caught on the edge of the protective running mat and sent her toppling. Grabbing the end of the soda fountain counter, she managed to regain her balance in the nick of time. A collective titter from the other students she didn't know rippled across the café and sent a shockwave of truth across her heart.

Lydia was going to have to face her ugly past.

THREE

G ut churning, Lydia turned back and met her fate. Ignoring Pierre, she forced her chin up and stalked forward.

This is your *café,* your *menu,* your *territory.*

Her rules, not Madame's. Not anymore. And wasn't it wonderful to see Elodie and Chloe again?

'Madame Delphine. What brings you to Buffalo?' If she ignored Pierre maybe they all could keep the past, and her brief almost-affair with him, where it belonged. Or at least most of it.

Madame took her time chewing before she swallowed. She must have called out to Lydia with her mouth full, completely out of character for the woman Lydia had studied under. Delphine Chenault was nothing if not impeccably mannered and dressed. Madame took a sip of water, a slice of lemon floating alongside the ice that *pinged* against the glass. Only after she patted her bright-red lips with the linen napkin did her gaze meet Lydia's.

'Lydia, *ma cherie*, of course I wouldn't miss the debut of my student's establishment. Perhaps you do not recall, but I made it perfectly clear in class that it's Madame Delphine's L'ecole du Cuisine's policy to support its students' future endeavors. Each and every one of my students. Past or present, certificate of completion or not.' She looked pointedly at Lydia, who'd left before completing the course.

Lydia gritted her teeth. Had Delphine come all this way to humiliate her in front of her students, in her own café?

Her hands fisted as Delphine continued, 'Pierre informed me of your new' – she sniffed, her lips pursing to the size of a pea as she deliberated on her word choice – 'venture.'

'We're lucky we found out about it, in fact.' Pierre spoke up. 'My college classmate mailed me this.' Pierre spoke as if he were defending a dissertation, his words rapid-fire. He pointed to the black-and-white print advertisement and coupon that Lydia had paid the *Buffalo Evening News* to run for two weeks. She remembered, vaguely, that Pierre had mentioned he had a friend from Buffalo who'd attended McGill University in Toronto with him.

'This coupon only applies on Fish Fry Fridays.' In truth she'd given the discount to anyone who brought the coupon in, but her heart was not open to extending the same grace to these two. As her mind raced, trying to keep up with her pounding pulse, a sudden, unexpected calm settled over her. The old feelings of failure that Delphine's presence had reawakened evaporated. She wasn't a student of Madame's any longer, and definitely not attached to Pierre in any way.

Thank you, Jesus, Joseph and Mary.

Madame Delphine waved her hand in front of her face as if a pesky gnat flew by. '*Pas de problème.*' No problem. 'Lydia, please sit for a moment, will you? I'm not here to critique, truly.' She patted the seat next to her.

'Isn't someone already sitting there?' A crumpled linen napkin lay to the side of a half-empty plate. But the fork and knife were also on the plate, in the classic 'x' to denote the diner was finished. It wasn't something she ever knew before living in Ottawa, and apparently a European custom used to signal the wait staff to clear the setting.

'*Non.* Jean was here, but he just ran off.' She pointed toward the front entry, where Lydia recognized Pierre's father, dressed in Bermuda shorts and a sport shirt, exit. Not surprisingly, he had a lit cigarette hanging from the side of his mouth. She recalled that Monsieur Chenault was a chain-smoker.

'Where is he going?' Lydia hoped it wasn't her food that had chased the man away.

'Who knows where he ever takes off to? His business appointments always come first.' Madame's impatience reflected in her distracted comment, but there was something more in her tone. Contempt? 'Sit down, Lydia.' Madame spoke more firmly this time, without the affectionate seat pat.

'Dad's working a very important business deal while we're in the States.' Pierre seemed intent to defend not only their presence in her establishment, but his father's, too. There was no need. The Chenault family's domestics weren't of interest to her. She'd moved on from her time in Ottawa; she was now living her dream.

'I'd love to catch up, but as you can see, I have many customers to satisfy.' And she did. Looking around the dining room, a solid third of the thirty tables were full. Not bad for opening early.

'Lydia, over here!' Chloe was still waving from three tables over, her smile bright.

'Shhh. Wait.' Elodie grabbed Chloe's arm and pulled it down, throwing Lydia an apologetic glance.

'I'll be right there!' Lydia's delighted tone wasn't feigned. She'd missed the two women.

'*Pffft.* Sit, Lydia.' Madame pressed on, refusing to be deterred.

Before she could open her mouth to protest, Lydia's reflexes had her butt in the chair next to Madame, opposite Pierre. The quick glimpse she allowed herself of the man she'd had nothing in common with except the pastry school and a most regrettable hot chemistry revealed that he barely resembled the man of her memories. Sure, he had the same bedroom eyes, the classically handsome profile that matched his longish dark hair that he wore in a ponytail under his chef hat. Today his locks were loose, and he looked quite the mess, in her opinion. But, much to her relief, she didn't feel any of the same attraction. What had ever possessed her to stick her tongue—

'There you go.' Madame patted her hand, and Lydia jerked at the woman's unexpected display of . . . affection? 'Now, listen to me, Lydia. Relax. I already said, I'm not here to throw stones. I always knew you were a good cook, and enthusiastic baker. Now, for certain you have created a business here with your special cultural flair. You haven't done anything I suggested regarding your cuisine, of course. Or your menu choices. But you have an excellent establishment nonetheless, Lydia. *Bien fait.* Well done. This is exactly the kind of fare I knew you were capable of!'

Lydia stared at Madame Delphine. Only she could make a compliment feel like a slice to the liver. But still, the approval was most generous coming from the woman who'd once criticized Lydia's methods with razor-sharp attention to detail.

'You . . . you like it?' Her words came out on a whisper and she mentally kicked herself. *You don't need Madame's approval.*

But she sure welcomed it.

'Oh, my girl, you haven't changed a bit! Always with the' – she looked to Pierre – 'how do you say . . .' The flood of French that the two exchanged was too fast for Lydia to follow. After five years of French from junior through senior high school, plus her time in Ottawa under Madame's tutelage, she'd been conversationally fluent in the language when she'd departed Ottawa. But that was almost a full year ago. Language skills, like baking or butchering, needed daily attention.

She attributed her language proclivities to hearing Polish spoken nonstop until she was three or four years old, when Grandpa Wienewski died and left the butcher shop to Pop. Pop, a second generation Polish American, understood Polish but never spoke it unless spoken to, as his first language was English.

'No more low self-esteem!' Madame's declaration shook Lydia from her musings. 'You must not do this to yourself anymore, Lydia. You have broken free of your past!'

'I sure have.' She shifted in her seat. The sooner she was back in the kitchen, the better. 'Thank you. I'm glad, and flattered, that you made the long trip here. What more can we bring you?'

'Nonsense. I always enjoy a chance to escape our simple life in Ottawa.' She giggled as if she were twenty years younger.

'Mother's being far too humble. We're pleased for you, Lydia, but that's not the only reason we're here. I take it you haven't heard the news?' Pierre looked from Lydia to his mother.

'I've, um, been busy since returning to the States.' Lydia was not about to explain how the café and bakery had been the smallest portion of her time since last December. How did you include the fact that your father and the family business had almost died, and that you found a dead body in the family smoker that you were initially considered a suspect of murdering?

'Tell her, Mother.'

'No, no, it's not important.'

Lydia gritted her teeth. 'Tell me what?'

Pierre beamed with pride as if he were the parent. 'Mother has signed a contract with a large New York city publisher for her very own cookbook. And it's not been announced yet, but—'

'Shh, *non!*' Madame swatted at Pierre, her gaze never leaving Lydia. 'Don't listen to him. Yes, I have a cookbook coming out next year. So have many these days, *non?*'

'Mother, not everyone gets their own television show.' Pierre admonished his mother with a false deadpan that made Lydia want to strangle something. Not a person, of course. She'd had enough of anything to do with murder in her lifetime. Her mind digested Pierre's words and incredulity blossomed.

'You're going to be on TV?'

'It's not a done deal yet.'

'If it wasn't they wouldn't have asked you to speak at the Chautauqua Institute, would they?' Pierre's smugness was less than becoming. 'Mother is going to be interviewed on *Good Day America* tomorrow. They're broadcasting from the institute's amphitheater all this week. Her publisher is most excited about the free publicity.'

It was hard to believe Pierre was such an adoring son when he'd been nothing but a hound dog during her time with him at the pastry school. All he had wanted was to become Madame's business partner – and to be on the teaching staff, too – and had vocalized his wishes aloud to anyone who'd listen. Madame had made Pierre work hard, and he hated it. One thing was for sure – he didn't have his mother's work ethic. But he had probably finally convinced Madame that he was up to the task of being on the school staff full-time. Lydia was all too aware of how charming and persuasive Pierre could be. He always got his own way in the end.

'Pass me my bag, Pierre.' Madame took a small, sequined cigarette case from him and busied herself with lighting a cigarillo. Lydia's stomach roiled at the anticipation of the familiar strong odor the woman's cigar would produce.

She had to get away from them.

'Something else you'll be glad to know, Lydia, is that Mother has been asked to be the guest judge of honor for the éclair bake-off, in the French category, as part of Buffalo's first international food competition!' Pierre beamed. 'We brought the students with us so they could experience the festival for themselves.'

So it wasn't Julia Child who was the surprise guest for the food festival. It was Madame Delphine. Lydia stared at the woman who'd gone from an ugly memory to the more positive, joyful person who sat in front of her.

'Please, do not use this phrase "bake-off." It sounds too rudimentary. I prefer to think of it as a cooking competition. I assume you've entered the Polish category's pierogi contest, Lydia, *non*?'

'I, uh . . .' She mentally scrambled for a better excuse than that she'd forgotten to enter.

'If your pierogi taste half as good on Saturday as these did today, I don't see how anyone would be able to beat you.'

'Thank you, Madame.'

She studied first Pierre, then Madame. Pierre must have sensed her observation because he looked up at her and held her gaze. He slowly, deliberately mouthed silent words at her. At first, she didn't catch his meaning. Until she did. *Je t'aime.* I love you.

Oh no.

Pierre hadn't come here for his mother, or for the festival or school trip. He'd come for her. She bit back a laugh but the sound forced its way from her airway, through her throat and out both her mouth and nose.

It sounded like she'd sworn.

Both Madame and Pierre stared at her. By the way the back of her neck was prickling, so were the rest of the customers.

'What did you say?' Pierre asked. 'Because it sounded like—'

'I know what it sounded like, Pierre. Like *mierde*.' The French word for crap, or dog poop, or . . . 'I meant to say "holy cannoli."' She pointedly looked at her watch. 'If you'll excuse me, *s'il vous plaît*, I've got so much work to do, and I need to say "hello" to Elodie and Chloe.' But when she looked for her friends, their seats were empty. She began to back away from the table. 'I'm sure you both understand. Thank you for coming, and enjoy the rest of your time in Buffalo. Good luck with your television appearance. And your cookbook, and—'

'Lydia, wait.' Pierre stood abruptly, his knee hitting the table with an audible *thud*. Madame Delphine's water glass tipped, and as she reached to stop its fall, her arm hit the taller glass on her left, filled with what Lydia surmised was loganberry soda, a local favorite. The bright purple liquid splashed over Madame Delphine's chic white sundress and sleeveless blue cardigan outfit, the full poplin skirt spread wide and now sporting a growing purple stain, and she pushed her chair away from the table.

'Oh, Madame, I'm so sorry.' Lydia went into full service mode, running back to the soda fountain for plain seltzer water and clean, absorbent rags. She returned to the table, where Pierre hadn't moved one iota to help out his mother.

'Give me that.' Madame Delphine grabbed the water and rags. She sprinkled the stains with salt, then poured the carbonated water over her skirt. Lydia took one of the dishcloths and attempted to soak up the stain.

Lydia felt all eyes of the remaining students burning through her back, along with a few regulars who certainly were getting more than they'd paid for this lunchtime. She knew that how she handled this would be remembered. Customers were forgiving of accidents, but it was all about how the service staff handled them. One surly waitress or waiter and they'd find another place for pierogi, kielbasa and Fish Fry Fridays.

'Please, come back into the kitchen with me. There's an employee restroom where you'll have more privacy.'

'Lead the way.' Madame nodded.

Once in the kitchen, Madame paused on her kitten-heeled electric blue pumps and took in the space. Lydia's stomach did a polka, she couldn't help it. It was a knee-jerk reaction, seeking her former instructor's approval.

'What did I tell you, Delphine? Lydia's a natural at this.' Grandma's arms were outstretched as if presenting the Canadian with a gift.

'Mary, you couldn't be more correct.'

Delphine? Mary? Since when were Grandma and Madame on a first-name basis?

'Relax, Lydia. Delphine and I got to know one another earlier.' Grandma winked. She always accurately read Lydia's facial expressions, even when Lydia thought she was keeping a blank one.

The service door burst open and Pierre plowed into her back.

'Ompf.' Lydia spun around and glared at him. 'What is your problem, exactly?' As she spoke, she noticed a young woman had followed them both into the kitchen. 'Excuse me, but patrons are not allowed back here. Sanitary reasons.'

Pierre followed her gaze. 'Cecile, please, go back to the other students.'

'I want to make sure you're OK first, Pierre.' Her purring was a complete contrast to the ugly look she shot Lydia. 'We're returning to the hotel soon.' She kissed him on the cheek, close to his ear. To Lydia's amusement, she then blew into his ear and Pierre's cheeks reddened.

'Leave at once, Cecile. You have no right to be in Lydia's kitchen,' Madame Delphine snarled.

Cecile held Madame's gaze; the tension between them was palpably ratcheting. Lydia didn't see anything but contempt between the two women. Was Cecile Pierre's girlfriend, as she'd intimated? Lydia cast a glance at Pierre, whose awkward stance reflected a desire for the floor to swallow him whole. Lydia suspected that Madame wasn't on board with this fling or whatever it was between the pair. After witnessing Cecile's aggressive and possessive behavior, Lydia didn't blame her former instructor.

Finally, Pierre spoke. 'You're going to have to wait for the taxis because we only have one vehicle at the moment, Cecile. Dad took the Buick to his appointment. And the Acorn Bay Hotel is too far to walk.'

As Cecile stared at him, her lower lip protruding in a dramatic pout, Pierre offered her a quick kiss on the lips.

Some things never change.

'I'm fine, Cecile. This doesn't involve you. Go back into the dining room, please.'

'I'll wait for you.' She shot Lydia and Madame Delphine a murderous glance before turning away.

Pierre waited for Cecile to exit the kitchen before he spoke again. His doleful expression turned desperate as he grasped her shoulders. 'Lydia, I was such a fool to ever let you go. I understand you had to leave the school, this is what you were born for. Your kielbasa, those pierogi,' Pierre looked heavenward and inhaled deeply, 'are divine. So was what we shared. I want to start again. We made magic together.'

'So did you and Olivia. And Eva, and Juliette . . . and now Cecile, it appears.' Really, there was no end to the notches on Pierre's Canadian oak bedpost.

'Cecile, eh.' His Gaelic shrug was impressive. 'You know me, Lydia. I can't help myself when it comes to women. So I flirt a little, eh? But it doesn't change how I feel for you.'

'That's one of the many differences between you and me, Pierre. The definition of commitment, and flirting.'

'What the hell, Lydia?' The baritone that rolled across the kitchen like thunder over Lake Erie plucked her heartstrings. She jerked out of Pierre's grasp and turned to see Stanley, yet another carton of eggs in his arms, glaring. Not at her, but at Pierre.

'Stanley!' His unexpected visit had happened at the worst possible time. 'We have some surprise guests today.' She rushed over to him and took the extra eggs he was carrying from his death grip, gave him a quick peck on the cheek, thought better of it, and planted a full kiss on his unmoving lips. *Did you see that, Pierre?* 'Remember I told you about Madame Delphine—'

'Yeah, let me guess, you're Pierre?' Stanley still hadn't taken his attention from her former, for one time only, thanks to Jesus, Mary, and Joseph, fling.

'*Oui.*' Pierre stood up straight, faced down Stanley. Tears filled Lydia's eyes, but she couldn't tell if they were from self-hatred for ever getting involved with Pierre in the first place, or pride in how Stanley made it clear that they shared no secrets, or sheer relief that she and Stanley had found their way back to one another.

They had, hadn't they? His stormy gaze wasn't reassuring her at the moment.

'Lydia, I need your assistance *maintenant, s'il te plaît,*' Madame Delphine yelled from the bathroom doorway, in full in-charge mode again, never mind the hideous Rorschach loganberry stain on her dress.

'Coming!' Lydia bolted to the bathroom.

As soon as she closed the door on the plain but roomy space, Madame whirled on Lydia and batted away her attempts to help with the stain.

'If you're going to serve such a potent staining liquid, make it a cabernet, at least!'

Lydia gasped. The woman had morphed back into the Madame Delphine she remembered all too well.

Madame closed her eyes, pinched the bridge of her nose through several breaths. Lydia stood in silence, watching her former nemesis. Or maybe not 'former' after all.

After what felt like hours but couldn't have been more than a minute, Madame opened her eyes again and assessed Lydia with calm detachment, except for the tiny sparkles that turned her green eyes aquamarine. Compassion? Or was Madame plotting to make Lydia's life miserable again?

'Lydia. Please. Forgive my impetuousness. That was meant to be humorous but in my usual manner it came out as an insult. I've not had a clear conscience since you left my school. I wanted to make amends to you, but a letter or phone call weren't enough. When I received the invitation to judge the éclair competition, and then the TV interview, Pierre mentioned that you'd opened your café and bakery here and I knew it must be fate. This is the only way I can show you what I always believed.' She sniffed, glanced away.

'Really?' A stinging sensation under Lydia's ribcage had to be a crack in the hardened wall she'd erected around the room in her heart. The room where Madame's constant criticism during pastry class had destroyed her self-esteem before she found a way back to it.

Could Madame truly carry guilt over how she'd treated her? Lydia had a hard time matching the contrite woman before her with the chef who'd haunted her most terror filled nightmares these past months. She'd even had thoughts of Madame while solving Louie's murder, for saint's sake!

'Yes, really.' Madame's shoulders lowered and her entire countenance exuded sincerity. 'Why would you think anything less of me?'

'It's not you, I mean, it wasn't totally you, Madame. It was me, too, how I acted. I . . . I am only just learning to have faith in myself, my own talents,' she explained. 'We didn't always see eye to eye, and I know I'm stubborn. And then when you found Pierre . . . Pierre and me, in your kitchen . . . well, it was embarrassing, is what I'm trying to say.' How else to describe the fact that Madame had seen Lydia in her birthday suit, atop the stainless-steel prep counter in the school's classroom?

'Certainly it was a little unsettling to find you and Pierre' – she waved her hand in a full circle, waggled her brows – 'in the throes of passion. I'm a mother first and foremost, so of course I was upset. But that's all in passing, water under the Peace Bridge.' She referred to the span that connected Buffalo with Canada. 'What's more important to me is that you brought a piece of what I taught with you back to your hometown. Am I making sense to you, Lydia?'

She nodded. 'Yes. And you did teach me a lot, especially the business part. I'm not a natural chef—'

'You are a gifted baker, Lydia. That's why your pierogi is exceptional – a dumpling is in truth a primitive pastry of sorts, *non*?'

Lydia didn't totally agree with Madame's comparison of pierogi to dumplings, as the former took far more time and experience. But it was nice to hear such shining praise from the teacher she thought she'd disappointed.

Was it possible that some, or maybe a lot, of the regret she harbored surrounding her time at the pastry school was because she'd been too hard on herself? She'd taken Delphine's criticisms to heart and challenged her, often rudely, instead of using the experience to push her forward as a cook and baker. Well, that wasn't strictly true. She had her own café now, after all.

'I never expected you to run a café so well, to be honest. But your decor is superb, and the cultural cuisine lives up to your menu's promise. You've mastered Slavic baking and savory cooking, too!'

'Thank you. As I was saying, Madame—'

'Please, call me Delphine. We are colleagues, no longer bound by the formalities of school.'

'OK.' She steadied herself with a deep breath. 'Delphine.' The first name felt like a new food in her mouth. Not unpleasant, but foreign. Exotic. Well, maybe not *that* fancy. 'I'm sorry about the way I left. You had every right to kick me out, you know. I behaved like a spoiled child.'

'You were very defensive about how to roll out mille-feuille.' Madame's brow lifted. 'You insisted I made it too thin.'

'I forgot about that. I couldn't imagine doing anything differently with puff pastry than how I'd taught myself to make a Napoleon.' Images of how she'd layered her too-thick puff pastry with cream while insisting she was correct assaulted her memory. As she remembered the incident, Lydia's embarrassment morphed to shame. 'And then it was so incredibly horrible of me to quit the way I did.'

'I was equally ugly to expel you in that same conversation, Lydia. We both had much to learn at that point. We were over-reacting to our passions.' Delphine's expression went from wistful to grave. 'I've spent too much of my life playing down my own talents and skills. Your confidence in opening the café reminded me that what I do is important, too.' At Lydia's silence, Delphine continued, 'It was easy for me to hide behind my stern instructor mask to my students. I've allowed life to go by without realizing my dreams. After you left, I took a long look at my teaching, the school I'd worked so hard to establish. I still want to teach, yes, but writing a cookbook was always my goal. And now, I have a shot at my own television program. I'll be able to teach hundreds, thousands of viewers in a single half-hour segment.'

'I'm very happy for you, Delphine.' Lydia meant it. 'Something you need to know is that I know now that I wanted the certificate from your school to validate my abilities. After I came back, I realized I never needed it. Not that it wouldn't have been a wonderful achievement, but I already had the skillset I needed to go after my dreams.'

Delphine nodded. 'I'm so glad you figured this out for yourself. I was a little rough on all of you. You in particular because you're so talented. I saw myself as your sculptor, I'm afraid. But you didn't need my tools. You'd already honed your own.'

'Oh.' Lydia blinked back tears at the heady praise.

'No crying, *ma cherie*. We are women with a passion few understand. We must support one another, like sisters. We don't need men for any of it, let me tell you! I love Pierre, of course, he is my son. But as much as I love my son, I know what he's like – he's his father's son through and through. Never happy with what he has, including women. And selfish.' Delphine's stark revelation sparked Lydia's compassion. Had the older woman stayed married to a philanderer all these years?

'You're better off with the American you kissed in this kitchen, Lydia. He is your lover, no?'

Lydia tried not to grimace at the old-fashioned expression. 'Yes, Stanley and I are together. A couple.'

'Wonderful! You must promise me that you will come to Ottawa with this Stanley and allow me to show you a better time than when you were in L'ecole. Promise?'

'OK.' Lydia thought about it. It wouldn't be in the near future, but she had enjoyed what little she'd seen of Ottawa proper. A romantic trip with Stanley sounded like heaven right about now. She nodded. 'Yes, we will come to visit you. I'll keep in touch. It might be a little while, as we're both swamped right now.'

'Enough of that. Look at you! You are living your dream, Lydia. Embrace it!' She leaned forward and Lydia couldn't help it – she stiffened and leaned back. Madame laughed, took her by the upper arms and pulled her forward. Giving her a kiss on each cheek, she exclaimed, 'You go after your dreams, always. No exceptions.'

'*Merci.*' French words came out reflexively, a holdover from her time with Madame. *Delphine*.

'No "thank you" is necessary. Indeed, I should be thanking you, Next year I intend to add in a class about different cultures and their cuisines, and I will include your pierogi. You must give me the recipe, *non*? I understand if you want to wait until the competition is a *fait accompli.*'

'Sure . . . but it is a family secret, Madame. Delphine.' The reminder of her absentmindedness over entering the contest made her fingers itch to get back into the kitchen. She may have messed up by not entering but at least she had a café and bakery to run.

'And it will remain that way, *cherie*, in my heart. Don't even write it down, just tell me what you do and I will incorporate it with my new students in the fall.' Madame was treating Lydia as if Lydia was a colleague. An equal. It was . . . exhilarating.

'Well, OK. Can we talk before you leave?' The cost of long-distance phone calls would make it worth the time to get together before Delphine returned to Canada.

'Certainly. Of course. But our schedule is so full. Let's see, we are returning to the Acorn Bay Hotel shortly, and going out for a local dinner tonight. Tomorrow, very early, I will take the students down to . . . how do you say . . . Lake Chautauqua? Where I'll be on the television show. Afterwards I've arranged for the students to provide a day-long French cooking class for the local attendees, and they'll attend the festival while I proceed to judge the éclair contest in Buffalo this weekend. We will drive back through here, on our way back to Canada, on Sunday.' She snapped her fingers in front of her face. 'I know! I'll have us all stop Sunday morning for your pastries and coffee, and you can tell me the pierogi secret recipe then. Now, you go and tend to your work, and I'll take care of this.' She gestured at her dress. The stain had faded with drying, but Lydia feared the material was ruined.

'OK. I'll see you back out there. Thank you, Delphine.'

Lydia left, feeling more confident about her professional choices than she'd been five minutes earlier.

But now she had a bigger problem than serving a crowd of hungry tourists. Stanley's grim expression hadn't changed, except for his single raised brow as he pointed to the door.

Was this the end of their recently rediscovered passion?

FOUR

'I don't want to know the details, Lydia. It's enough of a gut punch to know he's the one you were involved with.' Stanley spoke with quiet deliberation. They were in the old barn turned large storage building, and he leaned against one of two large commercial refrigerators that were stocked with a variety of café basics.

'Fine. I told you, it wasn't a relationship; it was a one-night stand. Not even. Barely.' She spoke at a near whisper, but she didn't know why. No one was around.

Stanley was right. He didn't need to know the details of her time in Ottawa. They weren't a couple then. They'd broken up before she'd left home.

'Right.' His reply was clipped, his stance guarded, but his eyes full of warmth as their gazes met.

She stood on tiptoe and kissed him, hung her arms around his neck. 'Thank you for making the trip out here. I know it's a lot with everything you have on your plate.' She didn't want to talk about Pierre ever again.

Stanley, never one to hold a grudge, pulled her fully into his arms. 'Nothing is more important to me than you, Lydia. You and me, that is. It's killing me that we don't have the time together like we used to, but we're both trying to make our break from the same old, same old.' He kissed her, and after she rested her head on his chest, his chin on her head. It was her favorite way to snuggle with him.

Stanley pulled back, touched his chin. 'Lyd?'

'Yeah?'

'Your head is bleeding.' He touched her temple, held his hand up for her to see the bright red evidence.

'Oh, it's just seeping a bit. I smacked it getting out of Grandma's car.'

'Ouch. That had to hurt.'

'I'm fine. Here, use this to wipe your hand.' She tugged a crumpled tissue from her apron pocket.

'That explains why your hair looks slicked back, though.' He chuckled as he cleaned off his fingers.

Lydia raised her hands and gingerly touched her temple and hairline. Her fingers met stickiness but she knew it wasn't from her gardenia scented hair mousse.

'Gosh nabbit.' She was trying to clean up her language, with owning her own place and all. 'No wonder all of Madame Delphine's students were looking at me like I had three heads.' She laughed. 'I thought it was because they'd heard about me—' Too late, she clamped her mouth shut.

'What did they hear? That you'd quit?'

'Actually, I know I told you I quit, and I did, but it happened to be just after Madame Delphine told me that it'd be best if I left.'

'Because of your relationship with Pierre?' To his credit, Stanley's earlier anger was gone. Law school had smoothed over the Stanley she'd left, polishing an already expressive guy into an incredibly articulate, logical man. His astute insight had helped her in solving a murder. Or more accurately, Stanley's warnings had kept her out of worse trouble than she and Grandma would have gotten themselves into.

Stanley always put her welfare first.

'I told you, it wasn't a relationship, not in anyone's reality or imagination.' Her words belied her thoughts, stuck on how emotionally reckless she'd been. The stupid part of her actions was that she'd allowed Pierre to convince her to go to his house – his parents' home – after their last pub stop that fateful night. They'd begun their dalliance in the same kitchen – an extra room off the family kitchen – where she and Madame's L'ecole du Cuisine spent all day, every day. Lubricated with booze and a devil-may-care attitude, they'd never made it past the school's work counter.

Madame had not been out of town, but had returned early from what was supposed to be a getaway weekend with her husband, interrupted by Mr Chenault's business. Lydia could still hear the sharply inhaled breath, the tone of disapproval in a litany of French accusations Madame hurled at Pierre. She'd ignored Lydia, as if she'd been a street rat.

It had been the most humiliating moment of her life. She'd known there was no way she'd ever be able to roll out pie dough on Madame's teaching counter again.

'Hey. You still with me?' Stanley asked.

'I am. But I'm still mad, Stanley. I don't like it that you for one second thought I knew Pierre was going to show up here, acting like the arrogant donkey he is, and not tell you.'

'You've been known to keep things to yourself if you're concerned it'll upset me.'

She knew he was referring to when she hadn't told him she and Grandma were in deep with investigating Louie's murder, or when she'd found herself in a pickle that could have cost her life.

'True. But you showed up in time to save the day.'

'I did nothing of the sort. You're the one who brought down the killer in the end.' Stanley whistled. 'I'm glad you're not dealing with that anymore. I was never more terrified than when I thought I was going to lose you for good.'

Warmth flushed over her at his words and she stood on her tiptoes to give him a quick kiss. 'Never. Now, I'd better get back to work.'

'Yeah, I've got to get back to the case files the partnership gave me to study. But I'm available later tonight, if you are. Please?' The flicker in Stanley's eyes made several parts of her flicker with desire.

'Grandma's supposed to be going to her ballroom dancing class with Nowicki. We'd have the loft to ourselves for a few hours. Unless you want to meet me out here again?'

'Honestly, Lyd, I prefer meeting you here. It's like we're camping out, and definitely more private. Until we each get our own place, it's the most alone we can get.'

'OK, well, then I'll either meet you here, or if I get home before you do, we'll drive back out here together.' She didn't add that she'd slept out here last night. Stanley worried too much about her as it was.

'I think you might need stitches, hon.' He stared at her forehead, his brows drawn together.

'Naw. It's clotting up OK, or I'd look a lot worse. I'll be fine. Stop worrying.'

'I'll never not worry about you, Lydia. I love you.'

'I love you, too.'

His overprotectiveness was touching, sure, but unnecessary. The solitary nature of the lakeside community seemed eerie to Stanley

because, like her, he was used to having his neighbors geograph-
ically close by, and regular suburban street activity on the other
side of his windows. But as far as she was concerned, the quiet
at her café location was a godsend, a real peace amidst the chaos
of summer visitors from places as far flung as New York City.
And Ottawa, Ontario.

Stanley drove off and Lydia turned back to the café, ready to get
back to work. The outside kitchen door burst open as Chloe and
Elodie spilled out onto the stoop, laughing.

'Chloe, Elodie!' Lydia jogged up to them and all three
exchanged embraces. 'I've missed you both so much.'

'Really? We wouldn't know it from how often we don't hear
from you.' Elodie spoke the words with a smile, but Lydia heard
the hurt.

'I know, I'm a terrible pen pal.'

'You didn't even let us know why you'd left, not really.' Chloe
tossed her long blonde hair over her shoulder, her grey eyes a
match for the lake water.

'I thought I told you I was rude to Delphine. I decided to quit. It
was a decision more about my stupid pride than anything else.'

'So it had nothing to do with Pierre?' The quick glance she and
Elodie exchanged caught Lydia off guard.

'No, not at all. And for the record, as much as I knew I had to
leave, Delphine had asked me to go too, in the same conversation.'
After her chat with Delphine in the restroom it was important to
her that she own up to her side of the mess.

'Pierre never got over you from what we hear.' Chloe sniffed.

Lydia could understand their hurt at her not confiding in them
fully before she left the pastry school, but they suddenly seemed
very immature. They were younger than her by several years, but
she remembered having long, meaningful talks about life with
them that lasted into the wee hours. Had they changed, or had
she? 'Pierre and I were nothing more than a fling. I'm back with
my boyfriend, Stanley.' It didn't seem enough to refer to Stanley
as her boyfriend since they'd gotten back together, but they weren't
engaged. Yet.

'That's wonderful, Lydia. I mean it.' Chloe nodded enthusiastically.
Elodie didn't react.

'It is. And you both knew I wanted to open my own place.' She motioned at the building. 'I have. What have you been up to? You'll be finishing pastry school in the fall, right?'

'I will. Elodie has to stay on to retake part of the course.'

'What? I can't imagine . . . you were the best in our class, for heaven's sake.' Lydia had envied Elodie's cool demeanor, her ability to whisk, roll, boil or bake no matter the stress imposed upon her by Delphine or the other students.

Elodie snickered. 'Let's just say I didn't agree with how Madame wanted her profiteroles filled.'

Lydia turned to Chloe for more information. 'As in cream puffs?'

Chloe mock shuddered. 'Don't ever tell Madame that cream puffs, éclairs, or profiteroles are the same thing. You should know this, Lydia. Don't tell me you've forgotten how unreasonable she is?'

'Yet you've both stayed in the school.'

'Not everyone has a family business to go back to.' Elodie's sharp tone brought Lydia up short. She'd told the women about her family, about Wienewski's Wieners & Meats. She never thought of them as anything but working class, but belatedly she remembered that Elodie had been raised by a single, hard drinking father. The pastry school had been Elodie's ticket out of a life of poverty, thanks to an anonymous scholarship she'd received with the pastry school's acceptance. Now Elodie's chance at a better life seemed to be under threat from Delphine over a batch of profiteroles.

'No, you're right.' Lydia didn't have the inclination or time to fill the women in on all that had transpired after she came back. Pop's stroke, the days wondering if he'd live, much less recover. The months she'd fought to keep the shop open, ready to let go of her café and bakery hopes.

And then, she'd literally stumbled upon a murdered corpse in their family's backyard sausage smoker.

'Elodie will finish up, and I'll stay in Ottawa while she's still at school. Then we're both going to move to Toronto together and get jobs at the best restaurants!' Chloe's excitement was infectious.

'What? Wonderful!' Lydia high-fived each of them, then looked at her watch. 'I'm so sorry but I have to get back inside. Madame said she's coming back through here with your group on your way back to Canada on Sunday. Let's sit together and have coffee like we used to, OK?' No way was she going to call Madame 'Delphine' in front of Elodie again.

'That sounds great, Lydia. I can't wait!' Chloe gave her an impulsive hug. Elodie offered her a nod and they went back to where the group was waiting for their taxis to arrive.

As Lydia reentered the kitchen she couldn't help but wonder what was really going on with Elodie and Chloe, and the fall-out that must have occurred between Elodie and Delphine. Her friends seemed so different from how she remembered them, far less chummy for sure. Elodie's slam about Lydia's implied nepotism had stunned her. Was the profiterole drama just the tip of the iceberg? Maybe she'd find out when they spoke over coffee in a few days.

After Delphine's group left, the entire Lydia's Lakeside staff worked straight through the long, unseasonably warm afternoon to provide meals an hour past closing time, another first for the café. Lydia had to wonder if the visibly full parking lot at lunch had helped spread the word that her place was worth a try.

Now, to prep for tomorrow.

'Teri, can you make the cookie sandwiches for me? The cookies are cooled, and there's a jar of raspberry jam in the refrigerator.' Lydia wiped her hands free of rye flour with a towel. It had been a long day, and they'd closed almost an hour ago. Grandma had left two hours earlier, and she'd sent Freddy home an hour ago.

'Sure, but I'm not done putting out the fresh linens for tomorrow yet.'

'I've got it.' Lydia did quick mental math. 'I'm going to run out of napkins, though, if we don't do a load tonight. Will you please take them home for me, throw the red napkins in their own load on hot, and I'll get to the whites . . .' She stopped. If she and Stanley were going to stay out here tonight, she wouldn't be able to bleach the white tablecloths herself.

A sly grin worked its way across Teri's pretty face, accentuated by her glossy peach lipstick. 'You're not going home, are you?'

'Maybe. Maybe not.' Lydia and Teri were close, but Lydia had never been comfortable talking to her sister, ten years her junior, about her sex life.

'You know, I've told you about me and Johnny. You can stop turning red whenever I ask you about your love life with Stanley. We're all adults here.' Teri had always been wise beyond her years but her youthful appearance belied her proposal. Her recent spiral permanent wave made her naturally straight, fine hair into a mass of blonde half-curls, which she had pulled back in a low ponytail and shoved under the hairnet Lydia and New York State health codes required. Technically Teri, as a waitress, didn't need the net but the last thing Lydia needed was for a customer to find one of Teri's corkscrew hairs adorning their scoop of potato salad on Fish Fry Friday.

'Well, the fact is, Stanley and I haven't had a whole lot of time together. It's hard, with both of our schedules.'

'Plus you live with Grandma. At least I can either sneak Johnny into my room through the window or we use his basement bedroom when his parents aren't home. Although his mother is pretty nosy, and very judge-y. She looks at me like I'm a seductress. As if her little boy would never partake in such sinful acts of lust.'

'Stop. No shame around your sex life. Mom never meant for us to be ashamed of having sex, if you ask me. She was only raising us the way she'd been, and she was terrified we'd get pregnant, or that Ted would make her a grandmother too soon. Grandma would have your *dupa*, too, if she heard you. Like she says, our sexuality is to be celebrated!'

'Hey, I'm all for that. High five!' Teri held up her palm and Lydia smacked it with her own. 'Is that why you have the stash of clean clothes, toothpaste, and blankets in back of the coat check?'

Lydia paused. 'When did you have time to find that?'

Teri shrugged. 'I wanted to see how far you'd gotten with the bakery display case.'

'And what do you think?' She'd already had a refrigerated display case that could double as a serving counter installed next to the large coat check room at the entry, and used it to store desserts that needed to be kept cold.

'You've done good, sis.' Teri-speak for 'excellent.'

'Thanks.'

The café had started as a general store with a soda fountain back in the 1930s, then evolved into a fully-fledged, upscale dining establishment. Lydia planned to install a long coat rack for the winter months, and convert the roomy coat check room and ticket counter into her bakery area. She'd sell all of the desserts and breads she served on the menu, plus seasonal items like Polish coffee cake, placek, and her family's beloved Christmas cut-out cookies with her Aunt Dot's frosting. In addition to the classic Polish American fare, she made several fruit and cream pies and tarts that customers already ordered to take home. So far the most popular was her coconut custard, followed by lemon meringue. Belatedly she realized that her time at pastry school under Delphine's tutelage had inspired the latter.

With the constant talk of pierogi, she realized that adding a display of them alongside the sweets might not be a bad idea. She'd need a separate, smaller refrigerated display case. Which reminded her that she didn't have the revenue to support such a purchase. The prize money from the pierogi cook-off would have been a nice windfall.

Needing a distraction from beating herself up all over again, she turned her thoughts to what she could afford, for now.

'Why so quiet, Lydia?' Teri displayed an ability to empathize every so often, offering a glimpse of the woman Lydia thought she'd grow into. After she got through her current 'it's all about me' phase.

'Ah, no reason, not really. Just the usual to-do lists running through my mind.'

'Your old teacher's visit upset you, didn't it?'

'I'm fine.' Lydia wasn't ready to talk about her conversation with Delphine yet. That was something she'd save for Grandma. 'I've been thinking of lots of things I'd like to change around here, is all.'

'Like?' Teri prompted.

'I'm going to trust you with something, Teri. You can't mention it to Mom or Pop.' Lydia hadn't even told Grandma about this particular plan yet. 'I'm going to eventually make the small cottage out behind this building livable again. Not this season, but hopefully by next year. That way Grandma can have the loft apartment to herself and I can be right here for my baking days.' Which were Monday through Thursday, beginning at two-thirty a.m. She'd gotten away with her cheat method of raising the bread dough – making it at night and putting it in the refrigerator to slow the yeast productivity – but it wouldn't work once they opened for breakfast and had the full-serve bakery display case.

'Then I can share the garage apartment with Grandma!' Teri's eyes sparkled as she verbally nixed the idea of Grandma having the place to herself. 'You like living with her, right?'

'I do, she's the best roommate ever, but maybe think about that. Grandma would be better moving into your room, on the main floor, if you're serious about taking the loft.'

'Oh, I get it. So in case she ever has a stroke like Pop—'

'Don't even say that! She's in great health, anyway.' It was true. Mary Romano Wienewski looked more like thirty-five than her actual sixty-five years. Her figure was still girlish thanks to the super-duper lifting bra she swore by. When Lydia had once commented on the lingerie's impressive architecture, Grandma hadn't blinked before replying 'you gotta haul the titties up after a certain age, honey bunny.'

It was only upon close inspection that the fine lines between her brows and around her lips were visible, that one noticed the arthritis that had crept into her knuckles.

She and Teri worked together for the next hour in their comfortable, familiar way, until Lydia ran out to the dining room to gather the remaining dirty linens. She cleared the salt and pepper shakers and floral centerpiece from Delphine's table onto a stainless-steel utility cart, and placed all the napkins in the center of the table and wrapped them with the tablecloth.

Something hard pressed into her palm through the linen.

'What the heck?' Digging through the fabric she discovered a small navy-sequined and beaded cigarette case. Delphine had forgotten it. Remembering that Delphine and her students were staying at a lakeside hotel less than a mile away, she dropped the bundle of linens back on the table and walked over to the dining room phone that sat atop the former soda fountain counter. She pulled the phone book from the shelf below and flipped to the yellow pages.

'Hotel . . . there you are.' Lydia dialed the number.

'Acorn Bay Hotel, Candy speaking. How may I help you?' the receptionist answered.

'May I please be connected to Mad— I mean, Delphine Chenault?'

'Hang on and I'll put you through.'

Lydia waited through a couple of loud clicks and two rings before Madame answered.

'*Alo?*'

'*Oui*, I mean, Hello Delphine, it's Lydia Wienewski. You forgot your cigarette case at the café. It's navy blue. It is yours, correct?'

'Oh, *mon Dieu*! Yes, it's mine. I thought I left it in the car. In fact, I was on my way outside to get it when the phone rang. I have more cigarettes here in my suitcase, of course, but that case is special to me. It was my mother's, you see. She passed away last year.' That would have been when Lydia was still a student under Delphine, yet she'd never known about it. Delphine had never discussed her personal life with her students.

'I can drop it off at your hotel if you'd like, or you can get it either tomorrow on your way to Chautauqua or when you stop back here for pastries and coffee in a few days.'

'No, please don't bother. I'll stop by and get it later, after the class returns from their late-night snack. The students want to try Buffalo chicken wings, and some local ice cream. I am not a fan of deep-fried fare, to be honest, and my hips do not need the rich dairy.'

Lydia didn't bother defending her hometown's best fare – next to her pierogi and Wienewskis' kielbasa, of course. She was anxious to get ready for Stanley's visit. As grateful as she was for mending fences with Delphine, she wasn't about to lose precious time with Stanley.

'We're closed. No one will be here.' The lie came easily.

'There's no money in it, only the cigarettes, and your café is in a safe area, *non*? Can you leave it on the front porch or in a post box, perhaps? I'll swing by and get it when I can. Either later tonight or early in the morning.'

'Sure thing. Tell you what, Delphine. I don't trust leaving it out front. There's a milk delivery box on the stoop at the back employee entrance. The kitchen door you went out of earlier. I'll put it in there. Does that work for you?' Lydia sent up a silent prayer that

Madame wouldn't come until the morning, because by nightfall she hoped to be in a blissful snooze after some alone time with Stanley. She didn't want anything waking them up.

'Marvelous. I thank you again, Lydia. You are a gem and I already miss you. *Au revoir.*' She disconnected.

''Bye,' Lydia spoke to the receiver, then hung up the phone. She needed to take the small case out to the dairy box, before she forgot. She crossed the kitchen, holding up her hand to Teri. 'Hang on, be right back.'

The sturdy tin dairy box was the size of a milk crate and located on the back kitchen door's stoop, at the base of the steps that led to the deck. Lydia opened the hinged cover and placed the cigarette case inside. She hadn't used the box at all since Mr Gorski had her order delivered while someone was in the café, or she brought it in herself from Cheektowaga.

She took a moment to daydream about how nice it would be to be able to serve the deck customers from the kitchen by using the back steps, without having to go through the dining room. Maybe she should consider moving ahead with the deck repairs sooner than she'd planned. If they had a warm summer, her sales could make up for the expenditure in one season.

Once back inside, it was time to let Teri go for the evening.

'Are these all of the linens? And don't worry if you don't make it home tonight. I'll make sure they get into the dryer. And because you're being so nice to me, I'll fold them for you and bring them back with me tomorrow.' Teri stood next to two large plastic bins containing dozens of stacked raspberry sandwich cookies. 'I'm ready to head home.'

'Great.' Before she thought twice, Lydia walked over to Teri and gave her a quick hug and peck on the cheek. 'Thank you, sis. I owe you one.'

'You owe me nothing. Just make sure you make the night worth it for yourself. And Stanley.' Teri shot her a wink and erupted into giggles.

'Thanks, sis.'

Teri left out the back door.

Finally Lydia was alone, with plenty of time to set up for tomorrow's menu before Stanley arrived.

It was actually beginning to feel like a date night.

FIVE

The next morning, the scent of freshly brewed coffee woke Lydia an instant before she felt Stanley's lips on hers.

'Good morning.' He waited for her to sit up before handing her the white porcelain mug. 'I hope it's OK that I used a café cup. I couldn't find anything else.'

She took two full sips before she replied. 'That's fine. I do have a stash of employee dishes but they're on a shelf next to the linens, all the way in the back of the cubby. You wouldn't know to find them unless I told you.'

He offered a quiet smile. 'I didn't get that far. I was hoping to get the coffee made before you woke up. It's hard to leave your side. Last night was a treat.'

'Even on a hard pallet?' She shifted to lean her head on his shoulder.

'It's a heck of a lot more comfortable than camping, or—'

'In the back of the Gremlin.' They both laughed. Lydia's backside ached just thinking about the many inventive ways they'd had sex over the years. 'I haven't told anyone else but Teri yet, but I'm going to fix up the cottage here. It's time for me to get some space from my parents and I need to be closer to the bakery for the earlier jobs.'

'But you'll be further from me.'

'Please. We hardly have time together as it is. And this gives us way more privacy, right?'

'Right.' He smiled. 'Let me help you with the fix-up.'

'I'm counting on it.' Lydia wielded a good paint brush while Stanley had completed several home renovation projects alongside his father. 'We're a good team.'

'We are. But Lyd?'

'Yeah?'

'You'd better be absolutely certain you're ready to be apart from your grandma.'

'We'll never be apart. We work together every day.'

They enjoyed their coffee for several long minutes, the camping lantern the only illumination in the back of the dining room. Instead of setting the pallet up between the soda fountain and back wall, they'd opted for the far corner behind a built-in room divider that held the sound system left by the former owner.

'Will you let me make you breakfast?' Stanley asked. 'If you'll trust me in the kitchen, that is.'

'Well, if you insist . . .' she teased. 'Are you kidding me? Yes, of course!' She jumped up, wrapped herself in the hand crocheted Afghan. 'I'll go get dressed while you cook. I have to open the butcher shop today. Pop's got his six-month check-up with the neurologist.'

'Has it been that long already?' Stanley mused. 'It seems like it was yesterday when you came back home just before his stroke.'

'I know.' She sighed. 'A lot has happened since then, hasn't it?' Including taking over the butcher shop while Pop recovered, doing all the preparation to open her café and bakery, and of course, solving Louie's murder. 'But the most important thing is that you and I are back on track, wouldn't you say?'

'Definitely. And you're making your career dreams come true.' He took her empty mug, gave her another kiss, and stood. 'Meet me in the kitchen in ten.'

Lydia smiled as she watched him walk through the swinging door, her gaze lingering on his dupa, Polish for bottom. Even in bulky grey sweatpants, Stanley's sexiness was undeniable.

She plucked her clothing from the various places it had landed last night: the floor, the soda bar, one of the artificial ficus trees; her bra always ended up in the strangest places when she and Stanley made love. As she headed for the swing door to get to the employee restroom a pale sliver of light caught in her peripheral vision. It was the back door to the balcony. She looked at her watch. She didn't have long, not if she and Stanley were going to enjoy breakfast together. But a few moments of staring out across the water was better than none.

Dressed in a thin-strapped, white satin camisole and jeans, she put on her favorite sweatshirt and slid into her white leather sneakers, firmly fastening the Velcro ankle straps that were the latest trend. Grandma called it a 'silly fad' but Lydia disagreed.

Aerobics exercise videos were all the rage and she didn't envision physical fitness ever going out of style.

She trotted over to the door, and smiled at the way her stomach still shimmied with excitement as she opened it. Her dream had really come true. She stepped onto the wooden deck, inhaling the fresh air as the waves lapped softly on the beach below, against the café's foundation.

Giving up the comforts of the garage apartment to deal with faulty plumbing and iffy electricity in the adjacent cottage was a fair trade for this view.

Focused on the water and ever-brightening horizon, Lydia almost didn't see the broken railing. Lucky for her she glanced down at it before she reached the very edge of the deck.

She blinked.

There was a small gap where the railing had broken in two. The two-by-four that had served as a railing had been shaky ever since she bought the place, but Lydia hadn't expected it to break so soon. She figured she'd have it fixed before the first snowflakes flew, in October. How had it broken? It was still in one piece yesterday morning when she'd grabbed a few minutes with her coffee out here.

Her stomach sank at the prospect of the needed emergency repair. The insurance agent had made it clear that Lydia had to meet all safety codes at federal, state, county, and local levels 'in order to keep your establishment open for business.' She wasn't using the deck for serving, and kept the back doors closed and locked for this exact reason.

Except for when she wanted to go out on the deck, like now.

She decidedly ignored the railing dilemma for the time being, but she was careful to stay to the left of the broken section. This was her few moments of peace each day, the single time her brain was able to shut down its constant activity.

Lake Erie wasn't the Atlantic – she'd seen the ocean once, as a kid, on a trip to Long Island to visit Pop's cousins – but it was close enough. As far as Buffalo was concerned, it was the only body of water that mattered after the Niagara River and Falls. When the lake was calm, all was well in Western New York.

This morning the water was dotted with frothy whitecaps as far as she could see, the breeze brisk. The warm summer air fought with the colder gusts that whipped her hair around, blowing strands in her mouth as she stared out at the horizon.

'*Cawwww!*' The brown mottled female seagull screamed at her as it careened by, doing an extra circle no more than five feet above her before it landed atop the rusted weathervane pointing northwest. The goosebumps on her forearms were accurate; rough weather ahead.

'I hear you, Dolly. Where's Kishka?' And for that matter, where was Pacha this morning?

A flash of bright white punctuated by a spot of bright yellow flew past her, solving one mystery.

'Kishka, I didn't forget you, boy.' She had her back to the water as she stared up at the pair. Seagulls mated for life and while she didn't know a whole lot about them, working and eventually living here she hoped to watch them raise several generations of chicks.

'*Caw.*' Kishka was more to the point than Dolly, staring down at Lydia from his perch next to his mate. Lydia had no problem with the pair, as they were making their nest on a corner of the large storage shed roof. She'd enticed them there with day-old bread, sometimes soaked in gravy when the weather was on the harsher side this past spring. Pop thought she was nuts for feeding wild birds, but he'd thought the same about Luna and her brood when she finally told him she'd fed the cats behind the butcher shop this past winter.

'You'll get your bread in a bit.' She had to be careful to feed them when no one could observe her – the last thing she needed was for someone to report to the board of health that she was encouraging wild animals to set up shop alongside her food establishment.

Kishka let out another harsh cry. The large web-footed avian puffed out his chest and cocked his head as he stared at her, as if to ask where the heck his breakfast was. Pacha had made zero attempts at stalking the bird since the cat's relocation from Cheektowaga, and Lydia didn't blame him. The gull was capable of serious damage with that beak, she suspected.

'You're going to have to wait, Kishka!'

'*Caw.*' Kishka was nonplussed by her shout.

She'd fallen for Kishka the first time he'd approached her, on day one at the lake, alongside his mate, Dolly. According to the previous owner, the pair had been the bane of his existence, returning year after year to build a nest on either the café roof or nearby barn. Lydia had decided then and there that she'd befriend the pair. Dolly's mottled plumage reminded Lydia of a doll she'd had as a girl, that had a brown and white polka dot dress, hence the gull's name.

Grandma had picked Kishka for the male, after the sausage delicacy made with pig's blood. 'Because he's a tough one, that bird,' Grandma had observed.

Lydia looked at her watch. 'Dolly, tell your man to stop cawing at me. You know it's not feeding time yet.' They'd be waiting until almost sunset, and she'd feed them on the beach or closer to where they nested atop the old barn. As much as Lydia loved animals, customers didn't appreciate them, and the board of health even less.

Soft pats sounded on the deck stairs to her left and she turned to see her favorite bundle of peach fur make his way toward her.

'Good morning, Pacha.'

The large orange tabby wound himself around her legs, his purrs insistent against her calves.

'Come here, sweetie pie.' She lifted the soft fluffy cat and hugged him to her.

'*Meow.*' He wriggled to be let go but she held on, not releasing him before she managed to kiss his pink nose. At his indignant grimace, she laughed. Pacha jumped out of her arms, raced away.

The wind that frothed the wave tips was a constant reminder that she was indeed lakeside and not twenty minutes inland, in her hometown of Cheektowaga. It was mid-June, which might mean almost-summer on the Roman calendar, but Buffalo abided by its own weather. Her skin broke out in gooseflesh at the bit of a chill that remained in the air, a reminder that literally five weeks ago snowflakes had swirled in the same space. She'd walked out on the deck and had found it hard to imagine it ever being warm enough to serve patrons al fresco here.

The French door opened again as Stanley stepped outside, holding two mugs of coffee.

'I'm sorry. I've taken longer than ten minutes out here, haven't I?' she asked.

'I'm glad you're relaxing. You deserve a break.' He handed her the mug with the lighter coffee. Stanley always knew how to make hers with the perfect amount of half and half.

'Thanks.' The warm ceramic felt good in her cold fingers.

'Who were you talking to?'

'Dolly and Kishka.' She pointed at the birds, who perched together and pointedly ignored the humans below. 'And Pacha, but he took off.'

'Right.' He slugged down half his drink and turned to the water. She followed suit. The waves were almost nonexistent with the tide out, and the water's surface reflected the blue sky. Lydia knew she'd never tire of this view.

'You've got a little problem with your railing, Lyd,' Stanley observed.

'I know.' She sighed. 'The wind was stronger than I realized last night. It needed to be replaced, anyway, but now I'll have to get it done sooner. It's a safety issue.'

'Only if you allow patrons out here.' He replied in what she was coming to recognize as his lawyerly voice. 'Good thing you have the chains up with the warning signs at the bottom of each stairway.'

'And inside the dining room doors.' She pecked him on the cheek. 'Thanks to my personal attorney.'

'Not yet. Don't jinx me.' He was so superstitious about getting his law degree.

'Stanley, you're the smartest person I know. You're going to ace your finals and the BAR exam.'

'I'm still a year out, Lyd.'

'Perfect timing. You'll graduate and I'll have the cottage completely redone by then. It'll be a full-time house and not just a summer cottage.' Her dream might be verging on fantasy, but with a little luck and a lot of revenue, it could happen by next year. It would be so nice to be able to move out here sooner, though.

'You'll make more money if your customers know they can eat outside. It's a big draw, waterfront dining.' He sipped his coffee as he leaned against the building, next to her. Neither of them were keen on heights, something they found out on the Comet rollercoaster as teenagers. Lydia had cried, tears streaming down her face the entire rickety ride on the wooden coaster on the Canadian shore of Lake Erie. Stanley had barfed the moment the ride ended. She giggled and snuggled up to his side, wrapping one arm around his waist.

'What's so funny?' He smelled of coffee, minty deodorant, and pure Stanley. She knew no place she felt safer.

'Remember when you threw up your bright blue cotton candy at Crystal Beach?' She referred to the amusement park.

He groaned. 'Don't remind me. I feel that nauseous before every single exam right now.'

'I'm sorry. But it was funny.'

'Yeah, you and I have come a long way, Lydia.'

'We have.' They kissed.

'So back to your business. When do you think you'll get the deck fixed by?' Stanley motioned toward the unprotected spot.

'I was hoping by Labor Day, at least.' The beginning of September was less than three months away. 'It's going to depend on how well we do over the next month. We're just starting out here, you know.' Of course he knew but Stanley's brain was focused on the law, not balancing books.

'Isn't that when you're going to close for the season?' He pushed back from the wall, finished his coffee.

'It was, but I was thinking that maybe I'd keep the bakery open, or at least going, through the fall, maybe even all winter. I'm not sure yet. I can sell the baked goods and pierogi out of the butcher shop, either way. It's an easy way to keep my cashflow going if I do have to close down in the winter.'

'Smart thinking.' He stared off at the horizon and they stood there in happy silence until the railing's ragged break beckoned her forward. Unable to tamp down her curiosity, she slowly stepped to the end of the deck planks and peered over the edge.

'Careful.' Stanley wasn't being patronizing, not in the least. In fact, he knew Lydia down to her bones and often reminded her that she had a penchant for throwing caution to the wind. Like when she'd put herself between a pistol and Grandma two months ago, facing down a killer.

Stop thinking about murder.

'I promise, I'm not going to do anything stupid. I like to see what washes up at low tide, is all.' Usually it was nothing more than seaweed and empty aluminum beer cans, the odd glass soda bottle. She stopped a couple of inches before the edge and peered down.

All thoughts of the deck, the railing, her café shattered into oblivion at what lay before her.

Twenty feet below the deck, on the concrete pilings and boulders where the waves swished against the shore, lay a body.

A woman with long brunette hair. Wearing a white sundress, navy blue cardigan, and with one electric blue heel on her left foot. She was lying facedown but recognition was instant. Lydia blinked. She wanted to crawl into the safety bubble of denial, pretend it couldn't possibly be whom she thought. Lydia had watched her eat pierogi in the cafe mere hours ago.

Madame Delphine.

Lydia's blood morphed to cold plasma before she began gasping for her next breaths. The mug dropped from her hand and fell through the wind to land with a crash on the rocks below, several yards to the right of Delphine's head. Which was the problem. While Delphine's body appeared relaxed, as if she were taking a facedown rest, the sickening angle of her head left no doubt that Madame Delphine Chenault was no more.

She was dead.

SIX

The guttural cry ripped from her throat before she had a chance to turn back to Stanley.

'Lyd? What is it?' Stanley stepped up next to her, following her stare. 'What the . . .' He took in the scene with amazing alacrity. He grasped her shoulders, turned her away from the horror. But it was too late for comfort.

'She was eating my pierogi not long ago, Stanley.' Her voice sounded hollow, as if it belonged to someone else.

'Lydia, go inside and call the police. I'll go down to the beach and wait with her.'

'No! Wait! Maybe she's still OK.' Denial was a baffling monster. Her brain knew that there was no way the body below was alive, but her heart hadn't caught up to the facts yet. 'Let me go check.' She shrugged out of Stanley's embrace and raced down the stairs that were perhaps ricketier than the shattered railing.

Please, please, let Madame only look like she's dead.

'Lydia, stop!' Stanley bellowed, his steps heavy behind her. She heard a loud crack but didn't – couldn't – stop. Not until her feet landed on the sandy beach and she'd climbed over the massive slabs of slippery concrete, crawling the last bit to reach the woman she'd only too recently mended ties to.

She needn't have bothered. The unnatural position of Delphine's neck bone reminded Lydia of the hundreds – thousands – of chickens, geese and ducks she'd helped Pop with at the butcher block. A dark stain had seeped onto a rock next to Delphine's head, and down by her waist there was a second pool of what she assumed had been Delphine's blood. There was no doubt she was staring at the woman's corpse.

The tide was still out, but it had begun its resurgence. A detached part of her thought that what remained of Madame Delphine was in threat of being washed away, bit by bit, with every wave of the slowly rising tide.

There was no use feeling for a pulse, but she had to, on the

off chance that poor Delphine still breathed. Her shaking hand
stilled against the cold skin. There was no movement under her
fingertips.

Lydia straightened and turned back, seeking comfort where she
knew she could always count on it. But Stanley wasn't right behind
her, and she had to stand up straight to be able to see him. He sat
on the bottom step of the deck's stairway, holding his ankle.

'Stanley!' She made her way over to him, but he waved her off
before she reached him.

'No! I'm fine! I just need a sec. Go back inside and call the
police. Use the kitchen door, I unlocked it when I made breakfast
and fed Pacha. Now, Lydia!'

Stanley's urgent tone was exactly what she needed to get herself
into gear, to shake out of blanket of shock that threatened to
overwhelm her.

Keeping her feet solidly under her was the priority. She couldn't
afford to slip on the algae-coated rocks so she focused instead
on putting one sneakered foot in front of the other until she
reached where the sloping dirt path met the rocky beach and
began her climb back up to the parking lot. Once she'd climbed
up the embankment, her breath coming in brief bursts, she ran
through the thin grove of pine trees, needles from low hanging
branches of the trees scratching at her. The hooded sweatshirt and
jeans protected her from the worst of it. Sweat dripped from her
forehead and there was an annoying sting above her left brow
where she'd hit her head yesterday.

It felt like an hour but it couldn't have been more than a minute
or two before she cleared the trees and ran out onto the café's
graveled parking lot.

Lydia stopped short at the sight of a car parked smack dab in
the middle of her path, blocking her from the kitchen door. She
hadn't noticed the station wagon when she'd run from the deck
stairs.

It wasn't some random stranger's car, though, it was Grandma's.
The long, unwieldly hulk of a car was parked perpendicular to the
lake front, the driver's seat empty. Relief washed over her cold
shock. Grandma would know how to handle this. She took off at
a run, intending to round the back of the wagon, assuming Grandma
was inside preparing for opening.

Peals of laughter rang out from inside the car and cut through her labored breathing. Lydia halted mid-stride.

What the heck?

'Oh, Harry, you are too funny.' Grandma's voice tinkled from the back of the wagon, from which she and Harry Nowicki were climbing out. More like unfolding out of the space that was roomy for seated passengers but cramped for two senior citizens. Narrowing her eyes, Lydia saw that Grandma had put the seats down to allow for a completely flat space.

'Here, give me your hands, Mary dear.' Nowicki, clad in only boxer shorts and a white sleeveless T-shirt, emerged first and turned to help Grandma, wrapped in the cotton quilt she kept in her car at all times for 'weather emergencies.'

'Grandma?' Lydia's query sounded more like an accusation thanks to her shortness of breath and frenzied state.

Nowicki whipped around to face her. Belatedly, Lydia realized his undershorts were covering more than his bare dupa. She'd bet her bottom dollar that wasn't a length of kielbasa tenting the front of the detective's paisley print boxer shorts.

Jesus. Mary. And Joseph.

'Well, good morning, honey bunny. Were you catching the sunrise, too? Wasn't it beautiful?' Grandma spoke as if her frosted peach lipstick wasn't smeared all over her face, as if she didn't look like Lydia's worst clown nightmare. As if she weren't naked under the quilt. Lydia knew her grandmother was naked because she spied a pile of pink clothing inside the opened back of the wagon. Grandma looked past Lydia to the café's kitchen door.

'Oh, good morning, Stanley!' Grandma waved at him. Stanley lifted a hand more in confusion than acknowledgement. Lydia jerked back into action.

'I . . . I can't deal with this.' She held up her hands palm-out in front of her. 'We've got an emergency. I can't talk. There's a dead body in the lake, or I mean, on the beach, oh I don't know! I have to call the cops.' She threw the words over her shoulder as she took off for the café.

'Hang on, Lydia!' Nowicki's demand boomed across the parking lot.

At his commanding tone, Lydia stopped, turned back.

Nowicki was shoving a leg into his trousers, thank the Saints above, but he paused, one leg in and balancing on the other, and gave her a hard look.

'Did you say "dead body?"'

She nodded. 'I have to call the police.' Belatedly she remembered who she was talking to. Not only was Harry Nowicki Grandma's boyfriend, he was a Cheektowaga Police detective. 'Unless . . . unless you can handle it?' Nowicki was a very good detective. He'd know what to do.

'Where is it, Lydia? The body? Show me.' He pulled up his pants and buckled them as he switched from Grandma's Romeo to the Sherlock of Buffalo.

Lydia knew what Nowicki was thinking. It was the same thing that all of the detectives on the TV shows she and Grandma watched often brought up. Delphine was dead, so there was no urgency making the call in order to save a life. And Nowicki was a law enforcement official, thank heaven. If she could turn her sense of responsibility for reporting the tragedy ASAP over to anyone, it was Detective Harry Nowicki.

'It's over there, on the rocks. She's there, I mean.' She began to walk back toward the beach.

'Go ahead and wait for me. Don't touch anything. I need to grab my camera.'

Lydia walked past Stanley again, who stared at her with a mix of confusion and pain in his eyes. 'What are you doing?'

'Detective Nowicki's going to take a look, probably so we can call it in right. I'm going back down there with him.'

Stanley's pained expression briefly smoothed. 'That's a relief. That Detective Nowicki's here, I mean.' He stood up on the step and she noted the smallest glimmer of a wince as he applied weight to his injured ankle.

'Oh no! You've really hurt yourself. Let me help you into the kitchen first.' She looked over her shoulder, at where she'd left Grandma and Nowicki. Nowicki was quickly closing the distance between them, wearing a jacket and camera bag slung over his shoulder.

Stanley shook his head. 'No, no. I'm good. I need to catch my breath is all. You go with Detective Nowicki. Go with him, Lydia, and . . .' Reluctance turned to resignation, then decisiveness.

'And what? What is it, Stanley?'

'I was going to tell you to stay out of it.' His laugh came out like a bark, no doubt due more to his sore ankle than the tragedy on the rocks. Stanley knew how to keep his cool. 'But your curiosity is a force of nature.'

'What are you hoping to find out with photos that you can't see standing right here?' Lydia spoke her thoughts, needing to understand what Nowicki wouldn't be able to answer. Why Madame Delphine, why now, why here?

Grandma had run into the kitchen to get ice for Stanley while Lydia and Nowicki stepped carefully across the rocks to Delphine's corpse. This close to the body the rocks were beyond slippery, thickly covered in the slimy green algae, and again, each step had to be premeditated. When he didn't reply right away, she continued. 'At least it's low tide, so the evidence is intact.'

Nowicki finished with a series of half a dozen or so snaps, aiming at Madame's head and neck, her back and abdomen, and the dark stains next to both. He'd instructed Lydia to stay back, closer to the seawall, but she'd crept within a few feet of Delphine as he worked.

'A camera lens is as objective as it gets, more so than our gaze. The first photographs will always be the most accurate, before time and Mother Nature disrupt the scene. Minutes matter. Trust me, Acorn Bay PD will be grateful for these.' He continued snapping for the next several minutes. When he paused to peer at the bits of ceramic on the rocks, Lydia quickly explained that she'd dropped her coffee mug.

He rested the camera against his belly as it hung at the end of a worn leather strap around his neck. His thick brows were drawn together and under his mustache his lips were a thin line.

Nowicki didn't think this was an accident. Not if his expression meant anything.

'It's possible she had a bad fall, all on her own, right, and landed on something that caused the wound?' She had to ask, had to hope. The thought of a killer being near her café, on her deck, was too dark, too sinister to contemplate, even if her gut instinct about Delphine's terrible fate was taking her in that direction.

'I doubt it.' A brief shake of his head.

'Why?' Her teeth began to chatter and not from the light breeze.

Dread and apprehension mixed with validation that her hunch was correct. Delphine hadn't slipped from the deck. She'd been killed.

'Look, I'm not sure. It could be an accident, or suicide. There's no way to determine the cause until we have a full autopsy and forensic report. This isn't my jurisdiction so I'm not going to move the body to see if something foreign caused the abdominal bleeding. I'm already overstepping a bit by taking these photographs, but they're necessary.'

'Do you think it was a bullet to her abdomen?' Lydia had seen evidence of a bullet wound before, but hadn't recognized it for what it was at first glance.

'Or a knife.' Nowicki's face took on the impenetrable expression he'd worn like a Halloween mask when he'd come into her and Grandma's life at Easter. He was in full detective mode.

It was futile to try to pull any more information from him at the moment. Not with direct questions, anyway.

And one question kept throbbing against her mind in time with Lydia's ragged pulse.

Why had two murdered bodies crossed her path in such a short time? Ever, in fact?

She shook her head as if it would clear the menacing thought and stared at Nowicki.

'What exactly are you taking photos of, besides the obvious? I mean, what do you want to find?'

'I'm hoping to capture the way the blood has pooled on this side of her body, without disturbing the scene. If I move her head I might be able to see if the head injury caused her death. If I tilt her body the slightest bit I could confirm if the blood here,' he pointed to the rock her middle rested upon, 'is from a bullet wound. I can't make out an exit wound, either. Not with the way her dress is bunched here and there. But I can't risk contaminating the scene. Only a forensics team is equipped to handle this properly. All I can do is make sure I've photographed every last millimeter of this scene for Acorn Bay PD to analyze later.'

He expertly wound the cannister of film before opening the back of the camera and replacing it with a fresh roll. Once again, he aimed the thirty-five-millimeter camera's lens at Delphine's head, then moved the lens down the length of her too-still form. The *click* of the camera's button and *whirr* of its lens were inaudible this close to the water, but Lydia imagined hearing the sounds just the same.

'You think it's foul play, don't you?'

This time Nowicki didn't avoid her stare or the query. 'I do, yes.' He paused, a muscle on his temple twitching. 'I've been wrong before, of course. And I don't have all of the facts yet. I'm going on my gut, which is based on years of experience. That's all.'

It was enough for Lydia, because she had the same foreboding sense that Delphine hadn't fallen by accident, and no way did she think the woman she'd spoken to yesterday would commit suicide.

Not again.

'Lydia.' His sharp tone broke her sorrow. 'Like I said, this isn't my jurisdiction. It's Acorn Bay PD's. Call nine-one-one and ask for Detective Klumpski. Tell him I'm already here.'

'Right.' Shudders began at her shoulders and she started moving before they reached her knees and made her unable to walk. 'I'll tell him you're with Cheektowaga PD.'

'No need. He knows me.'

Lydia clung to this one piece of solace in from Nowicki. It was going to be OK. He knew the Acorn Bay detective. It was a great distraction from the fact that she had what looked like a murder scene in her literal backyard.

Lydia stared out the dining room windows as she took a break from keeping the coffee pot full. The picturesque view from the café was ruined by three police cruisers, an ambulance, and several news reporters who had been ordered by the officers to remain across the street from Lydia's Lakeside Café and Bakery.

All of the dining room's drapes and blinds were open, to allow for maximum light. Lydia had seen to that the minute after she'd called the police from the kitchen phone. She learned enough from working on a murder case before that law enforcement needed a spot to ask all of the questions that were eminent.

The second thing she'd done was put on the commercial coffee pot. There was no such thing as too much coffee this morning.

'Who would have thought we'd be in a situation like this again, kiddo?' Grandma asked. They were both waiting to be questioned by either Detective Klumpski or one of his officers.

'Tell me about it.' Lydia hoped her calm demeanor was convincing. Her mind raced around its perpetual hamster wheel.

'It'll all be OK, honey bunny. Focus on the facts, the details. From what I'm hearing between your observations and Harry's, Delphine was murdered. He said there were signs of an abdominal wound? That sure sounds like foul play to me.' Grandma spoke just loud enough for only Lydia to hear. Her bright blue eyes were made all the more dazzling by her rose pink and sea foam green silk tracksuit, with a zippered jacket and matching pants. She'd bragged to Lydia that she'd found it for a song at one of the nicer shops in the Thruway Mall. The mall was a Big Deal in Cheektowaga, where the options for clothes shopping were more often limited to discount department stores, at least for Lydia's family and, more accurately, their budget.

Grandma always dressed in the current fashion with her own stamp of classiness. Today, with the ever-popular jogging suit that was a staple of Eighties' fashion she still wore her pearl stud earrings and gold necklace with the tiny charms held by a large hoop. Each charm represented something, from a grandchild's birth to the teeny tiny bingo card. Bingo was a favorite pastime, second only to reruns of *Police Woman*, and the new detective show *Cagney & Lacey*.

'I don't know. Not yet. I need time to process this, Grandma. Let me know if he tells you anything else.' Lydia glanced at Nowicki, who wore a canvas jacket over his polo-style shirt, and jeans. It was discomfiting to see him not in his usual dress shirt and tie, especially when she felt so exposed, so accused, by the on-scene police.

Why couldn't Nowicki have packed an extra suit in Grandma's station wagon? He'd look more official, at least.

Lydia wanted to question Pierre, Chloe and Elodie, the entire group that had been with Delphine. Had they all gone back to the hotel together? Did anyone know why Delphine left the hotel last night, that she'd planned to pick up her cigarette case? Lydia wasn't going to get any answers as long as she had to wait here at the mercy of the local police. She had to do something.

The milk box.

Lydia scurried to the stoop and quickly checked the milk box, silently praying that none of the on-scene police officers would stop her. Lucky for her, they were still focused on the stairs to the deck and the beach. She lifted the lid to the carton, and was greeted by sunlight glinting off the beaded cigarette case. Her fingers were mere inches from grabbing it when she stopped, let the lid fall closed. Evidence was evidence, and she had to leave this for the forensics team.

Back again in the dining room, Lydia joined everyone as they waited for Acorn Bay Police Detective Leo Klumpski to finish yet another call on the phone that hung next to the wall-length mirror behind the former soda bar.

'Oof.' Stanley sat next to her and was still in obvious pain from the wretched ankle sprain, but had refused her help back into the café and her subsequent attempt to put his leg up on a chair. He sat to her left, and Grandma was on her right at the eight-place table smack dab in the middle of the dining floor. It was next to the very table where Madame most probably had her last meal yesterday. Unless she ate the Buffalo chicken wings before she died.

Klumpski had told them all to sit together while he and his officers questioned Lydia, Stanley, Grandma and Nowicki separately in the former coat room. It had taken only an hour or so, tops, but Lydia's jaw ached from biting her tongue the entire time. No, she hadn't seen Delphine return to the bakery and café, and no, she had no personal conflicts with the pastry instructor. *Not anymore*. She'd told the investigators as much. But she left out the full details about her previous contentious relationship with the deceased. Her last foray into a criminal investigation had taught her well. The police would consider her and everyone she loved who was present as suspects until their alibis fleshed out. Lydia was honest but she wasn't a fool.

'What's taking your friend Klumpski so long, Harry?' Grandma asked.

'These investigations take time, Mary. You know that.' Nowicki grabbed one of the sweet rolls leftover from yesterday's baked goods as he replied. Lydia had placed a heaping pile of sweets on the table: rolls, doughnuts, and her specialty raspberry jam sandwich cookies. A carafe of hot coffee sat in the middle of their table. A much larger urn of the hot beverage and an even larger portion of the day-old treats was on the former soda bar.

Lydia observed her satisfied reaction to the officers helping themselves with a detachment fueled by her shock. It seemed no matter what the tragedy, there was always a need for sustenance, the sweeter and hotter the better.

'I want to know what the heck your pastry school instructor was doing on our property so late last night.' Grandma shot her a knowing glance. She'd slipped into her *Police Woman* mode, where she fancied herself as Buffalo's own Angie Dickinson.

'She left her cigarette case here and was going to pick it up,' Lydia commented. 'Except, as I told Detective Klumpski, it's still where I left it for her, in the milk box. I'm hoping that Acorn Bay PD will figure out what happened to her before her death gets announced to the public.' Lydia was shocked at her callousness, but wasn't it natural to worry about her business after seeing how Louie's murder had initially tanked the butcher shop's Easter sales? 'The Wienewskis can't afford another murder investigation. Who knows? Maybe we'll find out that Nowicki and I are wrong about our hunches, that it was a freak accident.' That would be a lot better than a second murder in less than three months.

'Hmph. Harry's gut is never wrong.' Grandma didn't sound like she would even consider the option of Delphine's death being an accident. Lydia didn't think her death was a cruel twist of chance, either.

'This won't take as long as Louie's case, right?' She posed the question to Stanley, but loud enough for the table to hear. It was her way of trying to reassure Grandma, but by the way Stanley stiffened next to her, definitely not in the same way as Nowicki had for Grandma, Lydia knew she'd picked the wrong tactic. Fortunately Grandma and Nowicki had begun their own private conversation, with Grandma furtively whispering to her paramour.

'What?' Lydia asked under her breath as she turned in her chair and faced Stanley. 'What am I missing?'

'I think that in this instance, it'll be best for you if it is determined foul play.' Stanley's attorney persona was firmly in place as he spoke to her just above a whisper. His breath smelled of cinnamon, and a pang of regret wrapped around her heart. What a lovely morning they were having before such an ugly reality encroached.

'How can you say that?' Fear scratched at her awareness. Was a murderer among them?

'If the railing was as rickety as you told me it was, you could be liable.' Stanley either didn't sense her sorrow or was ignoring it in lieu of staying on top of the situation. Which she needed to be doing, too.

'Liable?' Her tongue stuck to the roof of her mouth. She swore she felt the blood drain from her face, drop by frightened drop. 'But the café was closed when she was killed or fell. How can I be blamed? I left her cigarette case in the milk box, near the doors.' But Lydia's guilt at being responsible for Delphine returning to the café last night increased her grief at finding such a vibrant woman's life ended in such a harsh way.

'The law doesn't care about honesty, Lydia. It's about justice, what the facts show.' He must have seen her fear because he took her hand and squeezed tight. 'Before you go off the deep end, let's see what the Acorn Bay detective has to say.'

She glanced at the detective, still on the phone. His face was the color of her menu's red cabbage side dish, almost purple with what she had to believe was rage. His words grew louder until they boomed across the room.

'Well, find out!' Detective Klumpski huffed out the directive before he slammed the receiver on its hook. He removed a handkerchief from his tan wide-wale corduroy blazer pocket and wiped his very shiny bald head with it. As if he sensed her scrutiny, he looked up before Lydia could glance away. His close-set eyes were the epitome of 'beady' and she again fervently wished Nowicki was in charge of this investigation.

Calm down.

Tell her stomach that. It was flipping faster than Freddy's spatula when he made the breakfast crepes, in total freefall.

As Delphine had been in the moments before she crashed onto the beach.

SEVEN

'OK, folks. I appreciate you people waiting for my team to gather the facts.' Klumpski nodded at Nowicki. 'Harry. Long time no see.' Klumpski's gaze raked over the other detective's figure, lingering on the casual clothing. A smirk pushed through his frown before he resumed a neutral expression.

'Leo.' Nowicki returned the nod, but he was uncharacteristically subdued. Lydia had never witnessed the Cheektowaga PD detective as an observer to law enforcement activity. Of course, she'd only ever been involved in one police investigation, and Nowicki had been in charge. But like Nowicki wearing casual clothes at such a serious time, Nowicki holding his tongue along with his usually sharp observations was unsettling.

Klumpski cleared his throat. 'It's been a long morning and I'm sure you're all anxious to get on with your normal routines. You've all been very detailed in your descriptions and recounts of this morning's events, and your whereabouts in the hours leading up to Miss Wienewski finding the victim, which I thank you for. My team will be working 'round the clock until we're positive we've gone over every inch of the scene. For now—'

'What do you mean by "round the clock?" Is this going to affect my business hours?' Lydia blurted out. She couldn't help herself, not with all the cooking she had to do each and every day. And the still-recent sales drop that Louie's murder had caused her family's butcher shop was etched on her mind.

Stanley immediately reached for her hand again under the table. He gave it a reassuring squeeze. It was his way of telling her to take a chill pill.

'First things first, Miss Wienewski.' Klumpski's face was getting purply again.

Lydia remained silent. It wasn't worth the upset to inform Klumpski that she preferred Ms to Miss.

'Now, as I was saying, we're going to get through this

investigation the only way we can. I can't speak for how anyone else handles a suspicious death, yous know, like Nowicki here and the Cheektowaga PD, but *my* team dots all the "i"s and crosses all the "t's."' At the latter, Klumpski's exacting enunciation produced spittle that hit Nowicki in the face. Nowicki's hand trembled ever so slightly as he grabbed a paper napkin and wiped his cheek.

Odd. Nowicki was usually nothing if not a cool cucumber.

Was there some kind of competition between the Cheektowaga PD, where Nowicki worked, and Acorn Bay PD, the jurisdiction they were in at this moment? Or was the tension between the two men more personal?

More importantly, did Klumpski realize he'd confirmed her and Nowicki's thoughts about Delphine's death being murder by calling it a suspicious death?

'That's understood, Leo. And as I told your officer, I can vouch for each and every person here as far as their lack of criminal record and most unlikely involvement in anything suspicious. What more can we do for you this morning?' Nowicki asked.

'I'm getting there, Detective Nowicki. I called the Cheektowaga PD photo lab about the film you shot and they are awaiting your arrival, so I'll make this quick, like.' Heavy brows formed one as his thick fingers thumbed a battered palm-sized notebook. 'Whiles I appreciate your concern, you know as well as I do that I have to run a background check on everyone present.' Klumpski's use of the local idiom belied the intelligent glimmer in his eyes as he made a show of making eye contact with each person present. Lydia refused to look at anyone else in that moment as the risk of rolling her eyes was too great. The man's need to express his authority so overtly did more than tickle her hackles. His gaze moved to his notebook and then quickly returned to meet Lydia's stare, as if she'd physically touched him.

'Do you have a question, Miss Wienewski?' he challenged.

'No.' She bit her tongue to keep a sharp retort at bay.

She reminded herself that how law enforcement did its job wasn't her concern. But keeping her café and bakery open was. And a murder on its premises meant said murder needed to be solved before it hurt her sales.

Lydia had never thought she could be so detached, making her work the priority over a tragic death of someone she'd known. But she wasn't the woman she'd been leading up to her Good Friday discovery of Louie McDaniel's murdered body. This was an emotionally chaotic situation, no question, but life had to go on. Delphine would be the first one to tell her the same, just as Lydia's first priority besides the café's status was getting justice for her mentor. *Former mentor*. She blinked back stinging tears.

'All right then, Miss Wienewski.' Klumpski didn't bother to look at her as he read from his scribbles. 'You will keep your business closed for today.'

'But—'

He held up his hand in a 'stop' gesture and Stanley did that hand touch again. *Careful*. Lydia clamped her mouth shut.

'I cannot emphasize enough that with the discovery of the body on your beach, your entire property is a crime scene. Which means it can be shut down indefinitely. I'm asking you for one day, maybe two or three, that's all. Enough time for us to get all the evidence we need. I think I'm being very reasonable. Do you agree to closing your café until further notice, Miss Wienewski?'

'Smile,' Grandma whispered out the side of her mouth.

Lydia was certain that if she smiled the tiniest bit it would crack her skin. She nodded. 'Yes. Of course.'

'OK, now that we have that clear, all of yous,' the detective used more of the Buffalo vernacular, 'are not to leave town, meaning yous don't go nowheres. Not without explicit permission from me or one of my officers.' Klumpski took time to make eye contact with each of them. 'Am I clear?'

'Sure thing, Leo, but let's be reasonable.' Grandma spoke up, using her sultry TV show detective voice.

Lydia tensed. The last thing she needed was Grandma saying something to anger Klumpski. Two or three days of lost business was awful enough.

''Scuse me?' Klumpski wasn't used to being interrupted.

Grandma, unaware of Lydia's angst, kept at it. 'I don't see what Harry and I, or anyone of us sitting at this table, have to do with any of this. Harry and I were minding our own business a couple of hundred yards from the body, in my vehicle. Lydia and Stanley here were asleep, out cold. They both have very busy lives, you know. They never even heard us pull up late last night, just ask

Lydia. We sure surprised you this morning, didn't we, honey?'
Grandma stopped talking. She made a sudden little wriggle in her
seat, and Lydia wondered if Nowicki was using the same tactile
communication as Stanley had on her, grabbing her hand under
the table to keep Grandma from saying too much.

Lydia cast a quick glance their way and saw that Nowicki's
hand was indeed under the table, as was Grandma's. She returned
her attention to Klumpski, keeping her expression neutral, she
hoped, and a flash of brown leather caught her eye.

Nowicki's camera strap hung from his jacket pocket. He had
the camera shoved away. Forty-eight pictures of Madame Delphine's
body and the surrounding area were on two rolls of undeveloped
thirty-five-millimeter film. She'd love a chance to look at the
developed photos, but that was probably against the rules.

'Everyone has something to do with Delphine Chenault's death
until we prove otherwise, Mrs Romano.'

'Please, Leo, call me Mary. We're practically family, since you
and Harry are colleagues.'

'Right.' He grunted, but Grandma's words seemed to have
softened his harshest edges by the way a tiny dimple appeared in
the crevices of his cheek.

Stanley spoke up. 'You think there's wrongdoing?'

Klumpski waited a beat too long before he replied. As if he
wanted to put the fear of God into them all. Distaste roiled in
Lydia's belly. She much preferred Nowicki's no-nonsense
demeanor. Wasn't finding a dead body enough drama?

'I have to wait for the forensic photographs, and the coroner's
report. The death is officially suspicious.' He paused as if he was
done, but surprised Lydia with his next words. 'But I'm not ruling
out suicide, for reasons I'm not at liberty to talk about right now.'

Jolts of shock shot through Lydia's insides. It took every bit of
her will to stay silent in the face of what she found implausible.
Delphine Chenault had been argumentative, contrite, and supportive
to Lydia all in the same short time yesterday. But she hadn't shown
one iota of instability or despair. Certainly not depression. Was
both her, and Nowicki's, instincts off base?

You never know what someone's thinking underneath it all.

No, but she'd known Delphine long enough and worked closely
enough under her to know that the chances that the woman had

killed herself were minuscule at best. Of course, she'd made Delphine out to be an evil entity until their mutual amends in the kitchen and bathroom yesterday. Which begged the question: how well had she really known her tutor?

Klumpski ran a bear paw over what would be a smooth, bald head save for a long, stringy comb-over that Lydia suspected was kept in place with the clear pink hair gel her mother had used profusely to set her pin curls with for her First Communion twenty-two years ago.

'Miss Wienewski, do you have any recent photographs of the back of your property before the railing broke?'

'I, ah, maybe?' She'd taken some Polaroids when she first checked out the property with Grandma, who'd provided the down payment that was Lydia's ticket to financial freedom.

'What does "maybe" mean to you, Miss Wienewski? I need an answer. Yes or no. Do you have pictures of this building that predate this morning?'

'Any photos I do have are at least a month old.'

'Can you get me those now?' Klumpski asked.

'Ah, I can soon. They're at my apartment. In Cheektowaga.'

'I thought you said you lived here?' He flipped through his notebook, searching for what she'd told him.

'No, I only crash here when I have a long day, like yesterday.' It was none of Klumpski's business that she'd planned an overnight stay here with Stanley. 'I will eventually live here on a permanent basis, after I get my cottage that's next door fixed up. For now I'm working between here and my family's butcher shop, where I reside, in Cheektowaga.'

'We're roommates,' Grandma piped up. 'Lydia and me.' She threw Lydia a wink. 'Two girls living the life.'

'Call the station when you find the photos and one of my officers will pick them up.' Klumpski wasn't impressed with Grandma's comment and brooked no argument.

'Leo, I can maintain the chain of custody on Lydia's photographs,' Nowicki spoke. 'I'll bring in her photos of the café and property with the crime scene photos that I took.' At Klumpski's hesitation, Nowicki pressed on. 'Let me help with your manpower issues, Leo.'

Klumpski bristled. 'Maybe. This must be hard on you, Harry,

not being in your jurisdiction and all. You of all people know that I have to follow procedure, though.'

Nowicki didn't reply but Lydia saw the vein on his forehead throb. *Please don't have a stroke like Pop.*

Klumpski sighed. 'Fine, it's OK for you to bring both sets of photographs in.'

The wall phone rang and Lydia rose to go answer it, but Officer Sullivan, the rookie who had been present all morning, beat her to it.

'Detective Klumpski, it's the chief,' the young officer shouted across the room and Klumpski rose to his feet, but not before Lydia caught the detective rolling his eyes. Sullivan was going to get a verbal slap from his boss for his indiscretion, she suspected.

'If any of you think of more details, call the Acorn Bay PD ASAP.' Klumpski turned and stalked to the soda bar where he grabbed the phone receiver from Sullivan, whose ears had turned bright red. Compassion welled in Lydia. It was never easy being new, and a murder case was a tough way to become indoctrinated.

'What the h-e-double-hockey-sticks is wrong with your buddy, Harry?' Grandma issued her challenge in a low voice, not risking her words would carry across the café.

Nowicki let out a short laugh. 'Leo's a good guy, Mary. We have a bit of history, is all.'

'Is that what you call it when someone's being a dipwad?' Grandma's easy use of slang Lydia usually attributed more to Teri's age group punctuated her ire and made Lydia grin. 'He was so rude to you! Who does he think he is, when he's assigned to such a tiny department?'

'Now, Mary, none of this is worth getting yourself upset over. We'll resolve this soon enough.' He looked at Lydia. 'Lydia, you'd best comply with Leo's shut-down request. And make sure you find those Polaroid photographs as soon as you can. Do you have any idea where they are?'

Lydia nodded. 'Yes, actually now I remember, they're in a manila folder here at my desk just off the kitchen. Let me get them now, and I'll give them to the detective before he leaves.' She went into the kitchen and to her file drawer, retrieving the Polaroids, which she handed to Klumpski, still on the phone.

She returned to the table and faced Nowicki.

'Surely I can stay here to at least work in the kitchen. Baking and food prep, if nothing else.' She didn't ask about his undeveloped photos. Not here, not now. But she wondered if it'd be possible to get hold of the developed versions from the lab before they were sent to Klumpski, to go over every inch of the scene again, if only on paper.

He shook his head. 'Not until he gives you the green light. We both know you didn't do it, and we also both happen to suspect it absolutely wasn't suicide, but now isn't the time to do anything but comply with the detective's order. Leo's got the final call here, Lydia. Can't you use the extra time at the butcher shop?'

'She's got to keep her place open now, Harry!' Grandma protested. 'Customers aren't impressed by a "closed" sign on their first visit to a place.'

'It's OK, Grandma.' Nowicki was right. She didn't have a choice. Her gut sank with despair. Failing to enter the pierogi competition had become a bigger mistake than her forgetfulness. The competition would have been a way to try to keep the public focus on her food instead of what had happened at the café. 'I'll go help out Pop today, then. I can make pierogi and even some of the baked goods in our apartment or at the house.' She looked at Harry. 'I want your word, though.'

Nowicki's brow rose at the same time Stanley's hand jumped on her thigh. 'Word?'

Lydia stood up and leaned across the table until she was nose-to-nose with Nowicki, not wanting her demand to reach any other ears. 'You let Grandma and me see your photos right after you get them developed.'

EIGHT

'I'm not saying you can't talk to Harry like that, only that you shouldn't. Not if you want something he's not obligated to give you. And in this case, he probably shouldn't even think of giving you. I'm on your side, honey bunny, but for future reference, leave the sweet talking to me, OK?' Grandma's eyes glittered with anticipation and Lydia wasn't in the dark as to why. Unbelievably, they were working a suspected murder investigation again.

They sat in the front seat of Grandma's station wagon, and Lydia had left her passenger side window rolled down to dilute the heady scent of Grandma's perfume. Grandma held that like chocolate, there was no such thing as too much *L'air du Temps*.

It felt as though they'd already been working for twelve hours but in fact it wasn't even noon yet. She thought back to the last time the days and hours had melded together in such a confusing manner. Oh yeah. This past Easter, when she'd found her *first* dead body.

'Are you hearing me, Lydia? It's easier if I ask Harry the hard questions and favors. Especially the favors. Your manner is a bit more abrupt. Don't feel bad, it's just your generation. You didn't grow up watching Cary Grant sweet talk Irene Dunne like I did. My Aunt Rose took me to the picture shows every week.'

'I couldn't help myself, Grandma. I grew up on *The Sound of Music* and *The Graduate*.' Both depicted strong-willed women who didn't waste time sweet talking but asked for what they wanted.

'Touché.' Grandma frowned. 'Come to think about it, Irene was stronger than I'm making out.'

Lydia had zero patience for a trip down either of their memory lanes. Delphine's killer needed to be caught.

'What did Nowicki tell you, exactly? Did he say anything about why he thinks it's murder?'

Grandma made a motion as if to lock her mouth shut with an invisible key. Lydia didn't move. *One . . . two . . . three . . .*

'Oh, all right, I'll spill.'

'No, Grandma, never mind. Don't say anything you're going to regret.' Lydia kept her smile to herself. She'd learned from the best, i.e. Grandma, how to get what she needed. All she needed to do was wait out Grandma's resistance to giving her the goods.

'Listen to me, Lydia. We're in this together.' Grandma motioned between them with her hand, the bright red of her fingernails emphasizing her conviction. 'For some reason the Fates have picked us once again to be the soothsayers of truth and justice.'

'You went to Lily Dale with Florence again, didn't you?' Lydia knew that Grandma and her best friend enjoyed day trips to the small Western New York hamlet renowned for its plethora of other-worldly offerings. Practically Lydia knew – and believed – that there was more to this life than this life. But not as much as Grandma did. Lydia's penchant for supernatural happenings pretty much revolved around the Catholic faith she'd been raised in. Not a little bit of which she'd absorbed from Grandma. Grandma was her own person, though, always had been. She was able to converse on any and all things spiritual without batting an eye.

'What does that have to do with our God-given talents? Whether you believe it's from God, The Virgin Mary, or nature' – Grandma flailed her arms outward, toward the lake – 'what difference does it make when it all comes down to it?'

'So what does Harry think, Grandma?' Lydia didn't want to be sidetracked by a discussion of the supernatural. It wasn't anywhere close to Halloween.

Except for the corpse on your beach.

Grandma sucked in a deep breath and released an even longer sigh. 'Harry thinks that it's awfully suspicious that out of nowhere, your former instructor washes up dead at your feet.'

'Wait, what? He thinks I have something to do with Madame Delphine's death?'

'Yes, of course.' Grandma's eyes widened when she saw Lydia turn paler than pierogi dough. 'No, no, he doesn't think you killed her, Lydia. He thinks someone might have wanted to leave you this mess, though.'

'You mean like finding Louie in our family's private backyard sausage smoker?'

'Harry thinks that you probably didn't make any good friends while you were in Ottawa, or got on with Delphine. Otherwise, why run home the way you did?'

'Grandma! You of all people know why I came home early.' Grandma and Stanley were the only two who knew the entire story. Well, most of the entire story. She had never intended to share the conversation she'd had with Delphine. Some things were meant to be taken to the grave, in her opinion.

'How about you give me a refresher?' Grandma turned the key in the ignition one notch, so that she could open her window, too. 'I'm going to crack the back windows. We need a breeze with the sun getting so warm.' The back windows *whirred* down and the breeze that bordered on too chilly outside of the car provided the exact amount of relief from the sun inside. 'That's better.' Grandma turned the engine off and turned toward Lydia, leaning her back into the driver's door. 'Your turn to spill the beans, my dear granddaughter.'

There was an entire middle seat between them, complete with its own seatbelt, but Lydia felt as though Grandma was inside her brain with a flashlight, peering into every dark corner that Lydia was doing her best to forget about.

'Well, you know that I left to find myself.' Grandma would like this part. She was all about a woman finding herself. Mary Romano Wienewski prided herself on her activism, including most recently picketing the Federal Building downtown in support of the ERA. 'I didn't mean to be a jerk to anyone at the pastry school, but some of the other cooks were there on a whim, you know?' Cooking, and pastry school at the time, had been Lydia's lifelong passion.

'You mean they weren't as passionate as you,' Grandma said.

Lydia winced. 'Grandma, "passionate" in my generation means sexy.'

'It means driven. You have the fire in your belly to succeed, and you know what you want.'

'Yes. OK. Plus I'd saved for so long to go . . .' She didn't want to get into the financials. Grandma knew that without her help, Lydia wouldn't have been able to afford the down payment for her building. What Grandma might not be so smart on was that Lydia had taken what remained of her educational savings and poured it into Wienewski's Wieners & Meats, right after Pop had his stroke and she figured out the books were in the red. She wasn't any kind of martyr; family always came first, period. Which meant she didn't want Pop to ever know what she'd done. He'd work himself to death to pay her back, and he'd given her everything she had in terms of the ability to manage a business.

'It was hard to see spoiled brats playing kitchen when you needed it for your career goals. I understand,' Grandma said.

'I wanted to be the best student there. Madame Delphine had a job waiting for her top graduate at the best restaurant in Ottawa.' She couldn't help the pang of regret that twanged each time she remembered the millisecond she'd hoped it would be her. 'I always knew I wanted to come home to Buffalo, of course, but being the sous chef for a famous Parisian pastry chef for six months wouldn't have hurt.' Plus, she would have made enough money to refill the coffers she'd emptied on tuition. 'I figured out who I could trust, and they were the only people I spoke to.'

'Who were they?'

'My two roommates, Chloe and Elodie. Who weren't acting themselves yesterday. They wouldn't do something like this, though.' Would they? What was with Elodie's dark mood? Chloe hadn't been quite her usual self, either.

'People change, Lydia. Just look at how you've matured these last months.' Grandma's words peeled back the layer of denial Lydia had been wrestling since her conversation with Chloe and Elodie on the back stoop yesterday. Yes, she'd grown up a lot since Pop's stroke. And Louie's murder. How could she not? But in accepting that the year to date had included more than its share of learning, Lydia had to face a truth she didn't want to admit to.

She'd been incredibly immature for her years, and had acted more like a college co-ed than an adult woman seeking a certificate in French cooking. In retrospect it seemed obvious that a girl living at home her entire life would only get so far in terms of life experience.

What bothered Lydia most now was realizing what a complete pill she'd been to Delphine. And in turn, herself. She'd spent these last months since returning to Buffalo engaging in not a little self-recrimination.

'We must support one another, like sisters.'

The memory of Delphine's words to her made her straighten

her spine and throw her shoulders back as she sat next to Grandma. Lydia had to let go of her old self completely and embrace the woman Delphine had been so confident she'd become. It was the only way forward, the only way she'd be able to go ahead without reservation to figure out who had killed Delphine, and why.

'Yes, you're right, Grandma. We need to keep Chloe and Elodie on the table as suspects, because they came here on the trip with Delphine, of course, but also because you're right in that I might not know them as well as I thought I did. There is another person who has reason to harbor resentment against me, though. Pierre.'

'The one that Stanley was about to put cement shoes on and toss in the lake?'

'Yes.' Her cheeks burned and she rubbed them with vigor. She was almost thirty and hated that she had felt shame about her stupid life decisions for so long. *No more.* 'He thinks I dumped him, in a cruel way, I'm afraid. And to be fair, I did. I was in over my head with everything, from the constant battles with Delphine and how attentive Pierre was. Plus that French Canadian accent, it was so sexy! I wasn't thinking, Grandma. I let his slick flattery get to me. And, if I'm being brutally honest, which I know I can with you, he had a lot more experience than me, or . . .'

'Or Stanley?' Grandma chuckled. 'Experience between the sheets is overrated. It's the quality of the bang that matters. Remember when we read *The Thornbirds*? Not that I believe that priest was a virgin by any stretch.'

'Grandma!'

'I meant to say "fireworks."'

'Pierre's a playboy, plain and simple. And like I said, I just wasn't using my noggin.'

'When it comes to biology, we often don't. You know what I say about hard cocks not having a conscience, Lydia. It's the same with women. A wet hen isn't fussy about which rooster dries her off, you get my drift?'

'Ugh.' She so did not want to go *there* with Grandma. And yet, here they were.

'Hey, kiddo, I saw how Pierre looked at you and I heard what he said. I give it to him that he's very attractive, at first glance. I can see why you went for him. You were cleansing your heart of childhood attachments, spreading your wings.'

Thank you, Jesus, Mary and Joseph, that Grandma hadn't said 'legs.'

'Well, Pierre's very manipulative. But, I mean, he didn't have it easy with his parents both being workaholics and having to fight for their attention since he was a tot, at least according to him. And then when he asked to be part of the school, business-wise, Delphine told him he'd have to wait until he'd completed the course, just like everyone else. I'm pretty sure he's felt resentful toward her ever since.' Lydia shrugged. 'Pierre told me that the Chenaults never openly discussed any of this, not as far as the emotions go.'

'Some couples and families don't know how to get it out there. Lay it on the table, I say,' Grandma said.

'Our family has never had a problem with that. Remember Easter dinner?' Lydia looked at Grandma, who cracked into a wide grin.

'How could I forget? Your poor Aunt Dot.' Grandma referred to when Aunt Dot's famous cheesecake, ready for the dessert course, had become the target for Teri's ex's rage. It had been right when Teri began dating Johnny, after working alongside him at the butcher shop for several years.

'Yeah, Mom's still finding dried cream cheese on the wall.' Lydia gazed out at what was usually a peaceful water view, but at present marred by the crime scene tape and police officials crawling over the beach. 'I need to go see Pierre, Grandma. It's the least I can do, to pay my respects.' But if she were completely honest with herself, and her grandmother, it was for a more important reason than offering her sympathy to an ex. If Delphine had been resisting making Pierre her assistant or letting him have a greater role in the business, as he'd complained to Lydia about, could he have finally lost patience? But just then she had another thought. 'Oh my goodness! She's never going to see her cookbook when it's published.' Sadness washed over her, quelching her drive to solve the case for a brief moment. And the television show wouldn't ever happen, either. 'I am going to get to the bottom of this, Grandma. I mean, we are. We need to start questioning the suspects we have so far. Pierre, Chloe, and Elodie for starters. And the other students in the group who could have motives, too. There were two women I've never met, and of course, Cecile.' Lydia shuddered at the memory of Cecile in her kitchen.

'Let the police do their job, honey. Trust me, you don't want to be the one to tell Pierre his mother was murdered.'

'No, but I want to be there right after he finds out. That's when he might do something stupid, if he did it. Same goes with Chloe, Elodie, Cecile and the other students.' She met Grandma's gaze. 'No one's off the suspect list, remember?'

Grandma nodded. 'We have to assume the worst.'

The sound of rubber on gravel drew their attention to a cruiser, driven by Officer Sullivan, leaving the back lot.

Grandma didn't hesitate as she turned the ignition key and shifted into reverse.

'So we're doing this again?' Lydia asked. Grandma knew what she meant. They were roommates, grandmother and granddaughter, and once again, a formidable sleuthing duo.

'Try stopping us.'

NINE

Lydia and Grandma drove to the Acorn Bay Hotel in silence, doing their best to keep the police cruiser in view, but far enough in the distance that they wouldn't be pegged as following it. Lydia was in the passenger seat of the station wagon. It was a far smoother ride than her much smaller Gremlin and normally she appreciated the comfort. But not today. Instead she kept her eyes peeled for anything unusual. Her hackles had been up since finding Madame dead and coming to grips with the fact that it was in all likelihood a murder.

'I'll drive by the hotel this first run, then come back the other way and pull in,' Grandma explained.

'Sounds good,' Lydia replied, and she meant it, until her head snapped against the window thanks to Grandma's too quick, squealing tires U-turn a quarter of a mile past the hotel parking lot.

'I didn't say do something that could get you a ticket, Grandma!' Lydia knew she should have drove. The stink of burning rubber overpowered the lake's scent.

'No one's going to care out here, honey bunny. It's not Union Road in Cheektowaga, after all.' Grandma referenced the main drag through the suburb as she eased into the parking lot with aplomb, turning the large steering wheel with one hand while the other rested on the door frame. She parked next to the cruiser and killed the engine.

'I don't think parking next to the police is the best spot, Grandma. Aren't we trying to stay in the background?'

'Nonsense. Listen to me. It's like this.' Grandma motioned between them, in full undercover investigator mode. Except, they weren't in any kind of disguise and they weren't anything close to law enforcement. 'We're concerned. Your "lover's" mother has been tragically killed and you're desperate to comfort him.'

'Spare me, Grandma.' Lydia could do a lot of things to get to the truth, but to play lovey-dovey with Pierre? No thanks.

'No sparing anything, Lydia. I mean it. You have to go in there and act like you give a flying fig about the man. Don't let them know that your heart is really pumping piss for Pierre. Use it to your advantage.' Grandma looked at Lydia's chest. 'And for Saint Joseph's sake, take that matronly sweatshirt off!' Grandma disliked the maroon top imprinted with a pile of playful kittens.

'But I'm with Stanley now. I don't want to give the wrong impression here.'

'Don't even say his name, Lydia. Right now, our main objective is to get information. The only way the fuzz are going to let us hang around is if we're useful or needed. They're in there, right now, gathering facts that we can use, too. You're our ticket to the main event!'

'Grandma, Harry is a police detective. You can't use that word anymore.'

'Hogwash. I can say whatever the hell I want. Don't distract yourself with my word choice, focus on the role you need to play in there. Get us the information, Lydia!'

Lydia had never been interested in acting, and in fact had been rejected each and every time she'd ever tried out for a school play. Which had been each and every year. But maybe she hadn't had the right motivation.

'You're right, Grandma.' She shrugged out of the bulky long-sleeved kitten print top, leaving her in her white sleeveless camisole and high waist faded jeans. Grabbing her roller ball, strawberry-scented gloss from her pocket, she slicked up her lips. Not that she was planning to put her lips on anyone's but Stanley's. But if Pierre thought she might?

Whatever it takes.

Lydia looked in the visor mirror and finger-combed her hair. It was a mess, but maybe Pierre would think it was sexy. Bed hair was in style. She flipped the visor back in place and nodded. 'Let's go.'

'That's my girl!' Grandma nodded in approval.

Showtime.

They entered the hotel through a back door at the end of a long hallway to avoid being noticed coming through the main lobby doors. The hushed quiet of the carpeted hall dissipated as they

approached the central point of the building. At first it was the
hum of several conversations but as they neared the front desk
the noise became a riot of voices competing for attention.

The source seemed to be the single phone on the service desk,
at which Elodie spoke fast, urgent French. Lydia couldn't make
out much except 'terrible' and 'I want to go home now.' She
wondered who Elodie was speaking to as she recalled she was
estranged from her family.

'Come on, Elodie, we all need to make calls,' Chloe said in a
surprisingly aggressive tone Lydia had never heard her use
toward Elodie before.

'Chloe, are you and Elodie leaving town?' Lydia didn't waste
a second.

'Who wants to know?' Elodie glared at Lydia.

'I'm only asking to see if I can help. If you both need a ride
to the bus or train station, for example. I'm so sorry about Madame
Delphine.' Lydia prided herself on her quick thinking.

Grandma tugged on Lydia's arm. 'Take notes. I count seven in
line for the phone. This hotel doesn't allow international calls
from the room. Don't ask me how I know.' Grandma spoke in a
whisper from the side of her mouth, which was unnecessary since
not one single pair of eyes cast their way. Everyone was involved
in their own trauma, which Lydia had to assume was the news
that their fearless leader was dead.

'I won't ask, promise.' Lydia truly didn't want to know what
Grandma had done in this hotel, in the past or present day.

She strained to hear the two women furthest from them,
conversing in rapid-fire French in the far corner. They'd not said
one word to her during their entire time in the café yesterday and
no one had introduced her to them. It was impossible to make any
sense of their conversation. She shook her head in defeat. 'Let me
finish speaking to Chloe.' Lydia couldn't ignore the sudden bad
feeling between Chloe and Elodie.

Before Grandma could argue, Lydia took two steps up to Chloe
and tapped her on the shoulder.

Chloe turned and her eyes narrowed briefly before she quickly
regained her composure, softening her gaze. 'Oh, *mon Dieu*, Lydia,
I'm sorry I was so rude. But can you believe all of this? Is it true
that you found Madame?'

'Yes, I found her. Sadly.' Lydia remembered how the detectives in her favorite TV shows acted when trying to glean clues. It went against her usual garrulous nature, but she'd learned with Louie's murder that more listening and less talking on her part gave suspects more room to open up.

'It's just awful. We're all trying to get home now, and it's impossible with it being tourist season for the Falls and the international food festival.'

'Aren't you and Elodie going to go back together?' Judging by what she'd just heard, Lydia thought it unlikely. The pair had been inseparable in Ottawa, but now it looked like they were struggling to be in the same space.

Chloe stared at her in dismay, then looked away. What was she hiding?

'No. My family is vacationing at their summer lake cottage in northern Ontario, and I need to get there. Elodie . . . has other plans for her summer now,' she said frostily.

'I thought you were both going to stay in Ottawa until Elodie finishes her last class?' Lydia knew she was pushing the boundaries of compassion toward her former friends who'd suffered the same loss as she, but time was a-wasting. Delphine deserved justice and Lydia preferred to serve it quickly.

'Well, we were, like I said to you yesterday.' Chloe's English became heavy with a French Canadian accent, rare for her as she was completely fluent in both languages. Lydia's questions were clearly upsetting her. 'But now . . . Well, as soon as we realized there will be no more pastry school, and then Elodie and I . . .' Chloe's discomfort was palpable.

'Mmm.' Something had clearly happened between the pair since Lydia spoke to them at the café less than twenty-four hours ago. Did it have something to do with Delphine's death?

'What's with those two, Chloe?' Grandma broke up their conversation as she queried Chloe while pointing with her thumb over her shoulder at the two women Lydia didn't know.

'That's Marie and Miriam. They're twins and new students.' Chloe's tone was dismissive.

'How long have they been at the school?' Lydia needed to know their relationship to Delphine.

'Only for what, maybe two weeks? We were surprised that they wanted to make this trip but . . .' Chloe got distracted and Lydia surmised why as from the corner of her eye she saw Elodie hang up the phone and turn to them. One of the twins, Miriam or Marie, grabbed the receiver and began to dial.

'Oh no, I've lost my place in line!' Chloe's frown reached to her jaw.

'Chill out, Chloe.' Elodie spoke coldly with zero emotion. As if she'd had to make new travel plans for a flat tire instead of her instructor's sudden death.

Her murder.

'Easy for you to say, Elodie. You have your plans, am I right?' Chloe's acid tone made Lydia blink.

'You'll get home. Your family will pay.' Elodie snarled at Chloe before looking at Lydia. 'What are you doing here?'

Lydia was so taken aback by the tension in the room that it took a moment for her respond. 'We came to pay our respects to Pierre.'

Elodie snorted. 'Have fun getting past his guard dog.' Was she referring to Cecile?

'You really are a total loser. I don't know why I didn't see it sooner,' Chloe mumbled.

'That's rich – you, the epitome of untrustworthy, calling me a loser. I'm done with being nice to this crowd. The whole school was a sham from the beginning if you ask me.' Elodie turned to Lydia. 'Look, I'm as sorry as the next person that Madame is dead, and in such a sad manner. But I'd be lying if I didn't admit that I'm relieved, too. Pierre's agreed to give me a certificate of completion now, in light of the circumstances. I'm OK with it.'

'Of course you're OK with taking advantage of a grieving son so that you don't have to worry about making up the course you failed. You only care about yourself,' Chloe observed. Lydia's gut tightened at the bitter poison flowing between the two former friends and roommates.

They used to be your friends, too.

'Lydia, we need to keep moving.' Grandma spoke up and Lydia met her gaze.

'Right. Yes. Well, safe travels. Each of you.' Lydia nodded at Chloe and Elodie. Pretending they were still close friends was ridiculous. Death had a way of peeling away faux everything, in her opinion. She turned on her heel.

'Oof.' She took a step backwards from the person she'd bashed into.

'Ladies. Fancy meeting you here.' Detective Klumpski's jovial tone made Lydia's jaw clench.

'Detective.' She did not want to engage the man, not now. His tie was loose and his white shirt collar sported sweat stains on its edges. Nowicki wouldn't be caught dead looking so disheveled.

He cleared his throat and fiddled with the tie, as if sensing her disapproval. She forced her gaze elsewhere, hoping to throw him off her censorious vibes.

'Why, hey there, Leo!' Grandma turned on her charm.

'What are you two doing here? I released you to go home to Cheektowaga, period. Not make pit stops.' His mouth drew into a tight line.

'We're going home as soon as we can. But I had to be here for Pierre. This is a most traumatic event, Detective.' Lydia would have been shocked by how well she lied if she hadn't already decided to do whatever it took to solve this case. 'We knew each other well when I was at Madame Delphine's pastry school, in Ottawa, of course, and, well, you know. Miles can't keep true friends apart.'

'Friends or something more, Miss Wienewski? Tell me, what's your definition of "knowing" someone well?' He leaned back on his heels and put his hands in his pockets.

Lydia read the unspoken question in his narrowed gaze. *And why didn't you reveal this earlier when you were questioned?*

'Oh, Leo, come on now. Don't make her spell it out. This generation has their own way of defining a relationship. I don't care what she and Pierre say they share, I'm proud of her for standing by her man!' Grandma gushed.

Lydia's stomach flipped and she bit her lip. She wasn't going to blow her one chance to talk to Pierre alone.

'Yes, this is such an awful time for Pierre and his family. Since I couldn't be here this morning to talk to him, I was hoping to spend some time with him now. I take it you've informed the entire group? And it appears they've already been released to return home?' She pointedly cast her gaze around the students gathered into the small area in front of the service counter.

Detective Klumpski grunted. 'We informed both Pierre and his father Jean, and they are receiving the support they need at the moment.' He either didn't notice or ignored the question she was really asking. *Do you consider any of these students suspect?*

'I see it on your face, Miss Wienewski. The answer is yes, they are all making plans to leave but I've requested they remain in the area for at least another twenty-four hours. I expect the same of you two. Stay away until at least this time tomorrow, unless I call you sooner.'

Lydia wasn't going to argue with him, not right now. An extra day was gold, as far as she was concerned, and she had work to do here.

'Please, Detective, I have to see him. His mother was everything to him and I can't let him suffer alone!' Lydia placed her hand on his forearm. Too late, she realized he'd rolled his sleeves up and the coarse 'material' of his suit jacket under her fingertips was in fact his arm hair. *Eww.* She gulped and forced her hand to remain there a second longer than necessary. 'Please.'

Klumpski cleared his throat, grabbed at his tie knot as if he'd forgotten he'd already tugged it loose. 'Let me take you there myself.' He looked at Grandma. 'You, too.'

Score.

Lydia dropped her hand and smiled. 'Thank you, Detective. I really appreciate this.'

Lydia observed that there were two other corridors that fed into the welcome area. It wasn't a lobby so much as a service desk with old-fashioned letter boxes on the back wall, and a brass service bell that had seen shinier days. Klumpski turned and Lydia, followed by Grandma, headed into the hallway opposite the one they'd entered in.

Pierre's door was ajar and Klumpski pushed it fully open as he entered. He stopped short of the bed, where Pierre sat next to Cecile, who was rubbing his back, her breasts pressed firmly into his shoulder. Officer Sullivan sat in a chair opposite, notebook open, pen at the ready.

'Mr Chenault, these women insisted on seeing you.'

Pierre looked up with dull eyes until he saw Lydia. '*Mon cherie!*

I knew you'd come.' He leapt from the bed, which forced Cecile to fall back in surprise.

Lydia's silent judgmental rant was cut short as Pierre threw himself around her, pressing her tightly to him. Her nose was assaulted by the competing odors of alcohol, Pierre's cologne that was heavy on the sandalwood, and a sweeter scent she concluded was Cecile's perfume imprinted upon Pierre's shirt sleeve.

Ick.

She fought every urge to one – pull back from her worst mistake, and two – remind him that she wasn't nor never had ever truly been his *cherie*. Instead, she leaned into him, patted his shoulders, and murmured '*je suis tres descendre*,' what she thought she remembered meant 'I'm so sorry,' over and over.

A peek over his shoulder as he clung to her revealed Cecile glaring at her with utmost contempt. Was it because Cecile saw her as competition for Pierre, or was it something more? Just how close were Pierre and Cecile? Close enough to plan a murder together? Was Cecile as ambitious as Pierre? Could the two have plotted to take over Delphine's business?

Detective Klumpski stood awkwardly next to Grandma, who was murmuring mews of consolation as if she'd known Delphine and her family for decades. When their gazes met, Grandma gave her a strained wink before dabbing the same eye with a tissue.

The motion tickled Lydia deep under her ribcage. No, she wasn't going to laugh. Absolutely not. But her entire body shook with a sudden urge to . . . giggle. *Damn it, Grandma!*

She bit her lip and inadvertently hugged Pierre tighter in her efforts to maintain her role of concerned pretend girlfriend. He responded with a hug so tight and so fast that it *whooshed* the air from her lungs as it flattened her breasts, an accomplishment as like most of her Polish relatives Lydia's breasts were the size of ripe cantaloupes. A sound something akin to a sad cow's *moo* came out of her mouth.

Just great. Her act would be over before they found out anything helpful.

Except that Pierre let loose his own loud, low keen, and his body began to shake.

Jesus, Mary and Joseph.

Pierre was sobbing. Was Lydia relieved that Pierre's distress had inadvertently covered her almost screw-up? Yes. But it didn't prevent her from reacting the way any decent human being would in the face of such grief.

Lydia stiltedly maneuvered Pierre back to the bed and helped him sit down, squeezing herself next to Cecile, who shoved a bony elbow into her ribs.

As Pierre's sobs eased into quiet gulps, Lydia glared at Cecile. As if she really still cared for Pierre. Which, admittedly, a tiny part of her heart felt awful for him and his tremendous loss.

Unless he murdered his mother.

'Can you give us some space, Cecile, *s'il vous plaît?*' she whispered.

'Oh, I'll give you space, all right.' She stood and had the decency to pull her skirt down far enough to cover her dupa cheeks. 'For the record?' Her eyes were slits of rage. 'Your French sucks.' She trounced to the door and disappeared into the hallway.

Lydia blinked. Mentally reviewed what she'd said to Pierre. *Crap.* She'd used the wrong adjective. Instead of saying she was sorry, she'd told Pierre she was 'coming down.' *Double crap.*

'Pierre, I meant to say I'm sorry for your loss. My French is still pretty awful.'

Pierre nodded as he wiped his eyes.

'We're going to leave you two for a bit, honey,' Grandma said.

'I'm staying,' Detective Klumpski sputtered.

'No, no, Leo, give them some time. Come on, now. Let's go get ourselves a cup of coffee.' Grandma touched his back, gently urging Klumpski to exit. She murmured more words that Lydia didn't try to discern. She didn't want to risk blowing her pseudo cover with a spasm of giggles.

'Officer Sullivan, step outside, please.' The rookie followed Klumpski into the hallway and the door clicked shut behind them. A crush of quiet descended and slapped Lydia's better sensibilities to life. What was she doing? Where was her decency?

Get to the truth.

She couldn't stop now, no matter how gross she was being, taking advantage of Pierre during what had to be the worst time of his life. She was on Delphine's side, seeking answers.

'Pierre, I am very sorry for your loss. It's a shock, I know.'

'It's terrible. Did you know she died alone, Lydia? She killed herself. With a gun.'

Alarm bells clanged in Lydia's mind.

'Who said she died alone?' And why was he so sure it was suicide? Had she heard him wrong, mistaken a French word for English?

'My father said that's what the detective told him. Chumpski.'

'Klumpski.'

This didn't make sense to Lydia. If Klumpski had left the café and bakery and come here to inform Pierre his mother had died by suicide, he'd have had to determine the cause of death before he left the café, yet when he spoke to them, he thought it was suspicious but seemed to be keeping an open mind.

Pierre didn't realize it, but he'd confirmed Nowicki's thought that Delphine's abdominal wound could have been caused by a bullet.

'Are you certain that's what your father said?'

'Yes. At least, I think so . . . everything seems all jumbled right now.'

'Was, did Delp— Did your mother show any signs that she wanted to kill herself, Pierre?'

'My mother is not the impetuous type, Lydia.' He blew his nose, making a foghorn sound in the small hotel room. 'She was at your place for some reason I don't know, but I will find out. As far as I know my mother has never, ever held a gun, much less fired one. Which explains the bad aim. She has suffered from melancholy in the past, yes, but I thought she was in a better place these past days. Being on the trip, the judging, the TV show, even visiting your café. Until . . .'

'Until what, Pierre?' Lydia couldn't believe that Madame had committed suicide.

Pierre rubbed his eyes, leaned back, and moaned. 'Ohhh, this is so awful. She, she lost everything, Lydia. When we got back to the hotel yesterday she got a call from the TV company. They'd decided not to go ahead with the show so the CBC dropped her from their fall lineup. Worse, shortly after she'd hung up the phone with the TV producer, her literary agent rang. The publishers aren't happy with the book and were even considering asking for her advance back! Plus *Good Day America* cancelled their interview with her this morning at the Chautauqua Institute. Don't you see? In less than fifteen minutes she lost everything. Everything.' Pierre began to sob again. Were the tears really for his mother, though, or for himself?

'This all happened after I spoke to her.' Lydia thought aloud before she could retract the words.

'*Pardon?*'

'She left her cigarette case on your table, at lunch. I called her late yesterday afternoon, and caught her here at the hotel. She said she'd come back and pick up the cigarette case in the evening or this morning. You were all going to Lake Chautauqua today, then you were going to stop for pastries and coffee on Sunday when you were supposed to drive back to Canada.' And she was going to give Delphine the secret Wienewski family recipe for pierogi. Lydia paused. 'Pierre, didn't anyone notice that your mother was missing last night, or very early this morning?'

'That's how I knew something was wrong. We decided to leave for home early, of course, and told the five other students we had a family emergency back in Ottawa. I couldn't possibly tell them the truth, not yet, and it wasn't a complete lie. Mother was so distraught and I agreed that getting back home immediately was in order. She planned to tell the food festival committee that she was pulling out of judging this morning; I'll have to do that instead now. We were all waiting in the lobby, ready to go at dawn. But she was nowhere to be found.'

Could Delphine have come to collect the cigarette case in a state of distress at the news, and decided she couldn't face going back to hotel, instead choosing to take her own life in the peaceful surroundings of the lake?

'Did she say why they decided not to go ahead with the TV show?'

'I asked when she told me, but all she said was that it was all over, that the truth had come out. Later, she said she had to go somewhere, and that's the last I saw of her.'

The doorknob clicked and Lydia looked up to see not Officer Sullivan, but the man she'd watched leave her café yesterday and had only met a handful of times while living in Ottawa. Jean Chenault, Pierre's father and Madame Delphine's husband.

He's a widower now.

Spying Lydia on the bed with Pierre, he came up short, his mouth agape.

'Lydia? Lydia Wienewski?' He held a paper drink carrier with two lidded Styrofoam cups, and a white paper bag that had grease stains on the bottom.

She stood and walked to him. 'Here, let me help you.' He allowed her to take the food from his hands and she placed it on the varnished dresser that did double duty as a television stand. Only then did she notice the TV was on a local channel with the sound muted.

'It's kind of you to comfort Pierre at this time, Lydia.' Jean Chenault had aged drastically since she'd seen him last. What had appeared as distinguished silver strands in his mutton chops were now white and wiry. He wore a dress shirt, open at the collar, sleeves rolled up, under a navy suit vest that had seen better days with at least one missing button and matching slacks with frayed cuffs. His dark eyes lacked any of their former sparkle, only made more drab by his overall pallor. Was he sick? Or was it simply grief at losing his life partner?

'I'm so sorry for your loss, Monsieur Chenault.' As the words left her lips, she realized that it was real sympathy that poured from her heart. Pierre and Jean had lost their family's anchor. Could she really believe either one of them were responsible for Delphine's death? She knew that Delphine's marriage wasn't a blissful one – Pierre had said that his father was often away from the house on business, and Delphine worked long hours. Not such an unusual occurrence in hard-working families, though. And unlike Pierre, Lydia had no motive for Jean killing his wife, let alone for doing so on her café property. No, whoever had killed Delphine had probably just followed her to the café and waited for their opportunity, making it seem as though Lydia had been framed. Still, none of it made sense.

He sank into the single easy chair, opposite the bedside, and nodded. 'Thank you. It's . . . it's unbelievable.'

Something was nagging at Lydia's awareness yet she couldn't quite grasp it. There was an air of . . . detachment between the two men. It seemed odd that Jean had left Pierre so soon after finding out about Madame.

'Ah, when did you realize Delphine was missing, Mr Chenault?' she asked.

Pierre looked to his father, who looked out the window for a moment.

'About eight o'clock.'

Pierre shook his head. 'We were all waiting in the lobby at six o'clock. Then I tried knocking on the door. You were still sleeping until I woke you at seven.'

'Yes, yes, you're right.' Jean shot Lydia an apologetic glance. 'Forgive me. I'm not myself.'

'It's OK. This is a terrible day.' Lydia hoped her expression wasn't reflecting her thoughts. How did Jean sleep through Pierre knocking on the door? Unless . . .

'Do you each have your own room?'

The Chenault men stared at her.

Pierre recovered first. 'Yes, of course. I'm an adult Lydia, I don't still share a room with my parents.'

Jean's face took on a pale pink hue. 'Ah . . . Delphine and I haven't shared a room in a while, I'm afraid. And of course she needed her own room here, to prepare for her TV appearance. It will never happen now.' He ended on a whisper.

'If only I'd realized she was gone sooner,' Pierre continued. 'I should have never listened to you when you said I was over-reacting!' He spat the latter at Jean.

'Put it in context, son. I said that, knowing your mother, she went on a last-minute joyride. It's always been a way to clear her mind of her melancholy.'

'But the car was still here this morning,' Pierre insisted. 'That was our first clue that something was very wrong.'

Jean didn't reply as he issued a long sigh and shrugged, as though everything in the world currently overwhelmed him. Lydia didn't envy either man their long road ahead. Grieving wasn't easy.

'I'm sorry I missed you at my café yesterday, Monsieur Chenault. You were on your way out when I arrived.' She'd been focused on Madame, and Pierre. 'Madame and Pierre mentioned that you had business in the area.'

'Yes, that's right. I had an appointment in Niagara Falls.' He spoke so mechanically it reminded her of a children's clay figure stop-motion television show.

'Dad brought down the family Buick, plus we rented a car, so that we had a seatbelt for each of the students and ourselves, when we crossed the border,' Pierre filled in.

'Oh, I see.' Lydia recalled seeing the vehicles in the café's parking lot.

'It doesn't make sense to me. Both the rental that Mom drove and Dad's car were in the parking lot this morning when I discovered mother was missing. So she didn't drive herself to the café or both cars wouldn't have been here. Who would have taken her to your café? Would she have walked that far last night, alone?' His voice, heavily accented, cracked and his red rimmed eyes filled with yet more tears.

Poor Pierre, he really was beyond upset. He'd never slipped into his native language in front of her before. In fact, he'd prided himself on his English, how 'American' it sounded.

'This is what Detective Klumpski is going to figure out, hopefully. It's just awful, isn't it?' Lydia wasn't acting – she meant it. She'd never wish anything like this on any family, and was determined to find out the exact circumstances behind Delphine's death.

'Yes, well, life isn't meant to be fair. Poor Delphine. Nobody but me, Pierre, that detective and now you two' – he looked across at Grandma – 'know, on the record, that Delphine has had depression on and off for many years. She didn't want anyone to know. She was suffering with it again lately, and her career success was all that was keeping her going. When she got the news that it was gone, well . . .' Jean stopped and tried to regain his composure.

'Depression? How can you be so sure? That she killed herself?'

If Delphine's family was so quick to accept this explanation, was she wrong to think it absurd?

'Detective Klumpski's team have determined . . . well, they found a pistol near her with her fingerprints. It was a family heirloom, passed down from the war. I didn't know she'd snuck it across the border. It's a shame she wasn't caught.' He sighed, ran his fingers through his hair. 'Combined with our corroboration of her state of mind these past weeks, I believe the police will close the case once the autopsy is complete. She killed herself. We all failed her. I most of all.' Jean Chenault's weary tone conveyed what he and Pierre had been through and what she'd not been aware of. 'There's no doubt, I'm afraid.'

Lydia's gut churned in time to her racing thoughts. *No* . . . if Delphine had a weapon, why hadn't she or Nowicki found it?

'This makes no sense. She was so . . . yesterday . . .' Lydia couldn't say the words. She was *so full of life*. And Madame had made her promise to come back to Ottawa with Stanley. Was that the action of a woman who was in a deep enough depression to kill herself right after disappointing career news?

'This is the way with Delphine's family, you see. There is a long, sad history of mental illness. One moment they seem fine, but underneath, what is really going on, can be sheer hell for them,' Jean revealed. His evident torment and sense of helplessness on his face when talking about his wife's depression reached out its tentacles and tore at her heart. Tears spilled over and coursed down her cheeks.

Mental illness hurts the families just as much as the sufferer, Lydia thought. Both Pierre and Jean bore the signs of weariness she'd solely attributed to their grief. Maybe they'd been dealing with a woman who suffered from failing mental health for a long while. What had caused her struggles? Had that been why Delphine had been such a tough teacher?

'Too young, and so tragically. Ah, Delphine.' Jean bowed his head. A mournful silence descended on them and Lydia wasn't sure what to do next. Sure, Grandma had left her in here to get information, but intruding on the grieving family at this point was beyond her definition of pale.

Suddenly every word Delphine uttered to her took on a secret meaning. Had she encouraged Lydia in her business because she'd felt a failure in hers, despite her most recent success? The dropped TV show and problems with the book could have made these thoughts of failure too much to bear, especially in front of her students. Had she meant 'come visit my grave?'

No. How had Delphine's personality been so positive, ebullient, yesterday if she was fighting off life-threatening depression? Lydia had more questions than she'd come to the hotel with, but was more determined than ever to get answers.

A large growl rent the silence.

'Sorry.' Jean placed his hand over his stomach. 'My body has not registered that I cannot bear to think of food at this time.'

Lydia disagreed; his defeated posture and reddened eyes reflected a body that was well aware of the breadth of his loss.

'You two need to eat. I know it's probably the last thing you want to do right now but you must keep up your strength. Please know that I'm right down the road. Call me anytime, at any hour, with whatever you need.'

'*Merci*, but we'll be going back to Canada immediately after the twenty-four hour hold on our travel is over,' Jean declared. 'We have to make arrangements.'

'Not without Mom, Dad,' Pierre insisted. 'I'm not leaving until . . . until . . .'

'Of course not, son.' Jean turned to her, his frailty uncharacteristic for a man of his age. Pop had had a stroke and appeared stronger, more full of life than Pierre's father. 'Lydia, do you know this detective who is working with us? He told us it will take up to a week, three or four days, minimum, before we will be able to bring the body back home. Maybe you can see if he can speed up the process?' Jean's gaze pleaded with Lydia, as if he was asking her to protect his son from the harsh reality of the condition of the body. His skin had a sheen of sweat over his pallor and his yellowed teeth aged him further. She'd never noticed these details when she'd met him a year ago. Poor man.

'Of course, I'll see what I can find out for you.'

Lydia inwardly winced. Madame Delphine's body wouldn't be released until an autopsy was complete. That wouldn't be by tomorrow, surely?

Once again, her thoughts turned to why Detective Klumpski had misled her and, more significantly, Nowicki, about the cause of death. Klumpski had said he thought Delphine's death was suspicious, and while he wasn't ruling out suicide, made it clear they were all suspects.

Why, if he'd found the family pistol and the fingerprints? She hoped there was a good reason why she and Nowicki had overlooked the pistol, because the acute sense of failure as an investigator stabbing at her pride wasn't something she wanted to carry forever. She was nothing if not a detail-oriented person, as she knew she demonstrated with her cooking accomplishments.

Lydia and Grandma made their goodbyes short and left the room, walking silently down the corridor. But before they reached the lobby, a room door opened and Cecile stood in their path.

'We need to talk, Lydia Wienewski.' She pronounced Lydia's surname with a heavy French accent, but her contempt was still clear.

'Oh?' Lydia knew she needed to play nice, get whatever information she could, but Cecile's overt dislike toward her was tiresome. 'What is it?'

Cecile took a step closer. Her perfume filled the space between them.

'Ladies, let's all be nice now. It's a hard time for everyone. And women need to stick together!' Grandma's interjection unwittingly reminded Lydia of Delphine's near final words to her, about women sticking together. The fight deflated from Lydia's attitude.

'My grandmother's right.' Lydia sighed. 'Please, Cecile, help us if you can. What do you think about everything that's happened?'

'I don't think, I know. Poor Pierre has been working himself to death, trying to keep the pastry school going, to be the best associate to his mother. She was very busy landing the book and television deals, which left the pastry school entirely on his shoulders.' She mewled and tears spilled from her eyes. Grandma shoved a lipstick-stained hankie at the woman.

'Here, honey. It's not clean but it's just lipstick, no snot, promise.'

Cecile plucked the handkerchief from Grandma's hands and delicately dabbed at her eyes. 'Pierre has been through enough. I don't like how the police spoke to him, asking questions as if he would have anything to do with anyone's death, much less his mother's. That's all I'm saying here.' She took a shaky breath. 'But you, Lydia, you broke his heart so very completely. Please don't tease him now with any hope of reconciliation. No one will love him like I do.'

'I'm sure you're right, Cecile. Has Pierre been Delphine's business partner, then?'

'Partner? More like he's the boss. He has been running the school almost completely on his own for the last few months without so much as a thank you or any recognition of his hard work from his own mother. Delphine wouldn't even listen to his ideas to make the school an even bigger success.'

Lydia nodded. 'That sounds very difficult. Thank you for telling us your side of things. And I wish you and Pierre all the best.'

Cecile nodded and disappeared back into her room.

'Ready to go?' Lydia looked at Grandma, who didn't hesitate. 'Let's get outta here.'

But as Lydia and Grandma entered the lobby, Candy the receptionist called them over with a furtive motion.

'I overhead you talking to the detective who's just left. I recognized your voice from the other night, when you called to speak to Mrs Chenault. Are you helping to investigate Mrs Chenault's death?'

'Not officially, no. Delph— Madame Chenault was a close colleague.' As Lydia spoke the words, her heart confirmed that she meant it. 'She meant a lot to me, and I'm trying to find clues as to what happened to her. Do you know something?' Lydia couldn't be certain if anyone else knew Acorn Bay PD had ruled the death a suicide and didn't want to influence any information she might glean.

Candy stared at Lydia as she bit her lower lip.

'Did Detective Klumpski speak to you already?'

'Yes, yes, he did, about an hour ago. But I haven't seen him since, and I think he needs something I have.'

Lydia waited, trying to appear patient while all she wanted to do was shout 'tell me now!'

'Whatever information you have I will get to Detective Klumpski.'

'Maybe this is nothing; I do tend to overreact to things, but, well, here. The maid found it in Mrs Chenault's room and gave it to me a few minutes ago.'

Candy shoved a piece of notebook paper across the reception desk. It had been ripped from a wired notebook.

Lydia picked up the paper and couldn't stop the dread that washed down her spine when she read the message written in bold block lettering.

You're finished.

TEN

By the time Lydia and Grandma left the hotel, Lydia's watch read noon. She had myriad emotions vying for her attention and analysis, but her brain was too fried from the events of the morning to sift through them right away. The threatening note had been the final straw. Which made it the perfect time to head home to Cheektowaga. She would use the time with Grandma this afternoon to dissect what had transpired at the Acorn Bay Hotel. There was always the chance they'd discover a clue they'd overlooked.

Lucky for them, Klumpski was still in the parking lot as they left the hotel and Lydia handed him the note. Then she and Grandma drove back to the café to get her car. They drove away from Acorn Bay separately, agreeing to touch base later, in their garage apartment.

Lydia was happy that the drive home was quick, even for the late lunch hour. It wasn't always the case, as she was going in the direction of many Western New York commuters, toward down-town Buffalo, until she exited the Thruway onto Union Road and drove the few blocks home.

She parked the purple Gremlin at home, opting to walk the two blocks to the butcher shop. She needed the five minutes to herself. Summer was evident in the fully leafed maple and oak trees, the darker fruit tree leaves having bid farewell to their full blossoms weeks ago. Mrs Haas's tulip bed had yielded to peonies, and there were tight buds on her prized rose garden.

Lydia's fingers were crossed that Pop hadn't heard about Delphine's death yet. There was no reason he would have; Teri had gone to the college library to study for her summer course, and neither she nor Grandma hadn't spoken to anyone in the family this morning. Someone could have phoned them, but Lydia was hoping not. She'd let them know soon enough, and wanted to be able to tell them in person. They'd no doubt flip out over it, and tell her she jumped into her own business venture too soon. But was there ever a good time to launch a new life?

Pop would figure out something was off when he realized she was back at the shop several hours earlier than usual.

Lydia walked up behind Pop's four-year-old 1978 gold Ford Fairmont in the alley behind Wienewski's Wieners & Meats.

Plop.

Luna, Pacha's mother, greeted her by landing on the car hood and showing off the most exaggerated spine-stretch atop the sun warmed metal. Several other four-pawed family members darted between the main store building, the large adjacent commercial smoker building, and the storage shed alongside the drive.

'Hey, sweet momma.'

'*Meow.*' Luna jumped down and twined around her legs, her purrs similar to Pacha's. She allowed Lydia one scratch behind her ears before scooting under the vehicle.

'Pop already fed you guys, I take it.' If the cats were hungry they'd be mewing at her instead of prowling the premises for entertainment by the way of displaced baby birds from the huge maple tree that towered above the shop.

Lydia's suspicions that the cats had already been fed were confirmed after she let herself inside the back door. The deep sink was filled with a stack of empty aluminum pie tins that needed to be soaked in sudsy water. A large economy-sized box of cat kibble sat on the chair next to the sink, as if Pop had been called away from the task. Maybe he was on the phone in the office. The murmur of Johnny's low voice drifted in from the front retail area, where with a quick peek she saw he was waiting on a customer with three others waiting to be served.

Phew. Seeing the increase in business was balm to her crinkled soul. Stumbling upon dead bodies did that to her.

It was a marvel of Pop's stroke recovery that his demeanor had softened to the point that not only had he acquiesced to Luna's permanent residency, he'd taken in the two remaining kittens they didn't find homes for. In the past Pop had shown nothing but intolerance at the mere mention of having a cat at the butcher shop. He'd always proclaimed health code concerns but, thanks to the research she'd done before bringing Pacha out to Acorn Bay, Lydia knew several local food businesses kept outdoor cats, providing warm shelter during the winter, to keep pests at bay.

Much to her family's delight, Pop had melted when he met Luna and her seven kittens. Luna, along with Fern and Kippy, now almost full grown, remained free to roam the store property. Lydia had gotten them all neutered or spayed, and created a warm living area for them in the outdoor equipment shed, complete with a heater in the winter. As far as she was concerned, the cats were on the employee payroll. Their budget certainly benefited from the booming business they'd enjoyed since solving what she'd considered her only murder case at the time.

Lydia sighed. She had done a pretty good job of keeping errant thoughts about Louie's murder to a low roar. It was as if a floodgate had burst open with a surge of mental images and thoughts since she'd found Delphine dead.

She still believed Delphine had been murdered, no matter what Klumpski and the Chenaults believed. The note left in Delphine's room underscored her early conviction. She hoped Nowicki would get here sooner than later. Besides examining the developed photographs for more clues, Lydia wanted his take on all of it. The deft hand of a seasoned pro was much needed.

While she was at the butcher shop she'd try to shore up any extra tasks Pop needed doing and prepare a batch of kielbasa for him. It was just what she needed to put her grim thoughts on the backburner for an hour or two.

Until you tell Pop you found another dead body.

The scent of marjoram tickled her nose as she stepped further into the butcher shop. The ubiquitous ingredient in their fresh Polish sausage was essential to any self-respecting Polish American butcher as far as Pop was concerned. The strong aroma struck her as odd because they didn't have that much fresh kielbasa in the refrigerator this time of year, and she hadn't made any since last week. With the summer heat, customers were more interested in the smoked kielbasa, hamburgers, and pork ribs for their charcoal grills. Lydia had persuaded Pop that her addition of ready-made shish kebabs was a good idea, and to her relief they had been. The long wooden sticks of chicken or pork or beef chunks, separated by green peppers and onions, had sold well. So well that Pop requested she keep a good amount in stock through Independence Day, the Fourth of July, next month.

The strong scent of marjoram continued to tickle her nose. A quick glance at the workbench revealed the source. The two-quart glass jar they kept the dried herb in lay open on its side, half its contents spilled across the marred wood. As if Pop had been dragged away, unwillingly, by a very bad person . . .

Lydia shivered. Since finding a murdered body she'd been prone to more extemporaneous bouts of imagination than usual.

Make that two bodies.

To cure her dark thoughts she strode straight to the closed office door. She paused, straining to hear beyond the old oak door. All was silent on the butcher front. If Pop was on the phone, the person on the other end was doing all of the talking.

Lydia didn't want to invade Pop's privacy but her concern won out. She tapped on the door. 'Pop?'

More silence, which allowed her to make out the faint insistent echo of . . . the telephone's busy signal? No, not a busy signal, but the annoying clang the phone emitted to warn that the phone was off its hook. Anyone who tried to call the shop would receive a busy signal.

She sucked in a breath and opened the door. Pop's familiar profile was backlit by the light filtering through tattered aluminum Venetian shades as he leaned back in his chair, feet on the desk. It was his usual posture for taking phone calls.

Except the phone lay on the desk and Pop's limp arms hung from his sides. Lydia's heartbeat slammed to a halt.

No, no, no. *Not again.*

'Pop!'

Victor Wienewski sucked in a huge gasp of air through his prominent nose and open mouth as he jerked awake, his awkward movements sending the phone receiver across the desk toward Lydia, who caught the heavy plastic device before it put another dent in the front of the World War II era steel desk.

'Cripes, Lydia. What the hell do you think you're doing?' Pop bellowed with his trademark irascibility, but she saw the lack of true recrimination in his eyes, the same shade of blue as hers. Pop had recovered his neurological functions from the stroke but it had zapped a lot of his former high energy level, and not a little bit of his overall enthusiasm for the business.

'You OK, Pop?'

'Stop asking me that! Everybody asks that, every day. If I wasn't OK I wouldn't have been able to drive myself here early this morning and butcher the half pig you left hanging in the back of the cold storage, would I?'

'You did too much. I told you I'd finish the hog. You spilled the marjoram when you were making the kielbasa. Did we get an order for fresh kielbasa?'

'We did.' He ignored her criticism of his messiness and focused on business. 'Saint Stanislaus parish needs all we can give them for their lawn fete next week. I'm trying to plan ahead and prepare as much as I can for the shop now so I can start thinking about the fete next week. Whatever I can make and freeze, I will.'

Forgotten guilt stabbed at Lydia. St Stanislaus was also where the international food festival's pierogi cook-off was happening this coming weekend. The contest she'd neglected to enter.

'Why did they wait until now to order it? It's not like they didn't realize they were having their annual lawn fete.' Lydia's cheeks heated. It was just like a local parish that had a long history of good business with them to take advantage of Pop's previous reputation for always filling an order no matter how short on time or how many pounds of meat it required. 'You have to learn to say "no," Pop.' She tried to make her tone gentler as she finished.

'It's a lawn fete, Lydia. You only get this order once a year, and if they go to another shop, that's it. Kiss your future sales with them goodbye.'

Lawn fetes were second only to bingo games in how Catholic parishes in the Buffalo Metro Area raised money. They were always warm weather events, and boasted games of chance, delicious carnival foods, and of course the epicenter of any lawn fete worth its salt; the beer tent. Lydia had attended the crowded local festivals since she was tiny. First with her parents, when she'd prayed to the Blessed Mother that her ping pong ball would land in one of the small glass globes that housed half-dead goldfish swimming in water dyed blue to look like what her young child brain imagined was the ocean. It wasn't the lake; Lake Erie was more of a jade green.

She hadn't realized that small pet fish weren't made for lawn fete games, of course. Her fifth summer on the planet she became the proud winner of a small pale yellow fish she named Pretty Boy. Pretty Boy lasted three weeks before succumbing to a five-year-old's woefully inadequate care. She could still see the flimsy corpse spinning down the toilet bowl, ceremoniously flushed by her older brother Teddy.

'I don't back out of a business agreement, Lydia.'

'Maybe don't sign up for them, then. This is a big deal this year, Pop. St Stanislaus is one of the showcases for the Buffalo International Food Fest too, you know. They're hosting the pierogi cook-off just before the lawn fete.' She clamped down on her tongue. Dang it! She'd not wanted to bring up the very thing she had.

'I don't give a rat's dupa about some newfangled event or organization. A lawn fete is a lawn fete. My meat is the best in Western New York. Where's the issue?' Pop was unaware of her mental jaunt down lawn fete memory lane, where in her mind's eye he was twenty years younger. Physically sound.

'The issue is I don't understand why the food committee didn't figure out how much kielbasa they needed months ago.' Lydia prayed he'd overlooked her mention of pierogi.

'Trying to figure out what's going on in someone else's head doesn't add to my bottom line. I know I've told you this many times. The minute you worry about why, instead of saying "yes" and filling the order, you've wasted more brain cells.' His eyes sparkled and she knew he enjoyed imparting his hard-earned experience and wisdom. But not as much as she remembered from before he got ill, when a discussion like this was out of the question. It had been Pop's shops, his rules, no questions.

Guilt squeezed her heart, made her shoulder pinch. She needed to be more grateful. He was back at work, had been for almost two months. His recovery to date had been remarkable, maybe even the miracle her mother and Grandma attributed to the Blessed Mother. But Pop wasn't the man he'd been before he fell ill, and the nagging doubt that was her constant companion stoked her deepest fear.

Had she been too selfish with following her dreams? Had she opened the café too soon? Pop needed her here, in the butcher shop. She owed him. She wouldn't have the skills to cook and run a business without what she'd learned from her father.

'No question, Pop, you're absolutely right. I do listen to you, you know. I don't show it all the time, but I appreciate everything you've taught me.' She swallowed around the sudden, immediate lump in her throat. Tears burned her eyeballs and she started blinking like the battered doll with moving eyes that still sat on the bed in her parents' guestroom, her former bedroom.

Silence stretched between them until Pop broke it with one of his raucous laughs. He stood up and walked around the desk to embrace her. And she could almost pretend he'd never had the damned stroke, with how easily he moved albeit with the monstrous desk for support.

'Come here, my baby girl. You've got a lot going on, don't you?' He crooned into the hair over her ear, oblivious of how true his words rang. She allowed him to give her one of his trademark bear hugs, feeling a little foolish and a lot guilty at not telling him about Delphine.

How was she going to break it to him that her little girl had some kind of curse that invited dead bodies to crush the Wienewski family's business plans?

ELEVEN

'I'm fine, Dad.' She briefly hugged him back, then stepped away. 'This,' she motioned at her face, no doubt red from almost crying, 'is from my allergies. They're bad this year.' To prove her point she quickly grabbed a tissue from the box on the desk and blew her nose.

'Yeah, your mother's been sniffling and sneezing. Me, I never get hay fever. You've got to take your garlic.' He slapped her on the shoulder, the intimate moment dispelled.

'Gross. No thanks.' Lydia loved her pop but not his breath, which more often than not was stinky to high heaven thanks to his daily regimen of eating raw garlic cloves. He swore by the old school remedy for high cholesterol. Lydia thought he should rely more on an overall lean diet, but there was no telling him what had caused his stroke. He believed it was just 'bad genes.'

'One day you'll thank me for telling you the magic cure.' He looked at the clock on the wall, supposedly a war relic from one of his relatives who toured a Russian submarine after D-Day. 'Geesh. Where does the time go? I've got to get the front ready.' He moved from the office to the back work area and Lydia followed.

'Why don't we go over quantities for the lawn fete? While Johnny's handling the front end.'

'You don't have to babysit me, Lydia.' He walked to the sink, and she was relieved to see there was none of the wobble left from the stroke. But when he rubbed his weaker right shoulder, her stomach sank. Pop was in constant pain, she was certain, as his stroke had affected his right side. His leg was back at one hundred percent, but not his butchering hand. So as the doctors, including Teddy, had cautioned, other muscles and joints were compensating for the diminished strength in his hand. Pop held his knife fine, but relied on his shoulder and back muscles for the power needed to cut through bones and ligaments. The irony of his predicament wasn't lost on Lydia. Neither was the fact that

even with her assistance, Wienewski's Wieners & Meats was still
on shaky ground.

'I've got the smoked sausage for the next few days at the shop
done already. But I haven't had a chance to refill the front cases.
Johnny's been busy out there since we opened.'

'That's great, Pop.' It bothered her that he'd fallen asleep in
the back, but she chalked it up to the toll being back on his feet
cost him.

'Let's fill 'em up, then.' They made short work of it, filling the
front vendor refrigerated cases with fresh cuts and sausages.
Johnny nodded a quick hello but didn't interrupt his flow.

Lydia placed the last of the refrigerated trays atop a case.

'This is it, Pop.'

'OK, then. We're done. You're done. You can go back to the
lake now.' His pride shone through each syllable.

'Let me make a fresh pot of decaf before I go.' Lydia knew
Pop hated when she looked over the front refrigerator cases, as
if she didn't trust his abilities. So it was better to focus on the
other parts of the shop that weren't meat related but made a
difference to Pop's comfort, and hopefully, eventually, his
stamina.

She scooped grounds from the large, bright yellow and black
striped tin, her family's favorite brand since she could remember.
It wasn't until she was a teenager and had slumber parties at
friends' homes that she realized there were other brands of coffee
than what her family used.

'Tell you what, girl, sit with your father and enjoy a cuppa,
Lydia. You're always in a hurry. Don't make the mistake I did,
putting your work first.'

Lydia couldn't help the laugh that escaped her. 'Pop, it's not
putting work first as much as putting the family first. You did what
you had to do to keep food on the table.'

'Right. You don't have a family to worry about yet, so you can
relax a little. But not for too long, eh? Don't let me die before
you give me grandkids.' Pop rinsed out two mugs at the deep
commercial sink, then went on to clean the pie tins.

Lydia's jaw clenched at Pop's typical macho view of the world.
No matter how much he supported his daughters in doing whatever they wanted to, his old-fashioned sentiments, the way he'd

been raised, eked out. Even his own mother told him he was a chauvinist.

'Thanks for feeding Luna and the brood, Pop.'

He grunted. 'She's a good cat. Keeps the pests away. As long as she doesn't think she's ever sleeping inside. The board of health will shut us down.'

'The board of health will shut us down,' was Pop's constant refrain for keeping the store spic and span, and his main reason for being against Lydia's animal loving heart. Pop loved animals too; he was the main source of Stashu's affection. The family terrier terror enjoyed only the best scraps from the butcher block, thanks to Pop. But animals around his meat had never been tolerated before Luna.

'She's happy in the storage shed.' The small shanty adjacent to the shop was removed enough to be officially separate from the food but had its own electrical supply, which allowed for a small heating unit and heating pads in the depth of winter.

With the coffee brewing, Lydia did a quick check of the back storage room and the refrigerator. With the front cases full there was still plenty of inventory in the event there was a rush of customers later. One could always hope and pray that would happen, at least.

Satisfied that Pop didn't have to worry about anything but the most basic tasks – weighing and wrapping orders – she again sought out her father.

He was back at his fortress of a desk, chomping on an unlit cigar. Lydia stifled any urge to admonish his return to one of the habits that had precipitated the stroke. He wasn't smoking the tobacco, at least. Pop waved at the full mug of coffee he'd placed in front of the extra chair. He'd even brought in a small carton of half and half for her.

'Sit. Drink. Give me a few minutes before you go.'

She complied, adding a generous amount of the creamer to her drink. Stirring with the wooden stick Pop had placed beside the cup, she smiled. 'Thanks, Pop.' Maybe the stroke had changed him more for the better than she gave Pop credit for. Pop had never insisted they share a coffee break before. There had always been too much work to do.

'Did I mention that St Stanislaus offered us an extra special premium deal?' Pop's use of so many adjectives set off her internal alarm bells. He was up to something.

'No, unless, do you mean you gave them a good deal? As you always do. You've never ripped anyone off, ever.' She kept her tone gentle, not wanting to annoy him or hurt his pride. But post-stroke Pop sometimes mixed up his words.

'You need to clean your ears out, girl. You've got potatoes growing out of them.' He barked his frequently used expression with deep sincerity. Before she could get her hand in front of her mouth, Lydia spewed hot coffee across Pop's desk.

'C'mon, for cripe's sake, Lydia!' Pop faked being annoyed while she sopped up the mess with a tissue, her hand shaking from her laughter. She knew he loved nothing more than when he made her or her siblings laugh.

'I heard you, Pop, but—'

'But nothing. You think everything's about the stroke. I said what I meant to say, Lydia. The church gave me a good deal by paying top dollar for our kielbasa. They also threw in something else.' His eyes twinkled.

Lydia's nape hairs shivered. What had Pop gotten them into? 'Trade or a concession?'

'Yes.' He nodded and ignored distinguishing who got the shorter end of the deal. No matter what, he was going to couch it to her as their bonus. It's what Pop did. 'The pierogi cook-off is going to lead to more attention and money for the fete than ever this year and they want to give back to their long-standing fete vendors.'

'What, they're going to put a DJ in the beer tent, instead of a polka band?' Traditional live music was on the way out, with disc jockeys all the rage for big events. Lydia enjoyed both. There was something special about the oompah beat of live polka music, but she also had very modern musical tastes that live bands often had a difficult time replicating. The younger crowd wasn't as enamored with accordion and clarinet music blaring into the night. Of course, it depended upon how much beer one consumed.

'What's wrong with the polka band? You like to polka, ever since you were this high.' He lifted his arm and held his hand out, level with the desktop. 'You can't stop your toes from tapping on Saturday mornings.' He referred to the Buffalo Polish Hour, when

nonstop polka music blared from the AM/FM radio he and Mom
kept on the kitchen counter. Pop put the shoe-box sized radio on
top of the refrigerator every Saturday, so they 'could hear the beat
better.'

'Nothing's wrong with polka music, Pop. So what else did they
throw into the deal?' she prompted.

Pop chomped on the leathery paper of his cigar. 'I entered you
in the cook-off.'

Lydia stared at her father, hard. Were strokes hereditary? Because
if her blood pressure resembled her inner turmoil, she was about
to have one. 'Pop. Are you serious? The deadline to enter has
passed. It's too late. We've spoken about this already.'

'As St Stanislaus is hosting, and they wanted Wienewski's
Wiener & Meats kielbasa for their lawn fete, I had a word and
they spoke to the food festival organizers. They tell me the pierogi
contest has space for a couple more entrants, so you're actually
doing them a favor by entering last minute. I filled out an application for Lydia's Lakeside Café and Bakery and it was approved,
lickety-split. Simple.' Pop wiggled his brow at her.

Lydia's mind raced. Why *not* enter the contest if, in fact, she
was already signed up? She couldn't go back to her café for at
least a day or two, so she had time on her hands. *Do you, though?*
With trying to solve Delphine's murder? She mentally brushed her
worry away. She could use some good publicity right now, and
Delphine would expect it of her. Had, in fact.

'Follow me out to the kitchen, Daughter.'

Pop's expression sobered as he walked to the window over the
commercial sink and rested the mashed cigar in the aqua-speckled
ashtray she'd made him in eighth grade. He took his time turning
the spigots, rubbing the green bar of soap against his palms until
frothy suds formed. Washing his hands was Pop's way of mulling
things over.

'The family butcher business is going away, Lydia. You know
first-hand how much more meat I used to sell. But with the big
supermarkets gobbling up all of the cash, it's a matter of time
before we're gone. Poof! A part of history.'

Resistance reared in Lydia's gut. 'The grocery stores can't
compete with our quality, or come close to our variety of meats.
Show me where you can buy ready-made shish kebabs in the

grocery store.' She crossed her arms over her chest, crushing her sweatshirt's puff-painted kittens into an indecipherable ball.

'Quality's not the issue when you're feeding hungry mouths. None of us can compete with their prices. And the supermarket in the plaza has kebabs for sale. Half the size of ours, of course.' He shook his hands off and dried them with a paper towel. After he tossed the crumpled wad in the trash, he shoved his cigar back in his mouth. Pop wasn't going to waste one bit of the cigar, whether he could smoke anymore or not. 'We have to think about the Wienewskis' future. It's with your bakery and café, Lydia. With your pierogi. What do you say?'

Pop was ever the disciple of the Great Depression. When Lydia was growing up he never hesitated to remind her and her siblings to be grateful for all they had, because when he was a child in the Thirties his family had to survive on one meal per day. But they still managed to feed 'the hobos who walked two miles from the train station.' Grandma had taken the shop's leftover meats at the end of each day and added it to the ubiquitous potato soup.

'Think about how many more customers you'll get when you can put a gold medal sticker next to your pierogi on the menu, or on your front sign. "Best Pierogi in Buffalo." Maybe even best in the world, with this new international twist they've put on it.' Pop held his arms up and spread his hands apart as if unfurling a banner.

'I'll do it, Pop. Of course I will. But it doesn't mean it'll make much difference to my business. It might not make a bit of difference, in fact.'

'What the hell is that supposed to mean?' Pop looked at her as if she'd grown horns.

'I found another dead body, Pop.'

TWELVE

Holding secrets back from her loved ones always ended in disaster. So did revealing a secret. Pop's jaw dropped. So did his mushy cigar, right onto the tired linoleum. Johnny rushed in from the front. He stopped mid-stride, sensing the charged atmosphere.

Johnny's eyes were wide, and his wavy dark hair fell across his eyes in a sexy manner incongruous with his countenance. She saw what made Teri crazy for Johnny. The compassion, thoughtfulness, the polite manners he used to handle the unruliest customer. But it was panic instead of the usual calm reflecting in his brown eyes. His gaze bounced around the kitchen, from the butcher block to the walk-in refrigerator door.

'Is it in the fridge?'

'What?' Lydia stared at him and realization dawned. Johnny must have heard her. 'Oh no, not here. I found the body at my new place, on the beach. She fell off the café deck.'

'Who fell off what deck?' Amelia Wienewski sauntered through the back screened door as if joining a friendly neighborhood conversation, not walking into her daughter's most recent life-threatening, business-crushing ordeal. But when she took in Lydia's appearance, her shoulders sagged.

'Oh, no. Not again, Lydia! I knew it! There was a dead robin in the yard this morning, and I said to Stashu, "That's a bad omen, doggie."' Mom always had an ESP with Lydia and her siblings. She might not know what was going on in their lives moment by moment, but her ability to interpret their body language combined with her mother's instinct in a potent way.

Lydia let out a shaky breath. 'Yes. Again. But it wasn't anyone you know. Not personally.' She quickly filled all three of them in on what had happened, before Mom ran to the phone to ask her friends if any of them had heard and before Pop had another stroke. Johnny listened in until the shop's bell chimed, and he went out to greet the customer.

'Take heart, Lydia. It's not the best news, sure, but it's not the end of the world. You'll be fine. Bodies wash ashore all the time!' Amelia smiled. 'No one can blame you or your café and bakery. Don't make more out of it than it is. Are you free to play bingo tonight, honey?'

'No, no, I'm not free to play anything, Mom. Did you hear what I said? Delphine didn't "wash ashore." She fell there after she was shot. I've been up since before dawn, Mom, and now I have the pierogi competition to worry about.'

'I'm sorry, honey. But you won't be able to work in your place until at least tomorrow from what you said. I did hear you – you said the police had concluded their investigation and that you'd be back in the café soon enough, but you also don't believe it was suicide. Which means there's a chance the police will reopen the case, right? Just look how long Louie's investigation took. Settle in here, and enjoy a little time off before the pierogi competition. I'm worried about you, Lyd. You're pushing yourself too hard.' Mom's carefully drawn auburn brows knit together over her prominent nose.

Lydia gritted her teeth. 'I don't have time for time off. Besides the festival's pierogi contest, Pop's agreed to fill a last-minute order of fresh kielbasa for St Stan's.' Who was she kidding? She wouldn't be able to focus on anything until she knew exactly how Delphine died, and who did it. But this wasn't up for discussion with her parents. They'd been through enough with Louie's murder. She'd protect them from this case as much as she could.

'Well, hang in there, honey. You can prepare your pierogi at the house, of course. We'll make it a girls' night if you want.'

'Thanks, Mom, but I'll see what I can get done in the apartment kitchen. I'll come down and work in yours if I need to.'

Mom nodded, and her expression cleared. 'That's that, then. If either of you need me I'll be going over the books.' Mom poured herself a cup of coffee into a bright yellow smiley face mug and carried into the office, shutting the door with her foot.

Pop gave her a knowing glance. 'Her nerves can't handle all the truth, all the time. Don't push it. Let's get going on your kebabs.'

*   *   *

Lydia longed to immediately escape the butcher shop for her apartment but she couldn't leave Pop with all the extra work. Between the kebabs, kielbasa and pierogi for the cook-off, there was enough work for six people. Since she couldn't make the pierogi this far ahead of time, she focused on the kebabs for now.

'It's not good, Lydia. Your business is open for two weeks and bam,' the butcher cleaver *thwacked* through a lean cut of beef, 'you have another dead body on your hands.' Pop emphasized each word with a swing of his butcher knife. The stroke had left him weaker, his movements slower, but his blade placement and meat production remained spot-on. Unexpected pride made Lydia's eyes prick with tears as she carefully portioned and wrapped the beef filets, steaks and roasts Pop had already cut.

The lake view was a draw, Lydia admitted. But Delphine would have been careful to stay back from the railing.

Unless she'd gone to meet someone there. The person who'd written the threatening note? Was Delphine being blackmailed? Or had she unwittingly taken her murderer with her to the café to get her cigarette case? Which meant it was someone she knew, in all likelihood.

She could have been taking in the view before retrieving the cigarette case. But she wouldn't have missed the signs posted warning of the decrepit support inside the dining room doors when she was in the café earlier that day, either.

Pop put down his cleaver – never a good sign – wiped his hands on the front of his apron, then picked up a damp towel and began wiping the cutting surface. 'So this woman who died, your pastry teacher, you were involved with her son?' Pop's question came out as casually as if he were telling her the proportion of pork to fat in their locally famous kielbasa recipe.

'Who told you? And yes, we briefly . . . went together.' Lydia's cheeks heated as she used the idiom more familiar to Pop's generation. The thought of Pop ever catching her with a man, as Delphine had, was hellish.

He shrugged. 'It doesn't matter who told me, but Teri was worried about you when you first came back is all.'

Relief surged and smoothed away her ire, and that flicker of shame that lit whenever she recalled being attracted to Pierre in the first place. Teri may have spilled some of the beans but not the whole can. They were both good about keeping sister secrets when needed, which she appreciated.

'Well, it wasn't anything serious. Between Pierre and me. It was a fling, Pop.' She wondered if he'd ever had an indiscretion, a relationship he regretted. As far as Lydia knew, Mom and Pop had been a couple since the time glaciers covered Western New York.

'And you're sure Stanley's the one for you now?' Pop posed the query as a statement, his blade mid-chop.

'Yes.'

'So this,' he waved his free hand around in a circular motion, 'this worry I see on your face, it doesn't have anything to do with your former beau?'

'No, not at all, Pop. He was never a beau, or anything serious, honest. I'm wigged out over finding Delphine's body.'

'You didn't get along with that teacher, though. You left because of her.' Another bald statement that reminded her that while Pop was the quietest member of their immediate family, he missed absolutely nothing. Plus Grandma and Teri weren't afraid to keep everyone informed about whatever was going on with whomever. Lydia would never label them gossips, but when it came to the Wienewski family, if one member was hurting, they all were in pain until the problem was solved. It worked well most of the time, like when they had all pitched in and helped her older brother Teddy work through his anxiety so that he could study for the MCATs, to get into medical school, which he had. He was an orthopedic surgical resident at Erie County Medical Center, ECMC, these days. Or the way they'd all come together to keep the butcher shop running through New Year's, after Pop's Christmas Eve stroke, and kept it going no matter that Lydia had found Louie's body in the backyard smoker at the height of their Easter sales.

But there were times it backfired, and this was proving to be one of them, perhaps. Lydia loved Pop and his concern made her eyeballs burn worse than chopping ten pounds of onions did, it was so touching. But she didn't want her father to get too familiar with her most private affairs. The stuff she was comfortable telling Grandma, Teri, her high school girlfriends, and sometimes Mom. It was too . . . personal.

'I didn't leave because of Madame Delphine as much as I

realized I didn't need that fancy degree, Pop. You were right about that. You'd already taught me everything I need to know about making a successful business, and Grandma and Mom have taught me all my best baking and cooking secrets.'

Pop nodded. 'Yes, you're a born caterer, chef, baker, that's a fact. You're a good butcher, too, but you make pierogi your great-grandparents would be proud of.' He paused, pointed his cleaver at her for emphasis the way other people used their finger. 'And I have to tell you, honey, I like how you've put your own spin on what's in our blood, with a bakery and café. You're making it modern.' Pop piled sirloin steak neatly on the edge of the cutting board, unaware that his use of 'blood' made hers chill after what she'd witnessed on café's beach. 'Do you think I should sell these as is, or do you want to make a few more of your shish kebabs? The customers like them.' Pop's compliments were hard-won, and she refused to be embarrassed that even though she was a grown woman the soft spot under her ribcage swelled with pride.

'How about half for steaks and half for kebabs?'

'You got it.'

Pop immediately took half the stack and sliced the steaks into expert cubes. 'I still don't know how you do that, Pop. Your chunks are the perfect size, and all the same, every time.' Hers often resembled a hodgepodge of geometric shapes. She could butcher the largest side of beef no problem. It was the smaller details of the trade that she struggled with. Lydia knew how to wield a cleaver but was far more adept with mixing, kneading, baking, and frosting.

'It's time, is all. Years of experience.' He dumped the cubes into a nearby large stainless-steel bowl. 'There you go. All set for your secret seasoning.'

'OK, I'll get the meat marinating. I'll start on the fresh kielbasa while it sits.' She and Pop both knew her 'secret' was a bottle of commercial Italian dressing. She was one-eighth Italian on Grandma's side and one hundred percent American, which meant she loved convenience as much as she did delicious food.

Pop shook his head. 'Better yet, why don't you go get yourself some shut-eye? Take a nap. You can come back and put them together later tonight, or in the morning. No rush.'

'I'm not tired, Pop.' She fought from rolling her eyes as she lied. Her body ached from emotional exhaustion but her mind wouldn't shut off. Sleep was going to be minimal until she had justice for Delphine.

The back of her neck began to prickle in warning and she met Pop's watchful gaze.

'What?'

'I see it in your eyes, Lydia. You've got that same spark you had after you found Louie in the backyard smoker. You've got murder on the brain again. Do you know, I only finished cleaning the smoker out this week? Your mother made me use bleach. Bleach, taking away all that aged smoke.' He shook his head in regret. 'I'll never get the sausages to taste as good again.'

'Well, there *was* a dead body in there, Pop. Do you ever think you'd use it again, anyway?'

'No, probably not. It would be disrespectful. And we don't need it, to tell you the truth. Other than for making a little extra, or a family party here and there, we use the commercial smoker here at the shop. I probably should have knocked it down years ago. Let's face it, they've gone out of style. It's nothing more than a pile of old bricks now.' Since when did Pop give a smoked sausage about what was in fashion?

'But it was your connection to your father, Pop.' Lydia's grandfather and Grandma's husband of over forty years had helped Pop build the smoker when Mom and Pop moved from Buffalo proper out to the suburb of Cheektowaga decades ago. She had vague memories of Pop and his father, whom she called by the Polish *dziadzia*, amidst stacks of cinderblocks. 'I remember when you two built it.'

'Yes, you were all of three, Teddy was five or so.' Pop's smile was slow, full of joy and not a little bit of wonderment. Probably thinking about how fast time went. It was a constant theme of his.

'And Teri wasn't a spark in Mom's eyes yet,' Lydia added.

'You got that right.' He laughed. 'Who knew we'd become parents again so late in life? At any rate, don't change the subject on me. Now that you've got a second dead body associated with your name, best you take care of it like you did with Louie, so that your business doesn't suffer like mine has.'

Double ouch. He'd complained about his business, which was a double stab as far as Lydia was concerned. She thought of the shop as 'ours.' Since she'd been running it until Pop returned right after Easter, she viewed the revenue issue as her fault.

'But orders have picked up for you again, Pop. I saw the stack of call-ins for the Fourth of July. You're up to twenty-seven and it's only the beginning of June.'

He nodded, then stopped. His finger came up and he gave it one wave in front of her. 'Don't try to distract me. I had a stroke, not a lobotomy.'

'I'm not trying to—'

'Yes, yes you are. Look around you, Lydia.' Pop spread his arms wide, as if to encompass the entire butcher shop. 'I'm doing well enough. As good as I have in the past? No. Will I be able to retired extra early as I'd planned, maybe do something different? No. But not as bad as it was those days right after Louie died. I'm only saying I don't want to see you go through the same hell. My store's been here a long, long time. People are willing to overlook an ugly incident like Louie's death for me. But a new business like yours? They aren't attached to it yet, you know what I'm saying?' His words were taking on a slight Polish accent, the syllables more staccato, as they did when he was passionate about something. Grandma often recalled that Dziadzia, her dearly departed husband, went into Polish whenever he got riled up.

'I hear you, Pop.' She really wanted to get through this and start thinking about the pierogi prep. Suddenly the contest seemed as important as getting justice for Delphine. It was another way to honor her mentor.

'. . . and the only thing I need from you is help with the batch of kielbasa for the fete. You can knock that out at any time over the next day or two, sweetheart. I'll have the pork ready to go. We can ask your mother to grind it up for us, save you more time. Hell, let your mom and me do all the kielbasa. We can do it. Your focus needs to be on the pierogi. You're going to be the Pierogi Queen of Buffalo, Lydia!' Pop had moved on to the lawn fete planning, oblivious to her mental check-out.

'No, please don't ask Mom. She's got enough on her hands.' Recently finished with Pop's stroke rehab and all that it had entailed from hourly exercises to a specialized low-salt, low-fat diet, to thrice weekly trips to the physical and occupational therapy sessions, Mom was exhausted. She deserved a break.

Never one to balk at hard work, though, Mom had immediately stepped in to manage the books for Wienewski's Wieners & Meats, claiming Pop didn't need her as much. They'd recently lost their long-time accountant so the timing was perfect.

'You don't know what it's like to juggle as we did at your age, Lydia. Why, your mother took care of her parents, worked the front counter, and had a kid on her tit while she did it.'

'Stop talking about my boobies.' Mom stepped out of the tiny office where she'd retreated after Lydia's initial pronouncement that she'd found Delphine's body. Mom spent hours hunched over their electric calculator that competed with the single double outlet in which they plugged in a small lamp and the phone's answering machine, vital to early orders especially during the holidays.

Mom walked up to Pop and gave him a quick peck on the lips before hugging Lydia. 'Again, I'm sorry about your pastry instructor.' She pulled back and scrutinized her. 'You OK?'

'I'm good,' Lydia lied.

'You're lying, my dear daughter.'

Lydia sighed. 'How do you always know when I'm lying?' It had been impossible to get much past Amelia Wienewski as a teen, and her mother's true or false radar was still keenly attuned.

'A mother knows.' Amelia offered a small smile. Was that mascara and eyeliner? Mom hadn't worn makeup since diamonds were coal. Working in the shop with Pop again had put pep in her step, for sure.

Lydia shrugged, tried to keep her tone noncommittal. If Mom sensed that her middle child was experiencing any kind of angst, she'd try to fix it. She couldn't help herself.

'I just need to get the pierogi competition out of the way, then I'll be fine.'

Pop leaned his backside against the chopping block and crossed his arms, observing his women.

It was easy to imagine it was ten years earlier, when Pop was in full health and she hadn't found two dead bodies. She hadn't seen Pop so relaxed in such a long time. The months leading up to his stroke she'd been gone, still at Madame Delphine's L'ecole du Cuisine in Ottawa, and when she'd come home he'd alternated between being a pale, gray version of himself or an angry stress ball with a beet red face, until his stroke. Unexpected nostalgia sucker-punched Lydia and she sniffed.

'You getting hay fever, Lyd?' Mom stepped in and put a cold hand on Lydia's forehead. Lydia swerved away and forced a laugh to cover her emotions.

Mom laughed, and Lydia experienced a moment of relief. Finally, she'd pulled one over on her mom.

'That is the saddest imitation of a laugh I've ever heard,' Amelia proclaimed. 'Lydia, it's normal to be upset right now. You've got a lot on your plate.'

'I'm OK, Mom.'

'Here.' Mom shoved a rectangular box of tissues at her. 'Blow your nose.'

'Mom!' But she plucked out a tissue nonetheless. It was easier than verbally wrestling with her mom.

'She's going to be thirty, Amelia. When will you figure it out? The kids are gone. They're out of the nest.'

'Except for my baby, Teri,' Mom retorted. 'She'll never leave us.' She was joking. Lydia knew things about her younger sister that would forever keep Mom from referring to Teri as 'her baby,' but kept them to herself.

'Now, Amelia. Just take it easy, will you? Come here and give me a hug.' Pop opened his arms and her Mom went to them, hugging her husband of over thirty years tight. Until Pop's hand wandered down to her dupa. Mom batted his hand away.

'Knock it off, you old man.' She laughed.

Pop's way of calming Mom exacerbated Lydia's already over-wrought reaction and more tears spilled onto her cheeks. It was a beautiful balm, to have one area of her life be familiar, known.

Unlike not knowing who killed Delphine.

'Are you sure you and your father weren't talking about anything else? Something you might want to tell me?' Mom persisted.

Lydia immediately sobered. 'No. Well, I admit I'm not coping well with Madame Delphine's death, and I'm praying that the Acorn Bay Police let me back into the café soon. I need to manage the reputational damage to the business. But even if things change and they make me stay away longer, I'll just have to manage.'

'That's my girl! Stay on the positive side of the street. You know your father and I are here whenever you need us.'

'Thanks, Mom.'

THIRTEEN

'I don't like it that you both went somewhere other than where you told Leo Klumpski you'd be, and I like it less that he caught you there. It makes you look suspicious.' Nowicki had stopped at the small apartment Lydia shared with Grandma. He'd brought the developed photos, which he said were a duplicate copy of what he'd given Klumpski. Nowicki had a special relationship with his police department's photo lab and had been able to get the film developed, including duplicates for himself, in mere hours. To both Lydia and Grandma's delight, besides the photos he'd surprised them with a large pepperoni pizza and order of Buffalo hot wings, complete with celery sticks, and bleu cheese dressing for dipping the wings. When she'd lived in Ottawa she'd been dismayed to find out that Buffalo wings were truly a local specialty and unavailable outside of Western New York. When she'd asked her classmates about it, they'd looked at her in horror, thinking she meant a dish made with Bison meat. Chicken wings served Buffalo style were split in half, dipped in flour, deep fried, and then tossed in a special hot sauce and margarine mixture. Most taverns and restaurants served them at three levels of spiciness: mild, meaning little to no sauce; medium, the most popular; and atomic, with so much heat it made the consumer instantly sweat.

'But we found out some pertinent information,' Lydia persisted as she wiped cayenne pepper sauce-stained fingers with one of the crumpled napkins from the pile next to her paper plate. Desperate for all facts related to the case, she was eager for Nowicki to see her as a colleague.

Nowicki was the epitome of a professional, save for the times she'd seen him off-duty with Grandma, such as earlier today in his boxer shorts. She figured that Nowicki wasn't usually one to bend or break the rules when it came to law enforcement. It was fair to assume that sharing crime scene photos with her and Grandma was a definite breach of protocol.

'What were you both doing at the Acorn Bay Hotel in the first

place?' Nowicki asked, his tone edged with not a little annoyance. He sat next to Grandma on the sofa, with Lydia on the
easy chair opposite, the coffee table between them in the garage
loft's small but livable living room. It gave Lydia and Grandma
the perfect place to do their crochet and macrame respectively,
and of course watch their favorite detective TV shows. They
each had an aluminum TV tray in front of them with their meal
and drink.

'Now Harry, do we have to go through this again with this case?
You know from last time that we're going to snoop. It's in our
blood. And we happen to be very good at it.' Grandma offered
Lydia a reassuring smile. What was with her family's penchant
for all things blood related? 'Go on, honey. Tell him the kicker.'

'Look, we weren't looking to cause any trouble, or to impede
the case. We went there hoping that either Pierre, Jean, or one of
the five students in the group would reveal something useful. Two
of the women, Elodie and Chloe, were my roommates when I was
at pastry school, and they've had some kind of bitter falling out.
According to Chloe, the other two – twin sisters – are brand new
students, who I doubt are of much interest. They barely knew
Delphine and I can't imagine their motive. The third student,
Cecile, is having a fling with Pierre from everything I've personally observed.' Lydia paused. 'She's also bitter about Pierre having
to run the cooking school while Delphine was sorting out her TV
show and book deal, and about Delphine not making him a business partner. But there's something else, too.' She recounted how
Candy had presented the notebook paper with the threatening
message. 'I've been thinking of why Delphine lost her TV and
book deals. We found out from Jean and Pierre that Delphine was
suffering from depression, but it was a family secret. What if
someone found out and told the TV network? It might have given
them pause for thought, especially if they also said that she was
erratic and a nightmare to work with.'

'Remind me of the facts surrounding Jean Chenault. He was at
the café with Delphine and Pierre yesterday?'

'Yes, but he left on his own for a business appointment before
I was able to talk to him. I can verify this because I saw him go
out the front café entrance right as I arrived. I know Mr Chenault
from my time in Ottawa. I, ah, briefly dated Pierre. Jean

Chenault was never around during the day, while we were at the pastry school. The main classroom was a large kitchen off of their home. So I only saw him here and there, in the evenings.'

'OK.' Nowicki finished his last chicken wing, thinking as he chewed. He finished and wiped his mouth and hands. 'When you called Delphine about her cigarette case, did it sound like anyone else was with her in her room? Did you hear anything over the line?'

'No, she was the only one I spoke to, after the receptionist put me through.' Lydia thought for a minute. 'You're thinking that a husband is always the prime suspect, right?' Lydia knew from the crime TV shows that the spouse, or other close relative, was usually the first person law enforcement considered suspect in a murder. Lydia might have been inclined to agree if she hadn't witnessed Jean's grief and torment over Delphine's depression. Maybe Jean had used his work as an escape from how helpless he felt at his inability to fix his wife's illness.

'That's right. Good thinking, honey bunny.' Grandma, her crime-show viewing partner, agreed.

'Hold on, ladies. Remember, everyone's still suspect. What we're doing here is narrowing it down.'

'No, you hold on, Harry. Lydia, tell him the big whopper,' Grandma urged.

At Nowicki's silence, Lydia pressed on. 'There's another significant detail that Detective Klumpski didn't mention to us. Madame was killed by a gunshot, as you suspected, and he's determined it was suicide.' Lydia paused for dramatic effect but Nowicki didn't as much as stroke his mustache. 'According to Pierre and Jean, they have the gun she used with her prints on it. It was a family pistol from the war that she smuggled across the border. We somehow overlooked the gun when we were examining the body . . . but how is that possible? Is the gun in the photos?' She observed Nowicki carefully, but his closed expression remained in place.

Did Nowicki know something he wasn't telling them?

'Harry, tell me you didn't already know this and kept it from us?' Grandma read her mind.

Nowicki shrugged, casually stretched his arm across the back of the sofa behind Grandma and atop one of Lydia's hand-crocheted afghans. The happy neon pinks and oranges of the granny squares were incongruous to the subject they discussed.

'Leo called me at the PD earlier, and then filled me in with more details when I gave him the photographs. The reason Lydia and I never saw the weapon when I was photographing the body was because it had landed between two large boulders and slipped down between them. Leo's team almost missed it, in fact.'

'I can't believe we didn't find it!' Lydia wished she'd thought to do a more detailed sweep of the area. She'd been so focused on what Nowicki was looking at with the camera lens. Delphine's body. 'So now you believe it was suicide?'

'I didn't hesitate to tell Leo that I thought he was being hasty in his determination of suicide, but I can't publicly disagree, and I'm not going to personally argue with him. Not when he has a weapon with her prints on it. It's a World War I relic, not something I'd expect to still work without regular maintenance, but those sidearms were built to last. While this all sounds unbelievable, it's not impossible.' He grimaced and shifted in his seat.

'Pop has a World War I pistol in the basement, too. One of our relatives brought it back.' Lydia didn't mention that there were also bullets in the lockbox Pop had secreted in the basement rafters. Nowicki was a cop after all, and she wasn't certain if Pop had ever registered the weapon, or even if it was a legal requirement for such a relic. He'd shown it to her only one time, and allowed her to hold what she'd thought of as an ancient bullet in her palm. The small, time-dimmed metal object took on new significance when she realized that something similar had killed Delphine.

'A lot of people have wartime weapons; they get passed on as nothing more than memorabilia in most cases.' Nowicki didn't have to emphasize that Madame's use of the pistol hadn't stopped at souvenir status. 'It was found closer to the deck, several yards from where her body landed, and in between two rocks. It's feasible that it was knocked out of her hand when the bullet discharged, or during her fall, or right after. It could have ricocheted off the deck or a boulder and slid into the crevice. The rocks were still wet when we were out there, and the tide had only begun to recede at the time of her death. We wouldn't have found the weapon unless we'd had more time to search.'

'There's no way she killed herself. I feel it in my bones. Doesn't it make more sense that the weapon would have landed closer to her body if she had?' Lydia's anger hammered at her temple as Nowicki remained silent. 'So that's it, case closed, no further investigation?'

Nowicki nodded. 'Officially, and for Acorn Bay PD, yes. It's possible that Leo has more information that corroborates his determination that he's not willing to give up to us.'

Lydia noticed Nowicki awkwardly shift his position again, and that his tone didn't match his words. It was as if he knew something that Klumpski didn't want him to share. 'You mean to civilians like Grandma and me.'

Nowicki cleared his throat.

'You'll keep us up to date on anything more you hear from Leo, won't you, Harry?' Grandma was doing her best to keep Lydia from pushing too far by doing it herself.

'That's not enough, Grandma. Leo Klumpski needs to know what we've found out. I gave him the note – that should have made him think twice about his suicide theory.' Although, as she thought about it more, the note could be seen as what drove Delphine to suicide.

'I'll be sure to pass on anything we figure out. But we need to have a solid case.' He paused, gathering his thoughts. 'That brings us back to our suspects.'

'Starting with Jean Chenault,' Lydia interjected.

'Yes. Almost all the murders I've ever solved were committed by either a relative or very close acquaintance. But unlike your favorite detective TV shows, these things don't get wrapped up in an hour, and there are usually days, months, sometimes years of motive behind the killing. With a long-term marriage there can be so many secrets we may never be privy to. And secrets don't mean motives in most cases. Was there anything else about Jean Chenault that either of you thought odd?'

'Well, he looks a heck of a lot older than he did last year, but nothing abnormal, considering his grief and the shock of it all.' Lydia recalled Jean's sallow skin. 'Unless his business is stressing him out, too. He kept emphasizing that he was in Buffalo on business separate from Delphine's. They were even staying in separate rooms so Delphine could prepare for her TV show, but he also seemed genuinely upset when he mentioned that Delphine had been suffering from depression for some time. Pierre said she received a call from the TV company yesterday, telling her they'd decided not to go ahead with the show. That was the first domino, it seems. The *Good Day America* interview at Lake Chautauqua was cancelled quickly thereafter. Then her literary agent said there were problems with her cookbook.'

'Do you know what Jean does for a living?' Nowicki had pulled out his small notepad and was scratching notes with a worn pencil.

'No. It makes sense that he came with them to Buffalo, though. Pierre explained that Delphine rented a car for the trip, and Jean drove their family Buick down to provide the required number of seats with safety belts for the group, for when they crossed the border.' She knew she didn't have to explain to Nowicki that US Customs and Canadian Border agents were notorious sticklers for auto safety.

'OK,' Nowicki said, 'tell me more about Pierre Chenault wanting to be a business partner in the school.'

'He wanted to be in full partnership with Delphine, running the pastry school with the expectation of eventually taking it over, but while I was there she didn't allow him to do anything except participate as a student. He hated it, but agreed to play along for a while. Now he's apparently running the entire school, and has been since Delphine began to seek her book and TV contracts, but he still isn't a business partner, and Delphine wasn't interested in his ambitions for the business. At least according to Cecile.'

Grandma leaned forward. 'Don't forget, Pierre agreed to pass Elodie without her having to take her course again. He's definitely acting as though he's in charge, all the way. He'd have a lot to gain, becoming the new head instructor at the school. But it seems clear that wasn't going to happen while Delphine was around.' Grandma slapped her thigh, her coral nail polish bright against her tan skin. 'That's a serious suspect if you ask me. But awful to think about, matricide.'

Lydia nodded. 'I know. It seems the power has already gone to his head with him granting Elodie's certificate. The Delphine I knew would never have allowed that, and Pierre knows it. I can't think of a reason for a son to go against his so recently deceased mother's wishes, unless he's not as upset as he appeared?' Lydia thought for a moment. 'Except now, with the cancellation of

Delphine's cookbook and television opportunities, it looks like there may not be a secure business for Pierre to inherit.' Lydia stretched her arms over her head and turned her head to the right and left, releasing popping noises as she did so. 'Detective Klumpski would have inquired into life insurance and Delphine's will, right?'

Nowicki nodded. 'He no doubt contacted RCMP – Royal Canadian Mounted Police – for that part of the investigation. It's unlikely that he'd have all of the answers regarding this yet.'

'So we don't know much about Delphine's home life or her mental struggles, and it sounds as though Pierre and Jean's financial motives are a bit shaky, at least concerning the school.' Lydia pressed on. 'So until we can verify that Delphine didn't carry a large life insurance policy, I suggest we look at the students.

'Cecile is definitely over-the-top in her defense of Pierre. She had a confrontation with Delphine in the café on the morning of the murder and seems very volatile where Pierre is concerned. Obsessed, even. She was so angry about how Delphine treated Pierre, it's clear she thought Delphine was an obstacle to Pierre getting what he deserved – a shot at running the business. It's possible she could have decided to take matters into her own hands.' Lydia paused. 'They were together at the hotel, in his room, when I walked in. If Cecile came to blows with Delphine over her behavior with Pierre, who knows what else she might be capable of? I can see Cecile imagining herself running the business with Pierre and the two of them eventually becoming some sort of culinary power couple. Though I personally doubt that any relationship between them would last long enough for Cecile to benefit in any way, Pierre may have used her to accomplish his more nefarious objectives.'

'Hmph.' Nowicki grunted, a sure sign that he was in deep thought.

Lydia couldn't let go of how different Elodie and Chloe had seemed to her since her excruciating encounter with them in the hotel lobby. She said as much to Nowicki and Grandma.

'While it's not fun to have to repeat part of a course, I don't see how that's motive for murder.' Grandma validated what Lydia hoped was true. She didn't want to think of the two women as murderers.

'I agree with you, Mary,' Nowicki concurred.

'But it could be a motive for Elodie, since her plans had taken a severe knock. She needed a scholarship to attend the school, and struggled financially as it was. Finding out that she had to postpone starting work might have pushed her over the edge. I also find it interesting that Elodie asked Pierre for her certificate and got it without any issues. Why was he so willing to give it to her? Going back to Pierre's viability as a suspect, is it possible Elodie knew something about Pierre's actions that she could blackmail him over?

'Plus we're forgetting that Elodie and Chloe had clearly had some kind of falling out between when I spoke to them at the café yesterday and the discovery of Delphine's body this morning. The atmosphere between them in the hotel lobby was downright venomous. Chloe told me yesterday that they planned to travel back together, but by this morning they couldn't stand to be in the same space. You should have seen them throwing insults at each other – you'd never believe they ever were friends. We can't discount that they may have been involved in either Delphine's murder or the note, or both. Something's gone very wrong and it's compromised their friendship.'

'Maybe.' Nowicki frowned. 'What about the other students?'

'There are two, Miriam and Marie, who've just joined the school. I can't see how they would have taken against Delphine so quickly and severely to have a strong enough motive.' Lydia looked at Nowicki. 'I think it's time to look at the crime scene photographs.'

Nowicki took the photos out of their protective waxed envelopes and placed them on the table. The scent of photographic processing chemical cut through their leftovers, wafting from the recently dried images.

'The most effective way to do this is for us to each take our time looking at the pictures, maybe write down notes as we go, and then we'll individually give our interpretation of what we see.' Nowicki looked at Grandma, then Lydia, who both nodded.

The lurid details of Madame's demise were spelled out in the twelve photographs arranged at their knees on the rectangular coffee table.

'I thought you shot two rolls of twenty-four,' Lydia commented.

'Yes, and I have all of them with me, but these are the best of the batch. There are close-ups of all of them that we can look at as needed.'

Lydia couldn't stop staring at the photograph that revealed a partial profile of Delphine, her head wedged between two boulders. Her visible eye was open, as was the same half of her mouth. As if she'd been taken by complete surprise. Also, while Delphine's head had landed in the middle of two boulders, her entire lower body was atop a single, flatter slab of rock.

Grandma took her time looking at each photo, murmuring a low 'tsk' and 'ouch' every so often. Lydia met Nowicki's gaze and realized he'd been watching both of them. He'd already come up with his theory, she figured. Irritation at being played crawled up her neck.

'Tell me something, Detective Nowicki. Why are you even interested in our opinions at this point?' she asked. 'Klumpski's got the case all but closed. Unless you have something to convince him to reopen the investigation, we've already lost. No one wants to hear that Delphine was murdered.'

'Lydia, please don't be abrasive right now,' Grandma urged. 'We're crime-solving.'

'Not according to Klumpski. He says it's over.'

Grandma sighed in exasperation but Lydia kept her gaze on Nowicki. She raised her brow. 'Well?'

Nowicki shook his head in resignation, but she saw the hint of a smile on his lips. 'I know you two. You'll shake every tree you can until the right nut drops out. That's why I care about your assessment. I admire your tenacity, and your case-solving skills rival any professional's.'

'But?' Lydia wasn't fooled by his flattery.

'Not a "but" as much as a concern. The one thing you two don't have is years of experience. An investigation is usually boring and tedious. But if it goes sideways, it can be lethal in an instant. It needs the solid backing of time in the saddle.'

'Are you saying that we need your big gun, Harry?' Grandma giggled.

'There's nothing humorous about a risk to your lives, Mary. I know that I'm not going to stop you two from chasing this down.

But I want you to let me guide you through it. Let me keep you safe the best way I'm able.'

Lydia recalled his earlier edginess and couldn't stop herself from reading into his worried expression. He knew more about the case than he was letting on, as did Klumpski. But they didn't have all the answers. It explained why he was intent on keeping their activity under his unofficial supervision. Plus, she knew him well enough to believe he wanted to keep them out of danger, too.

'Aww, Harry, my dearest.' Grandma gave him a loud kiss on the cheek. 'I've known since grammar school that I can always count on you. Who else would have lied to Sister Teresa when I boobytrapped her desk drawer with my tomato soup?'

'My knuckles are still sore,' he jested about the ruler slaps.

Lydia didn't think there was anything funny about child abuse, and her nerves were stretched to their maximum.

'You know what I think? I think that you're letting us play along, in case we figure out something that you can use. We're more incognito than you are. Take earlier at the hotel. Klumpski would never have let you close to Pierre or his father, as the case is not in your jurisdiction. We're your undercover volunteer investigators,' Lydia remarked.

'Lydia! We talked about letting me do the sweet-talking.' Grandma batted at her forearm in a weak protest of Lydia's candor before turning her attention to Nowicki.

Nowicki rubbed his gray mustache with his hand, and let out a chuckle. 'You may be right, Lydia. I sure as sugar can't get caught with my hand in Detective Klumpski's cookie jar. He's got a lot going on.'

Lydia held back a grin. Only Nowicki would compare the machinations of a homicide case with a sweet treat.

'You bet I want to dig in, put my expertise to work on this case. Of course I do. But it would be a violation of the law, plain and simple. Please don't think I'm asking you two to do any kind of unofficial investigating on my behalf, though. I don't want to see either of you in trouble with Acorn Bay PD, or in danger generally.'

'But it wouldn't be any skin off your back if Grandma and I find more information, or figure it out. If Detective Klumpski catches us, we're two civilians being stupid. But if he catches you, you risk losing your job.'

He nodded, respect gleaming in his dark eyes. 'Possibly.'

'I'm all for Grandma and me figuring out what we can and letting you help us put the pieces together. Neither of us have any legal experience, like you said. Stanley has a great grip on the law but he's not a cop, either.'

Nowicki nodded. 'Now you're talking. But promise me you'll tread carefully.' He held out his hand to Lydia. 'Unofficial partners?'

She put her hand in his. 'Officially unofficial partners.' They shook.

'Finally!' Grandma cheered.

Lydia couldn't dismiss the distinctly familial feeling she had toward, and from, Nowicki. If the way he doted on Grandma was any indication, he wasn't going anywhere sometime soon. And he appeared to accept that neither were she and Grandma when it came to solving crime.

Especially a murder in our own backyard.

So what if they did happen to get caught with their hands in the crime-solving cookie jar? She had no doubt they could count on Nowicki to get them out of any trouble with Klumpski. Or any other law enforcement type.

'Now that we're all on the same page, let's figure out who did this!' Grandma's gaze darted from Lydia to Nowicki, and back to the photos. 'As far as I'm concerned, she was shot in the gut and bled out right there on the beach.' Grandma pointed to the photo of Delphine's torso. 'Whoever did this is a monster.'

'OK,' Nowicki said. 'Lydia, what do you see?'

Lydia nodded. 'I agree with Grandma. About how she died. The amount of blood alone is convincing. But the killer being a monster – I mean, aren't all murderers in that category? And look,' she pointed at the profile picture, 'she looks surprised. I noticed this when we were at the scene, too, before we knew for certain it was a bullet wound that killed her, but I'd forgotten about it until I saw the photos. She wasn't expecting to get shot. Not that anyone ever is, I imagine.'

Nowicki nodded with vigor. 'Good job!' He scratched his chin. 'Most rookies and even some seasoned officers wouldn't catch the facial expression. I'm impressed that you did.'

Lydia sat up straighter at his praise. 'So this suggests she was shot by someone?'

'Not technically. But the likelihood of her shooting herself in the abdomen seems slim, and then when you consider her expression . . .'

'You do see it as a clue?' Lydia pressed.

'It's more that I take note of it, along with the general sense I get at the scene. What else did you notice, Lydia?'

'I keep thinking about the deck railing. It was weak, fragile, rickety. Delphine was opinionated and very strong-willed. I know that I'm not a psychiatrist and we can never truly know what is going on internally with someone. But if you're going to jump, I'd think you'd want it to be a sure thing. Twenty feet above the lake, where the water could have been at high tide for all she knew, wouldn't offer a certain death. Plus, she would still have had to negotiate the railing, despite it being unstable. Wouldn't it have conceivably broken off in her hands, before she jumped? Finding her so close to where it broke, and the short drop to the shore, doesn't add up for me. And the gunshot doesn't help. Sure, she might not have needed to rely on a high drop to kill her if she planned to shoot herself, but then why do it on my deck? And as you say,' Lydia glanced at Nowicki, 'the gunshot location in the abdomen is odd. Plus, we don't know for sure whether the gun with her fingerprints on it was actually the one that was used. Klumpski's keeping everything close to his chest.'

'There's the Peace Bridge right up the road if she meant to jump, and it's five times as high. And deadly,' Grandma offered. She was correct. Sadly, the bridge spanning the US and Canada over the Niagara River had seen its share of jumpers.

'Exactly. I think she was shoved against the railing and shot, or was shot and then fell against the railing. It splintered, and broke away.' Lydia thought aloud.

'What does that tell you, about the moments before her death?' Nowicki asked.

'She had some kind of altercation with the killer before she was murdered.' Grandma spoke as though she'd read Lydia's mind.

'Is it possible that the family weapon, an heirloom pistol . . . isn't the murder weapon? Klumpski seems convinced it is.' Lydia knew little about guns or pistols, but she wanted to follow up on the gunshot.

'It's not impossible. But if it were my investigation I'd want forensics done on any found bullet casing, as a matter of course. The bullet that matches the weapon with her prints is a nine millimeter, which is consistent with the wound. But they have no casing, and there are plenty of other weapons that could have been used. It could have been any number of other pistols, antique or modern, that fired the nine-millimeter bullet that killed her.'

'How can you be sure it was a nine millimeter without the casing?'

'If it had been a forty-five-millimeter bullet, for example, it would have left a much larger wound. In fact, I don't think she would have made it off the deck in that case. She would have dropped right there.'

'Did they find the casing?' Grandma asked, leaning forward.

'Not that I'm aware of. But I will certainly try to find out.' Nowicki frowned. 'You have to promise me you won't do anything like going to the hotel again. Run your ideas past me, please. Leo isn't going to give you any leeway if he catches you snooping again. Don't make yourselves such easy targets, ladies. I can't guarantee that Leo will listen to me if I'm the one coming to your defense.' Harry's pronouncement made Lydia sit up straighter.

'And what about you? Why was he so rude to you when he first arrived on the scene?'

'He's being spiteful.' Grandma shook her head. 'And after all these years, to boot.'

'Will someone please tell me what the history is between you two?' Lydia didn't want to distract from the case but Klumpski seemed to be his own distraction.

Grandma and Nowicki swiveled their heads toward her, surprise on both their faces. Lydia laughed and shook her head. 'No, not between *you* two, but between Detectives Klumpski and Nowicki.'

'Ah.' Nowicki sat back and smoothed his palm over his bald head. 'It's all in the past, but suffice it to say it's about our career paths.'

'Cut the modesty, Harry dear,' Grandma exclaimed, then turned to Lydia. 'I finally got it out of him. It turns out that Harry was the top graduate at the police academy, and Leo barely made it through, even though his father and grandfather were both cops. These things run in families but in Leo's case, police talent ran the other way.'

'Now, Mary, please. That's not completely true.'

'Close enough,' she harrumphed. 'That man still has it in for you.'

Nowicki shook his head. 'So what if he does? It doesn't mean he's not doing his job right. There are so many layers to any investigation, and as a detective you have to go with the evidence on the table. I'm sure Leo's not thrilled that I was one of the first on the scene for a homicide in his jurisdiction. And while we can all be considered suspects, he knows me and does trust my professional judgement. I vouched for you both, and Stanley.'

'Thank you for that, Detective.' Just as Lydia still believed there were more layers to this case than she knew about, there were depths of Nowicki she'd yet to figure out.

'Please. I think it's high time you call me "Harry."'

'And you should call me "Lydia,"' she replied. A strange warmth invaded her chest, and she paused. Her relationship to Nowi— Harry – was no longer cursory, the by-product of Louie McDaniel's murder, or because he was Grandma's beau. They were becoming family. She cleared her throat.

'So what do we do next, Harry?'

FOURTEEN

'Hand me your snipper scissors, Grandma.' Lydia held out her free hand as she kept her crochet hook and yarn in the other, not wanting to lose her place in the blanket she'd been working on for Mom since she'd returned back to Buffalo. Cheektowaga, to be accurate. And now she had her own place in Acorn Bay.

That you're not allowed back to.

'Here you go, honey bunny.' Grandma placed the tiny antique scissors, rumored to have been in Great Grandma Romano's bag when she passed through Ellis Island, into Lydia's outstretched palm.

'Thanks.' Lydia clipped off the end of the burnt orange yarn and began a row of cream. The rippled pattern was a departure from the granny squares she'd grown up with, and she was excited to see it take shape.

The problem was that it was supposed to be Mom's Mother's Day gift, a month past already.

'What's going on, honey?' Grandma knew that getting Lydia to open up was the best way to get her out of the dangerous neighborhood that was her mind.

'I'm fine. Except . . . well, here I have a brand-new place I could be fixing up to live in, and I'm stuck here. Not that I mind living with you Grandma. You know I love being with you, right?'

'I get it, Lydia. Don't be fooled by my wrinkles. It wasn't that long ago when I was young, and I understand the need for your own place. Why do you think Harry and I were in the car earlier? I wasn't about to bring him here. Can you just imagine your father's face if he caught us?'

'I just wonder if I'm ever going to see my dream actually come to its full potential.' She hated the tone of self-pity that was creeping into her tone. 'Never mind. I'm being selfish, is all.' She still had a life to live, time to work toward her dreams. Delphine had none of that.

'Come on, honey bunny, we already went over your time in Ottawa. No experience is wasted in this lifetime. You found out you didn't need some fancy-dancy certificate or diploma to do what you already knew how to do, and you had a fling that made you realize that your true love is Stanley. Am I wrong on any of this?'

'No.' She had to hand it to Grandma – she knew how to get to the point. 'No, you're right on, Grandma. Tell me, does it seem as though the dead bodies are coming to us, because we won't stop until we get justice?' She gave it a minute, then side-eyed Grandma to see if she thought Lydia might be losing her grip on reality after their very long day.

But Mary Romano Wienewski's posture remained relaxed as she bent over a crossword puzzle magazine, having abandoned her macrame project on the folding card table for 'when it's brighter outside and my eyes can see it better.'

'You know I don't disagree with that. Everything happens as it's meant to. And when it doesn't, people like us get to the truth. No way was Delphine, or Louie, meant to be murdered. Not in my understanding of a loving universe.'

'But why us, Grandma?'

She paused, her pen hovering over the crossword. 'Because we're tuned in, is why. I've met a lot of people in my life and too many of them are sheep, I tell you. They don't want to take risks.' She shrugged. 'That's not a bad thing, necessarily. But makes for a boring life. You and I, we're go-getters. We're strong-willed, but with sensitive hearts. The combination isn't as common as you'd think. We feel things others miss. So it makes sense to me that we're being called to bring justice where it otherwise might be overlooked. Don't forget this past Easter and how the killer was so close to getting away with Louie's murder.' Grandma yawned. 'Any other questions?'

It was closing in on ten o'clock, and Lydia suspected neither of them would remain awake for the local eleven o'clock news tonight. They were both wiped out.

'I have one more question.'

'Mmm?' Grandma stared at her puzzle.

'What do you think Harry's keeping from us? Don't pretend you don't think it, too. My guess is that there's a bigger case going on that he can't talk about.'

'Hang on. What's a six-letter word for accomplish necessary steps, as in "take?"'

'Action?' Lydia replied.

'That's it!' Grandma filled in the boxes with blue ink. She never needed help with crosswords, hence doing them in ink. What was Grandma getting at?

After several moments, Grandma looked up at her. 'Yes, there probably is a bigger case going on. Isn't there always, these days? But we're interested in solving Delphine's murder, Lydia. Does it matter what Harry's keeping from us?'

'Well, yes, if it's at all related to this case. Even if it isn't. Maybe something that seems unconnected really is. We need to get this put to bed sooner than later. You know what'll happen if we take too long to solve a murder that's so close to our businesses.'

They both did. As Pop had so succinctly pointed out, the butcher shop's sales were still affected by the fallout from news that Louie McDaniel's corpse was found in their backyard sausage smoker. 'I mean, sure, the butcher shop is coming back out of the red, but we could have been so much further along by now if we hadn't had Louie's murder.'

'Take a chill pill, honey. What does it matter to us if Harry has a secret when we're going to do all we can to solve Delphine's murder, anyway? Whatever he knows, the case isn't completely solved or he'd have told us. Harry's on our side.'

'I know you're right.' And Lydia did. She was searching for clues and answers where she wasn't going to find them. It was time for bed, except she'd be trading in sleep for pierogi tonight.

'Trust me, Lydia, I did my best to butter up Harry to share whatever he knows, with no luck. But whatever Leo may have told him, he's not letting Harry see one dang thing about the investigation. Nothing, I tell you!' Grandma shook her head. 'It makes me so mad. Leo's being plain mean.'

'Hang on, Grandma. It may not be personal, to be fair. They are in different police departments, and I'm sure there's competition to solve a case. Plus, how often do you think Acorn Bay PD gets to work on a murder case?' Acorn Bay was a tiny village compared to Cheektowaga. 'Maybe that's why Klumpski called it a suicide so quickly. He just doesn't have the experience to see there could be more to it.'

'Maybe, but from what I know, what we've seen on TV, and what Harry's shared, cops from different jurisdictions often work together. Or at least they should. I'd say what Harry's holding back on is that Leo wants all the credit for this, and that's why he's being tight-lipped with Harry.'

'Talk about ego.' Lydia was grateful she'd fallen for a guy like Stanley, who put truth before his self-interests.

'Enough of the Harry and Leo drama. You get going with the pierogi filling and I'll write it all down. I'll make columns. Suspects, relation to Delphine, possible motives. We were too busy talking for me to write when Harry was here.' Grandma reached for the metal index file that they'd used to keep case notes last time and pulled out a blank index card. 'First up, Pierre.' Grandma scribbled on the card. 'He isn't on the up and up with women, so there's no telling what else he's lying about.'

Lydia began to peel the potatoes she'd use in the pierogi filling. She planned on making her cheese, potato, and sauerkraut pierogi – the one Delphine had enjoyed so much in the café – for the competition, but wanted to do a trial run first, just in case there were any small improvements she needed to make to the recipe.

'Pierre and Cecile could have planned it together. Or if Pierre's as good at manipulating women's minds as he is their privates, he may have convinced her to pull the trigger.'

'Grandma, that's good. Really good. I hadn't thought of that.' But she should have. Pierre's charm was his best asset.

'With Delphine out of the way, the pastry school business would be all theirs.'

'Yes. If we put aside the financial hit from the axed TV show and the book, the school itself has been doing very well. Do you think Leo has got any further with his enquiries into life insurance with the RCMP?'

Grandma clucked. 'They had to have at least searched her house and security boxes, and come up with nothing if he still says it's suicide. I suppose there could always be a policy that comes to light later.'

'I saw where they lived, how they lived, Grandma. I doubt there was any money there.' In fact, it had appeared as though Pierre would have needed a scholarship more than the one his mother bequeathed to other students.

'OK, on to the students. We've already ruled out the twins. Any more thoughts about Elodie and Chloe?'

Lydia frowned. 'I'm not sure. Elodie probably saw her dream slipping away when Delphine got tougher on her. Sometimes Elodie had a tendency to coast along and do the minimum requirements, especially if she felt she already knew how to do something. I was the same at times.' Lydia placed the peeled potatoes into her largest pot and filled it with water at their compact sink. 'I can't imagine either of them writing that threatening note, but when the stakes involve your future . . . Maybe Elodie found out about Delphine's depression and wrote the message to get revenge, and Chloe found out about it? Then Delphine turns up dead, and Chloe thinks the note triggered Delphine to kill herself, so blames Elodie for her death?'

'Then when Delphine's body was found, Elodie saw that Pierre stood to inherit the school and she knew she could get her way with him about the certificate. But we still don't know why, or how she found out about Delphine's mental struggles. Did she tell Pierre that she'd go to the TV network and share what she knew unless she got her certificate? But she did get it, so that doesn't make sense, unless she's particularly vindictive.' Grandma kept scratching notes with her stubby pencil, her data in neat columns.

'Wow, Grandma. It's awful to think someone I lived and shared a room with could be such a monster.'

'But if this theory about Elodie is true, and she sent the note, it doesn't help to solve who actually killed Delphine.'

'There's always the chance it was some kind of random shooting, too.' Lydia had read about bullets ricocheting off bodies of water. What if Delphine had simply been at the wrong place when a gunman fired from a boat?

'Possible but highly unlikely if you ask me.' Grandma yawned again.

'Hey, it happens. People have freak accidents all the time.'

'But when the victim is your former instructor that, oh by the way, you had conflict with, who came by to get her cigarette case out of your milk box, at your closed café, at night, on a deck that was cordoned off for safety reasons? Doesn't sound very "freak" to me.'

'Good points, Grandma.' Lydia paused in the midst of a double crochet, a fluffy strand of cream acrylic yarn hanging off her hook. 'But we've overlooked an important detail. We haven't been able to look at the scene ourselves. I haven't gone back up on the deck since we found her. I'd love to know if there are scuff marks or any other indication of a struggle.'

Both she and Grandma looked at the clock on the wall, then at each other. Grandma stood.

'I say we hit the hay so that we can be up before sunrise. We need to do some snooping around that deck, honey bunny.'

'Right on, Grandma!' But the police would recognize her Gremlin and stop them before they began. 'I'll call Stanley and see if the dairy truck's available for an early morning "delivery."'

Grandma set her magazine and pen onto the coffee table. 'Great thinking! I'll go lay out my prowling clothes.'

Lydia laughed. 'We're not prowling, Grandma.' 'Prowl' had a different connotation for her generation, apparently. 'We're . . . checking things out. And it's my property. It's not breaking any law to go there, just Klumpski's orders to stay away.' She knew she was twisting her legal facts and didn't care.

Not if they were getting closer to finding out who killed Delphine.

FIFTEEN

'We can't run our investigation on guesses. That's why we had no choice but to do this,' Grandma shouted from the passenger seat of the Gorski's Dairy delivery truck as Lydia drove them out to the lake the next morning. They had an hour until sunrise. She'd driven the aged vehicle several times, especially for one summer years ago. Lydia, seventeen, had been in a phase of teenaged rebellion and refused to work for Pop one summer. So Pop and Mr Gorski agreed to trade kids, and Stanley had worked a stint in the butcher shop.

Stanley had initially resisted her request to use the van when she'd asked last night, but relented when she promised it wasn't for anything illegal. He'd left the keys for her under the seat. She'd done the same with her car for him. She silently laughed at the vision of Stanley's six-foot-four frame folding into the cramped confines of the purple Gremlin, loading milk crates and eggs into the small hatchback for local delivery.

'Well, we have to be extra careful to not get caught this time. Harry's not in charge.' Lydia yelled her reply. They were having a hard time conversing over the aged diesel engine, and Lydia noticed that the stick shift required a heck of a lot more elbow grease than she'd remembered. A spring in the seat cushion poked at her buttock each time she pushed the clutch down and she had no doubt there would be a large bruise on her dupa tomorrow morning.

As they neared the café, she strained to see if the glow of police floodlights lit up the sky over her building.

'If the cops are still there I'm going to turn around and go home. No stopping,' she yelled.

'No. We have to get on that deck, Lydia. If the cops are there, I'll distract them while you run over for a look-see.' Grandma was on a mission from the Blessed Mother, Saint Teresa, or Padre Pio, depending upon her mood. Lydia didn't ask.

They both were, in truth, on a mission, a quest. Once Lydia

acknowledged that she'd found her second murder victim, she also accepted that since she didn't believe in coincidences, there was a reason dead bodies kept appearing across her path. Why it was happening was not hers to question, but justice was her aim. Maybe she was kidding herself, and this was a tragic coincidence, but at this point it didn't matter. Lydia was all-in.

'It'd be best if we inspected the deck together,' Lydia suggested. They each picked up on different types of details, which is part of what she felt made them a good team. 'It'd be better if it was in daylight, though. Maybe we should wait until sunrise.'

'No way! Each minute another gust of wind, or burst of a raincloud, or wild beast could clear away critical evidence. Our flashlights are as good as daylight, anyways. I've got an extra set of D's here.' Grandma patted the pocket of her lightweight jacket where she'd taken the last of the family's batteries from Pop's garage workbench.

'The cover of darkness is definitely our friend, Grandma.'

They needed to draw zero attention to themselves from anyone, including nearby home and business owners. The last thing she and Grandma needed was to get caught sneaking into the crime scene after Detective Klumpski had been so adamant that they remain in Cheektowaga until further notice.

'Park it across the street, over there.' Grandma's order cut through her worries and Lydia's gaze noted where she pointed through the windshield, to a group of several smaller commercial buildings. 'No one will think twice about this truck if they notice it in the body garage's parking lot.'

'Great thinking, Grandma.' Lydia smiled in the dark. Grandma was great at finding hiding-in-plain-sight spots. She pulled the truck into the small asphalt lot and parked in a row of other vehicles that were waiting for Sparky's Autobody to service them.

'Perfect.' Grandma spoke quietly once Lydia killed the engine. 'It's like old times, honey bunny. You and me on the prowl for a killer.'

'It's not like last time, though. We were in the thick of the woods by a creek, and it wasn't our property. No one had told us to stay away until called back.' Lydia knew they had to go against police orders if they were going to have a chance of figuring this out, but it wasn't her first choice.

'From what I've found out from Harry, Leo Klumpski is a big liar.' Grandma nodded. 'It's our sacred duty to find out the truth, and we can't trust him to give it to us.'

'What do you mean?'

'I told you that Harry finished ahead of Leo in the academy. Well, he and Harry served at the same time in the Buffalo Police Department. Let's say they each have . . . a different moral compass.'

'Be more specific, Grandma. We're risking getting fined or worse if we get caught tonight.' Lydia wished Grandma had opened up about this insight sooner.

'I don't want to betray Harry's confidence again, honey. You understand, don't you? Let's just say that Leo did everything possible to get ahead in his career, which included spreading malicious rumors about his colleagues.'

'But Harry is nothing if not morally upright. I'm sure no one believed Klumpski, right?' Since Klumpski was part of a much smaller department, it had to mean he hadn't succeeded at his ugly games.

Grandma's struggle with her conscience played across her face and Lydia silently waited in the dark. One, two, three—

'Oh, all right!' Grandma sighed in exasperation. 'I didn't know this myself until a few hours ago, when Harry told me. Leo was the man who broke up Harry's marriage.'

'What? Oh. My. Goodness.' Lydia sat up straighter. 'It has to be so painful for him to even see Klumpski again.' She thought back to how Nowicki had grown quiet around the other detective.

'More than painful,' Grandma admitted. 'I think that's why Harry's willing to give us whatever help we ask for, as well as looking out for us, of course.'

'Wait, what?' Lydia gasped. As Grandma had already emphasized, Nowicki was the epitome of a law enforcement professional. He'd admonished them many times for their interference in the investigation of Louie McDaniel's murder. Of course, that was before he knew them better. 'That doesn't sound like him.'

'He has a score to settle.'

'He said that?'

'Not exactly, no. Of course not. Harry's a gentleman through and through.'

'And didn't he get divorced, like, years ago?'

'Yes, but the soul never forgets. What we can't forgive we must forget, and what we can't forget we must forgive. Except in the case of someone stumping your wife.' Grandma slapped her hand over her mouth. 'Ermflsks.' Her muffled curse was incomprehensible, but Lydia didn't need much imagination to figure it out.

'Harry's secret is safe with me, Grandma,' she said. Harry was someone she'd got to bat for, she realized.

She must have sat there too long because Grandma patted her shoulder as if they were going strawberry picking and not murder evidence hunting.

'Don't you think we should get going?'

'Yes. Let's go.'

'Wait a minute, Lydia. Look over there.' Grandma put her hand on Lydia's forearm as they crouched behind a boulder that sat in the grass field adjacent the café.

'I see it.' A lone police cruiser sat in the café parking lot. Lydia's stomach dropped at what wasn't in the parking lot. Customers' cars. A stark reminder of what she risked if they didn't solve this before the news got out. The good thing about a murder in Acorn Bay as opposed to Cheektowaga or Buffalo was that Klumpski had been able to keep it quiet. So far.

Maybe he has an ulterior motive to keep it out of the press.

'No telling where the officer is.' Grandma interrupted her train of thought, peering through the clunky binoculars she'd kept in the clear orange and gold floral print plastic tote bag that she'd used for their previous surreptitious excursion.

'We should wait until he or she comes back to the car,' Lydia said. 'To play it safe.'

'Sure, and we can chat them up about who they think killed Delphine while we're at it.' Grandma rolled her eyes, the whites reflecting the pale ambient light from the half moon. 'Fortune favors the bold, Lydia. And we have these.' She held up a small square object with a metal stick attached.

'What is that?'

'It's how we're going to bust this case wide open. With our own communications capability.' She shoved the hard, smooth object against Lydia's sweaty palm. 'This is yours. I've already turned it on for you.'

'Walkie-talkies?' Lydia held her flashlight over the device. 'They're too loud. We'll get caught.'

'You've got to stop with the negative energy, honey. Your chakras need to be cleansed, is my guess. But no time for that now. Maybe say an extra rosary tonight after we get back, OK? Now, let's go get what we came here for. Evidence.'

Lydia ignored Grandma's familiar manner of juxtaposing various religious and metaphysical concepts into her own tisane of spirituality and steeled herself. Could she be the woman she needed to be in this moment? Grandma was right, of course. They hadn't dressed in dark clothing and parked across the street so they could play hide and seek. They were here for the Truth.

'OK. But no talking unless you have to. Keep the volume as low as you can,' Lydia instructed.

'I have to turn it up enough to hear it over the water,' Grandma said.

Lucky for them, the waves were splashing tonight thanks to the windy conditions, which provided a decent cover for any noise their not-prowling might create.

'OK, let's do it as we planned,' Lydia said. 'We'll go up to the front door and let ourselves in, as long as there's no sign the officer is inside. If you see him or her, duck.'

'Following you.' Grandma made a head start, forcing Lydia to catch up.

They scurried across the parking lot, toward the main entrance. The street was deserted, and it felt as though they were the only two beings on the planet. Lydia could let her imagination fly away with the lake wind, except it could lead to her and Grandma getting caught in the midst of doing exactly what Klumpski told them not to do.

She had a backup story prepared, just in case. There was plenty of unbaked bread dough in the commercial refrigerator. She'd plead a poverty defense. The bakery had to stay in business and there was no sense wasting thirty-six loaves of pumpernickel bread. It wasn't a story Nowicki would ever fall for, but she was counting on Klumpski not knowing her, or Grandma, as well. And OK, she'd already assessed that perhaps Klumpski wasn't the sharp investigator Nowicki was.

To her relief, she unlocked the front café door and they slipped inside without a hitch. She carefully closed the door behind them, keeping the wind from slamming it shut.

'Lydia, do you—' Grandma's voice echoed in the front entry and made Lydia jump.

'Shhh.' She had to let her heart and breathing settle, both of which were pounding in her ears. As she caught her breath, she heard Grandma's breathing beside her. After several more heartbeats the sounds evaporated into nothing. They were surrounded by darkness and silence, interrupted by the surf's rhythmic slaps against the foundation.

The only source of light came from the bakery display case in the coat check area – she must have forgotten to turn it off before Detective Klumpski had ordered her out until further notice. The shelves were bare, as she never stored food outside of the commercial refrigerators after hours. Her stomach growled and she shifted her weight on her sneaker-clad feet. Breakfast wasn't for another few hours.

Once their eyes adjusted, they glanced at one another. Lydia pointed to their objective and Grandma nodded her agreement. They headed straight to the back deck door and peeked through the blinds, past the deck.

No sign of an officer out there. *Phew.*

'So far so good, honey bunny,' Grandma whispered.

'Yeah, I think maybe we've lucked out.' Lydia's confidence added a spring to her step. The café and bakery seemed to be giving them a big hug, welcoming their return. It remained quiet with zero signs of an officer inside.

'It makes sense that no one is posted inside here, doesn't it? There's nothing to see or worry about; she died outside, after all,' Grandma observed.

'We still need to keep tabs on where the officer is. But yes, I agree. There's no reason for the police to keep someone in here, not after they swept it.' Lydia wasn't happy about this. It didn't seem right that anyone else was in her place when she wasn't.

Maybe the territoriality of the seagulls Kishka and Dolly, along with Pacha, had rubbed off on her.

'We'll be able to see from the deck, won't we? We'll stay low and look through the railing.' Grandma was focused on achieving their objective while Lydia was allowing her mind to wander.

'Yes, but let's double-check the cop's location first.' The reminder of the threat of getting caught made Lydia's stomach dip as if she was on her favorite wooden roller coaster that overlooked the lake, up in Canada.

'Good thinking.'

'We can try to see what we can tell from the kitchen window first. The car's right near the kitchen door.' Lydia hated delaying taking a look at the deck, but not getting caught was as important as finding evidence. There were a few places they could hide in the café, like behind the bakery case, or underneath the soda fountain. A cursory inspection by a patrolling officer might keep them out of sight. But once they stepped outside they'd be lot more vulnerable, especially on the open deck.

'Right behind you, honey bunny.'

Lydia would be lying to herself if she even tried to pretend that a big part of her absolutely loved this. The thrill of the hunt alongside Grandma. It would be too complicated to sleuth with Stanley, because he'd question the legality of everything she did and Lydia believed ignorance in these circumstances. Stanley was also a major distraction, with his sexy bedroom eyes and his hips. Mary, Mother of God, Stanley's hips . . .

They were going to have to plan their next rendezvous sooner than later.

Rendezvous, really?

She'd started thinking of her love life as part of a criminal investigation, too. More like a World War II spy novel.

A bright white beam stretched across the dining room to the kitchen door, only two feet in front of them.

'Grandma! Shut that thing off!' She reached forward and covered the lens of Grandma's flashlight.

'Sorry, honey. I was worried about tripping over one of the bar stools.' The serving bar ran three-quarters of the length of the back of the room, with a mirrored wall and shelves where bottles of alcohol had been displayed by the previous restauranteur. Lydia wasn't planning on getting a liquor license anytime soon, if ever. It was too expensive and came with a plethora of extra headaches including rowdy customers.

Lydia waited for Grandma to catch up to her at the kitchen entrance. 'OK, let's make this fast. Then we'll check out the deck.'

'I'm on it, honey.' Grandma held her flashlight as if it were a weapon. Lydia said a silent prayer that she wouldn't need it.

Pushing the swing door open, they walked into the kitchen. Ambient light spilled in through the back door's window as well as from the two sink windows and allowed them to maneuver around the stainless-steel worktable with no problem. They continued past a pile of empty wooden crates, a stack of commercially-sized cans of corn and mixed vegetables, and the trash can. Lydia's ire rose at the sight of crumpled donut boxes overflowing from the receptacle.

Just great. The police had supplied their own snacks after they'd finished all of her baked goods. A curl of displeasure roiled in her gut and there was no mistaking why. This was Lydia's kitchen, her café, her bakery. Her rules and her food should be all that anyone experienced here.

A shiver ran across her nape and down her forearms, raising gooseflesh under her sweatshirt. Maybe she was channeling Madame Delphine.

As she wrestled her emotions, a distinct rustling sound came from the pile of trash. Lydia grabbed the broom leaning against the sink wall and prepared to execute whatever pest emerged.

More rustling filled Lydia's stomach with trepidation.

'It's a mouse, Lydia!' Grandma cried and turned her flashlight on, aiming the beam at the pile of empty, sugared boxes. 'Kill it!'

'Turn the light off!' she hissed.

Grandma complied. 'I'm trying to help. I kept the beam low to the ground, don't worry.'

'I'm going to smash it.' Lydia clutched the broom handle with sweaty hands, knowing that the patrolman could be at the kitchen door in a matter of seconds.

A scary screech rent the air followed by a low growl. Two pointed ear tips came into view, then a familiar feline face as Pacha emerged from the donut wreckage, holding the disgusting pest in his able jaws.

'Eww!' Her exclamation was involuntary, but she quickly regained her composure. 'Good, good boy, Pacha.' Lydia reflexively moved to open the kitchen door to allow Pacha out, as she would in any other circumstance, but a hard slap on her hand stopped her.

'Are you kidding? You open that door and we'll get caught for sure!' Grandma snarled as if she was trying out for a role in *The Godfather*.

'OK, OK!' She regrouped. 'Come here, sweet Pacha.'

He complied, and did what she usually tried to avoid, dropping his offering at her feet. Before she could grimace or heave, Lydia quickly swept the deceased critter into the dustpan. 'I'll throw it off the deck, in the dark.'

'*Meeeeooooow.*' Pacha wanted out, scratching at the kitchen door.

'Shhh, no!' Lydia admonished. She looked out the window and kept Pacha from the door with her foot, all the time holding a dead creature, tiny paws up, aloft in the waste pan.

'What do you see, honey?' Grandma was a solid three inches shorter than her, and unable to peer through the kitchen door window without a step stool.

Lydia held her breath and looked out the window. Sure enough, the police car was no more than ten feet away, parked at an angle between the café and the back barn. The front seat was occupied, the officer's face hidden from view. A tiny red glow came into view, followed by a wispy cloud that the wind whisked away.

'They're taking a smoke break,' she reported.

'They? There's two?'

'No, no, just one. In the driver's seat.' Lydia turned back to Grandma. 'This is as good a time as any. Let's check out the deck now, before he's done with his cigarettes.'

SIXTEEN

They made haste back to the main dining room, and continued to the double French doors. Memories of carrying an egg on a spoon and racing to the finish line during school fairs tugged at Lydia as she somehow managed to keep from dropping Mr Mouse.

'You have two hands, Grandma.' She nodded at the door and watched as Grandma undid the deadbolt and doorknob lock. Without hesitation, they went outside, and as soon as they'd cleared the threshold Grandma shut the door and squatted down, tugging on Lydia's free arm. 'We have to stay low.' Grandma proceeded to prostrate herself on the deck, not unlike how Lydia's oldest cousin Peter had done during his ordination.

'Right.' As soon as Lydia was able, she tossed her burden from the deck. 'RIP, Mr Mouse,' she whispered, then put the dustpan down and lowered to her belly and elbow-crawled to be close to Grandma so they wouldn't have to speak above a whisper.

On her stomach, Lydia looked to the far left of what was left of the railing after forensics had finished with the scene, and saw that the police officer was still in the vehicle. Her eyes teared from the wind and as sporadic drops of rain began to fall she couldn't make out if he was still smoking or not. A sense of urgency gripped her. 'He could decide to come up here any minute.' She'd feel a lot better once they were back in the van and headed home to Cheektowaga.

'Naw. My guess is he'll walk around to the front first. Let's check the deck out, honey.' Grandma started a slow crawl around the wooden platform, running her fingers over the planking. 'I'm looking for any fresh marks or dents in the surface.'

'You get this part here, and I'll cover it from broken railing to the door.' Lydia copied Grandma's motions. Grit and grime scratched against her finger pads as she worked, but the beams seemed otherwise intact. She was grateful to realize that the deck itself was well built. If only the railing had held as well. But would it have made a difference for Delphine?

Until now she'd allowed herself to believe she'd make the cottage next to the café and bakery her new home, maybe hers and Stanley's first place. Now, she didn't think she'd ever look at the deck and not think of it as the last place Delphine had been. Funny how something like a dead body, and not just a random corpse but someone she'd spoken to only hours before their demise, could smother her dream.

No. She and Grandma would solve this, they *were* solving it, darn it. Lydia's Lakeside Café and Bakery would be all the stronger for it, too. If for no one else, she was going to do it for Delphine. The once-nemesis had gained Lydia's respect and admiration during her short trip and she'd never be able to tell Delphine in person. But she could do this one last, most important task for her.

Find her killer.

'Let's take a closer look at that railing, Lydia.' Grandma began to crawl across the deck again and Lydia followed. Rain drops splatted against her cheeks, and it wouldn't be too long before the deck got slippery. Grandma was in fantastic shape thanks to the workout videos she played on the apartment VCR, and the polka dances she attended, but Lydia didn't want her to risk a fall. Grandma's rheumatism was acting up, and her reflexes might not be as quick as usual.

It's OK. Grandma's fine.

The entire family had been on tenterhooks since Pop's stroke last Christmas. Who could blame them? Their main breadwinner had been stopped mid-pork chop. The last thing they needed was for their beloved matriarch to suffer an injury, or worse.

'Don't get too close,' Lydia said, and stopped at the edge of the deck. Waves raced up to the retaining wall fifteen feet below, and save for the bright yellow crime scene tape extending the length of the boundary it was easy to imagine that Delphine's body had never been there, that this was all a fever induced nightmare.

'We got trouble, honey.' Grandma's words were as effective as a gut punch.

'What?'

'That police cruiser's front seat is empty.'

Lydia looked and sure enough, Grandma's eagle eyes were right.

'Well, we didn't find anything here anyway. Let's go.' She went to crawl toward the deck's back steps, where they could easily run along the side of the building and cross the street before the officer ever reached the front entrance. Something poked her knee through her jeans.

She stopped and felt several scratches in the decking with her hands. 'There's something here. I thought I went over this already, but I have to turn on my flashlight.'

'Go ahead, but make it snappy.' Grandma took a turn at being the level-headed one.

Lydia shone her light on the area in question. Several definite gouges appeared in the beams.

'This looks like the dance floor after the last polka at a drunk wedding,' Grandma observed.

'They're fresh. Look – the wood is brighter inside. It hasn't weathered yet.' She'd never noticed these chips in the deck before, and she was certain she would have. She'd memorized every inch of the place since taking ownership.

'Madame Delphine was wearing serious kitten heels, but they were very pointy.' The mental image of the electric blue pumps flashed across Lydia's mind. 'And these divots are about the right size to be caused by them.'

'Which means she fought from being thrown over!' Grandma slapped Lydia on her shoulder. 'Good going, honey bunny. You knew there was more to it. This proves that she didn't come up here to jump off on her own.'

'Does Klumpski know all of this and still determined suicide?' Lydia gasped. Were they looking at some kind of police cover-up?

'Wait, honey, do you hear that?' Grandma's eyes grew wide.

A definite male voice reached them over the wind and steady rain. Lydia and Grandma flattened back to their bellies on the wet surface. Steps sounded on the main stairs that led up to the deck from the parking lot. Lydia held her breath and prayed for a way out. If they didn't skedaddle this very minute, there was only one way she and Grandma's excursion would end.

They were going to get caught.

* * *

'What should we do, Lydia? Go back inside?' Grandma hissed into her ear.

Lydia's mind raced. Which way to run, indeed? Back inside the café, or down the deck's back stairs? 'We have to go down the back steps. Get up, let's go!'

More footsteps sounded behind them as they made it to the darkest part of the deck where there were no motion detector lights ready to give them away. 'Quick, down the stairs!' Lydia nudged Grandma toward the steps, the threat of her slipping taking a lower priority. But Lydia made sure she came down ahead of Grandma. If she fell at least she wouldn't go all the way down.

The voices began to become distinguishable as more than one, maybe even more than two, as their feet left the last rickety step and landed on the graveled ground. Were there more than two officers on patrol?

Lydia faced Grandma and handed her the truck keys. 'You go around to the front, and get back to the truck. I'll meet you there as soon as I can.'

'Where are you going and why?' Grandma's stubborn streak wore on Lydia's already taut nerves.

'This isn't the time to argue, Grandma. I'm going under the deck to listen to them. You have to keep going.'

'No. I'm coming with you! But how will we get under there?' Lydia didn't have time to argue.

'There are two small doors in the lattice on either side.' The deck jutted out from the café's dining room and over the retaining wall by several feet, giving the impression of the café actually floating on the lake. But most of the structure was actually over what had originally been a backyard of some sort, years ago. Open work lattice had been added for aesthetic value, she assumed, but it turned out to be a perfect way create a storage area for outdoor items such as seasonal furniture and decorative concrete planters. The previous owners had mentioned it was a good place to store the outdoor furniture, but only in warmer months as the ferocity of the lake in winter could easily carry a folding table or chair away.

Makeshift access doors had been cut into each side portion of the lattice. A section of lattice had also been installed flush with the retaining wall, which Lydia thought a waste as it got pummeled by the waves during storms.

'Let's get under that deck. I'll follow you. Hurry!' Grandma insisted.

'Fine. But no flashlights!' Lydia grabbed Grandma's hand and tugged her toward the lattice door.

'Got it.' Grandma was in full *Police Woman* mode. All she needed was a set of fake eyelashes like Angie Dickinson's and she'd be set.

Lydia had to admit she'd have felt bereft without Grandma by her side, no matter how aggravating her elder could be. They were a team. Delphine's murder needed their combined brainpower to get solved.

Relieved that they didn't have to worry about keeping their footsteps quiet thanks to the loud waves rushing the retaining wall, they moved quickly to the underside of the deck.

A sharp gust of wind caught her baseball cap, flinging it through the air. Lydia didn't take the time to see where it went. If whomever was on the deck spotted it, hopefully they'd think it was simply windblown garbage.

She sidled up to the lattice work that hid the underbelly of the deck and reached for the latch of the small utility door.

'This is the spot.' A loud male voice sounded over the wind from the deck above. *Klumpski.*

Lydia froze. If he peeked over the far side of the deck they'd be in plain view, exposed.

'Don't stop!' Grandma spoke into her ear and poked her in the middle of the back. 'We'll be tits up if they catch us now!'

Lydia unlatched the door with shaking hands and slipped inside the pitch-black space, pulling Grandma in next to her and shutting the door. The musty smell under the deck combined with her practical blindness sent fear crawling across her nape, over her scalp. She needed her flashlight to see but had to somehow protect the light from shining upward.

'Can't see a damn thing down here,' Grandma muttered loudly.

It was incredibly difficult to hear too, as the relentless waves hit the wall, spraying water through the lattice. They were going to be soaked in no time.

Think, think, think.

Quickly shucking her black T-shirt, she made a tent with it over the flashlight. Her teeth began to chatter in time with her shivering but she ignored it all. Protecting Grandma and her from getting caught was the only priority right now. She clicked the light on and held her breath. Grandma's gaze met hers over the soft glow and she nodded. 'Good thinking.'

Lydia used the stealth lighting to see that they were standing in the midst of every kind of beat-up patio furniture imaginable. She grasped Grandma's upper arm. 'Here. Let's sit down here and listen.' They perched on the edge of wrought-iron chair frames.

'Don't scratch your legs on this or you'll get tetanus!' Grandma warned.

'Shhh!' Lydia's ardent reply happened at the same exact moment there was a pause in the pounding waves. *Oh no.* There was no way anyone didn't hear her.

Unless they were emotionally invested in their own conversation.

'It doesn't make sense. Why?' The pronouncement and demanding query reached through the quiet, through the deck slats. Lydia and Grandma's gazes locked over the darkened flashlight, both reflecting surprise.

The words, the voice, registered as well as it had at the Acorn Bay Hotel. Pierre was up on the deck, looking at the place his mother had died. Why was he here with Detective Klumpski, in the dark? At this hour? Unless, unless he wanted to come at the same time of her estimated time of death?

The wind picked up again and she missed whatever the muffled reply was. Sounds of shuffling feet, creaking boards, and splashing waves competed with the drone of male voices. She was getting soaked, but had to listen.

'Pierre, listen to me. You're grieving.' The man who replied spoke in French. Jean Chenault. Maybe they'd both asked Detective Klumpski to come out to the deck before they went back to Canada.

'Father, excuse me, but you're not in any better shape than I am,' Pierre responded in French.

'What the hellski are they saying?' Grandma didn't bother speaking quietly.

'Shhh.' Lydia strained to catch every word.

'Both of you, please, calm down. And speak English. I can't

answer your questions if you don't.' Detective Klumpski sounded annoyed.

A loud *plunk* followed by muffled cursing split the air in between all of the ambient noise and Lydia looked up to see that Grandma had dropped her flashlight into the large empty brass planter that sat beside her chair.

Lydia shut off her flashlight but didn't dare move as sheer terror coated her bare skin in layer of cold sweat.

'What was that?' Pierre had heard them!

'Hang on,' Klumpski barked. 'Officer Sullivan, that you out there?' Heavy footfalls over their head, to the edge of the deck. Peeking through the lattice, Lydia saw the beam of a flashlight swathe across the water's surface. And land on her ball cap, which had landed on the grassy strip of land to the right side of the deck, as if tossed from the top.

Please don't let them find us.

'I'll check it out in a minute. It's probably nothing more than another piece of the railing or the deck hitting the rocks. You can see where your wife fell. The gun was found between the rocks. A terrible tragedy,' Detective Klumpski explained.

A loud crackling rent the air.

Lydia heard the noise at the same time another wave hit the break wall and doused her with lake water. Her walkie-talkie made an unintelligible noise, albeit more quietly. *Crap.* She'd forgotten to turn it off.

'Is your walkie-talkie turned off?' The louder static had to be from Grandma's.

'Copy that, honey bunny,' Grandma whispered back, and Lydia let out a sigh of relief. Until a very loud burst of static emitted from Grandma's walkie-talkie. 'Oops, guess I turned it the wrong way.'

'That's either Officer Sullivan, or a nosy reporter. You two stay up here while I go check.' Klumpski was going to find them, she just knew it. Her worst fear was confirmed when his footfalls began to descend the same stairs they'd used to get off the deck.

'Stay with me!' She grabbed Grandma's hand and used her memory to get them around the derelict furniture, to the opposite side of the under deck. She dashed her toe against a cement planter, cobwebs grabbed at her face, but within seconds they were at the far latticed wall. She let go of Grandma and strained to see in the pitch-black with zero results.

Lydia felt her way along its length, all the time cognizant that there were two men over their heads and one who'd open the opposite lattice door at any moment.

A raw scraping sound sent her nape crawling until she realized it was Grandma, at the side hatch. She'd reached the door and the rusty hinges were complaining as she opened it. Light from the kitchen door's lamp reached into the first few inches of the space, allowing Lydia to see how she'd overshot the door's location while Grandma found it.

'Lydia!' she whispered, motioning with her hand. 'What are you waiting for? Come on!'

'There's someone underneath the deck!' Pierre shouted.

Crapola times two.

'Stay up there!' Klumpski ordered. A beam of light reached through the far lattice and Lydia was grateful she hadn't had that extra chug of water in the truck, because she was as close to peeing her pants as she'd ever been. Yet in some calm, clear-minded recess of her panicked brain, her reflexes took over.

'Grandma, get into the kitchen – go! I'll be right there.'

Grandma didn't argue this time, thank all the saints and martyrs. Lydia ran to where they'd been sitting, grabbed a chair, and lifted it.

'Oof.' Heavier and clunkier than she'd imagined, she ignored her screaming shoulder muscles and heaved it against the lattice door, just as Leo Klumpski unlatched it.

SEVENTEEN

ydia thanked the Blessed Mother for their successful escape and ruse, along with the fact that she'd spent day after day and long into the nights, in the café kitchen. It was why she'd been able to make it appear as if she and Grandma had been in here for hours, instead of three to five chaotic minutes.

She and Grandma had scurried about the kitchen more furiously than Pacha's rodent victim. Two dozen loaves of pumpernickel were arranged on baking sheets, the ovens were preheating. Flour, sugar, butter, eggs and raspberry jam were arranged on the worktable next to the commercial mixer, ready to become her secret recipe sandwich cookies. Well, actually Grandma Dot's recipe. Pierogi dough she'd made two days ago and put in the refrigerator was on a floured rolling board, with a large jar of sauerkraut next to it.

'OK, get ready to turn the lights on.' She cued Grandma, who'd stood next to the light switch waiting for Lydia's signal from her spot at the sink window.

No one was in view and the police cruiser remained empty, so her thrown chair ruse had worked. Pierre and Jean either went down to see what had happened with Detective Klumpski or they had remained on the deck. They hadn't come inside – she'd ran out to the dining room and locked the door, not risking a peek under the blinds to see if they were still on deck. The locked doors would be easily explained, as she'd locked herself out on the deck more than once.

But she always carried the key to the kitchen door around her neck, and that had saved them.

Voices sounded in the dining room. *The front door.* Klumpski had the keys, of course, and let them back in.

'Hit the lights, Grandma!'

The kitchen lit up as she usually had it at this time of day. She turned on the faucet and washed her hands, still sticky from working the cookie dough.

'Lydia, here, take this, you've got to—'

'Not now, Grandma!' She didn't bother turning toward her. It was imperative they give the appearance of being here for the best of motives. 'Start sprinkling cornmeal on those baking pans,' she instructed. There wasn't time, because the voices neared, and the swinging door opened.

Lydia stood as nonchalantly as she could next to the mixer, unwrapping a pound of butter. Which dropped from her lifeless hands as soon as she saw the gun pointed at her.

'Whoa!' She raised her hands in the universal signal of surrender. 'Detective Klumpski, it's me, Lydia Wienewski!'

He took in the scene, acknowledged Grandma next to the ovens with a quick glance. The door swung open again and Pierre, followed by Jean, barreled into Detective Klumpski.

'Well, I'll be damned.' Klumpski kept aim at her while Pierre and Jean stepped to either side of him.

All three men stared at Lydia, Pierre's face turning pink.

'I know you said I couldn't come back to work until you said so but, Detective, this is my means of a living, and I have employees to support. We're, ah, here to save my bread. I can't afford to have two days' worth of pumpernickel go to waste, and my customers show up extra early to get cookies and donuts, too. I thought since we saw you at the Acorn Bay Hotel, and that you don't think there was any foul play involved in Madame's untimely death, that you may have been too busy to let us know it was OK to come back.' She couldn't help the ramble, but at least it had one positive effect, as Klumpski lowered his weapon and holstered it. He cleared his throat.

'Miss Wienewski, is business so bad that you can't afford clothes?'

Lydia blinked, and looked down. She'd forgotten to put a top back on and was wearing only her bra and jeans. It was her black bra, the one with the fancy lace trim, because her two other bras were in the laundry. She looked back up at the men.

'Don't mind us, Leo.' Grandma stepped next to Lydia, holding the jacket that she'd meant for Lydia to don. Grandma wasn't dressed much better, wearing a camisole of sorts. 'It gets hotter than a smokehouse in here and it's long hours sweating over the stove. Don't worry, we normally wear aprons and keep our hair up.' Grandma smiled and Lydia grit her teeth. She tried to send Grandma a telepathic message to not try to flirt with Leo Klumpski.

Lydia let out a deflated sigh. Grandma turned to her and gave her a quick, private wink. 'Here, honey bunny.' Grandma was the picture of a concerned coworker, handing Lydia her fuchsia zip front silk jacket, the zipper the same shade of electric blue as Delphine's beloved shoes. Lydia slipped into the warmth, and protection from inquisitive male gazes, in silence.

Grandma didn't appear as self-conscious about her camisole, not at all, but she did don one of Freddy's white chef jackets that he liked to wear as he worked the grill.

Klumpski hadn't cleared them of a misdeed. Not yet.

'You two, weren't, let's say, just outside, under the deck? I can't say I noticed the lights on in here when I patrolled the rear of the building earlier.' Detective Klumpski offered a bold-faced lie as if he did it on the regular. He hadn't been the skinny officer in the patrol car, who'd been smoking.

A sharp knock on the kitchen door saved Lydia from having to answer immediately as they all turned to watch a uniformed officer, slim built and bringing the scent of cigarette smoke, enter the kitchen, his bloodshot eyes snapping to alertness as he faced them all.

'Officer Sullivan. Where were you five minutes ago?' Klumpski barked.

'I did what you asked, sir. I was out front, guarding the entrance. But then I thought I heard a commotion, and you didn't answer on the two-way, so I came 'round the back to check. Saw the lights blazing out of the kitchen and knew something was up.' His gaze moved from Klumpski to Grandma, and then Lydia.

Lydia, emboldened by being decently clothed once again, took a step forward. 'We had to save my baked goods, Detective.'

'Hang on there, Miss Wienewski.' Officer Sullivan held his hand up to stop her, as if she was going to attack him.

'It's OK, Officer Sullivan,' Klumpski stated in tired defeat. 'Ladies, what do I have to do to get you to let me and my team do our job?'

'I thought your job was over, I mean, you told Mr Chenault the case is closed. That Madame killed herself.'

'Yes, that's right. I brought her husband and son to pay their respects, on the spot where she took her last breath, only to have you two crash into the scene like a couple of jokesters! Have you no respect?'

'I'm sorry.' Lydia directed her apology to Pierre and Jean.

Grandma stepped next to Lydia. 'Of course you two can take as much time as you need. Would you like to go back out on the deck?'

Klumpski's mouth set in a grim line and he placed his hands on his hips. 'This is still a crime scene—'

'We're not trying to do your job, Detective.' Lydia's voice sounded as weary as she felt, and she prided herself on not admitting that it had been them outside. If no one actually saw them there, and if she and Grandma kept their traps shut, it'd be no harm, no foul. Maybe she and Grandma were being ridiculous, after all.

'We were surprised to see you all here, of course, but as you can see, we are here for a different reason.' She gestured at the array of baking accoutrements and offered her best smile. Sure, she was lying about their investigating but not about needing to keep the café and bakery open.

'I heard you under the deck!'

'Is it possible that you heard our cat, Pacha? The orange tomcat? He likes to spend a lot of time there.' She maintained eye contact with Klumpski as she told her bold-faced lie.

'Leo. You've known Harry for how many years now? Can't you let us work here if he vouches for us?' Thank the saints, Grandma didn't try to flirt with Klumpski the way she had with Harry that first time they'd all met, in the Wienewskis' backyard. Lydia recognized a miracle when she saw it.

'Well.' Klumpski relented. 'It just so happens that we're finished with the physical search of your property and the beach, so there's no reason for you to remain closed any longer.' He grunted. 'I was going to call you later this morning.'

Lydia looked at the large face clock that hung over the swinging door as a constant reminder to both Freddy and the waitstaff. Five o'clock. How had she and Grandma gotten into such a pickle in a mere thirty minutes?

'A bakery's day begins early, Detective.' Lydia looked at

Grandma, who'd opened the oven and sliding in the pans of pumpernickel.

'That's right, Leo,' Grandma agreed, 'we're usually at this no later than two-thirty.' Grandma wasn't lying exactly, but she hadn't been here at such a wee hour. Lydia had, though, and once she made the cottage her home she intended to begin her days early, instead of doing a lot of the work the night before as she did now.

'Hang on a minute, ladies.' Klumpski turned to Pierre and his father. 'Gentlemen, after you.' All three men exited into the dining room, followed by the officer.

Lydia and Grandma looked at each other.

'Holy Cannoli!' Lydia exclaimed.

'Holy . . .' Grandma used a more colorful noun. 'We did it, Lydia. They have no idea we were under the deck. And if they still think we were, they can't prove it.' Grandma closed the oven door and turned on the timer, her smile more than a little bit satisfied.

Lydia wiped her brow. 'I don't care if they know. It's my property and I can be where I need to be.' She wasn't sure where her newfound courage had come from but she was happy to have it. 'I don't believe for one minute he was going to call me this morning, for the record.'

'No, you're right about that. I'd say we wore him down but good.'

Lydia recalled the moment the men had burst into the kitchen, and giggled. Before she knew it, it turned into a full belly laugh. 'Grandma, did you see their faces when we were standing here in our underwear? And where did you get that cami, by the way?'

'I special ordered it. Remind me to give you the catalog. Your lingerie is lacking, my dear.'

'My bra is plenty sexy!' she defended herself.

'If you plan to live by yourself surrounded by a dozen cats, sure,' Grandma quipped. 'Give Stanley a thrill, why don't ya?'

The door hit the wall, cutting short their girl talk as Klumpski strode back into the kitchen unannounced. Alone.

Lydia didn't like his predatory mannerism, or the way he glared at first her, then Grandma. Her spine straightened and she lifted her chin. Just let him tell her she couldn't investigate her own property.

'Ladies, I'm going to take the Chenaults back to their hotel. And then I will return. We are going to have a much-needed frank discussion,' he announced quietly. As if he knew he didn't have to yell.

As if he knew they'd been scouring the deck snooping for clues. And found them.

'Have some more coffee, Leo.' Grandma held her hand out to Klumpski and he slid his coffee cup and saucer across the table.

'Thank you, Mary.' At least the man had manners from time to time, thought Lydia. The three of them were seated at a table meant for two, and she was sitting in a chair she'd pulled over from a larger setting. So far they'd discussed how sad it was for Pierre and his father to return to Canada without Delphine's body, and how tragedy could strike out of nowhere. Lydia was tired of the murderous small talk.

'Why didn't you tell us as soon as you determined it was suicide?' She shot her query at him. 'You were saying it was suspicious, that we were all suspects, and then less than an hour later you told the Chenaults that Delphine killed herself.'

Klumpski took his time sipping his coffee, and reached for a third slice of the pumpernickel she'd only pulled out of the oven ten minutes ago. With blunt-tipped fingers he picked up his butter knife, which appeared the size of a toothpick in his bear-sized hands, and slathered on a thick slab of Gorski creamery butter. Lifting the bread to his mouth, he suddenly stopped, and cast a glance at Lydia, who hadn't stopped staring at him.

'Oh, all right.' He put the bread on his plate and let out a sigh. 'I can't go into all the details, but let's just say my department is working a very serious, much larger case right now. That has had my attention. As tragic as your friend's death is, it's only added to my department's burden. As to why you think you needed to be informed, of course I was only ever going to tell the next of kin first. It's how we do things. We're professionals.'

'We're not questioning how you do your job, Leo. All we want to know is how you came to your conclusion so quickly, before the autopsy?' Grandma smoothly cut in.

'It's happened before, you know. Determining the cause of death at the scene.' His sarcasm pricked at Lydia's hard-won composure.

She could handle being treated like the civilian she was, but Klumpski's patronizing stance riled her deepest resentment. Especially since he was aiming it at Grandma, too.

Or maybe you're defensive over how he's treated Harry.

'I'm still confused,' Lydia offered, trying to keep her tone neutral.

'Well, that's understandable.' He opened his hands in what she was certain he believed was a magnanimous gesture. 'Let me explain.'

Lydia risked a glance at Grandma, who to her credit maintained her relaxed posture. The tiny indigo blood vessel that ran alongside her temple, making a perfect T with her penciled-in Jean Harlow eyebrow, was doing a serious polka. Mary Romano Wienewski was close to blowing her cork.

'It goes back to your relationship with Detective Nowicki, doesn't it?' Lydia kept pressing, as one does when you've cornered a rat. 'You didn't tell us because you wanted to keep the cards close to your chest. Heaven forbid you risk someone else figuring out that you made your decision too soon.'

'Without all the facts,' Grandma shot. 'You decided Delphine Chenault killed herself before you questioned her family.' Grandma stood then, and leaned over the table until she was nose-to-nose with Klumpski. 'Tell me one thing, will you? If the body found down on this beach had been male, would you have made your conclusion as quickly?'

Go Grandma, go!

'No, no, you ladies misunderstand me. And for the record, I took a full account of Delphine Chenault's mental health history from both Jean and Pierre Chenault before I made my determination. The UCMP was incredibly quick in getting back to me, too. Delphine Chenault's medical record backs their statements.'

Grandma sat back down and folded her hands on the table. She didn't offer him another cup of coffee.

Klumpski pinched the bridge of his nose with his eyes screwed shut. Lydia watched in fascination as he breathed through his mouth, the rasp of his breath the only sound save for her heart racing. What was he going to reveal?

He dropped his hand and his eyes burst open. Full of arrogance. Lydia stifled a groan.

'It was pretty clear cut to me, actually. A case any rookie walking in off the street could solve, and my superiors agree with my determination. Number one' – he held up his thumb – 'we have a body with a gunshot wound and a gun from the victim's house is found nearby, or close enough. Number two' – up popped his index finger – 'the bullet entered the front lower abdomen and exited the deceased's back. A bullet to the lower abdomen is a little unusual, of course. Do I have to remind you that your deck's railing was in poor shape? It's not inconceivable that she was wavering at the edge of the deck, getting up her courage to pull the trigger, staring out at the water. She finally decides to do it, but loses her balance at the same time and her weight against the railing breaks it. *Bam!* Gun goes off as she's falling and the bullet could go anywhere other than her target, which would likely have been her head. Or, if you want to think the best, she didn't mean to shoot. She was toying with the idea and playing chicken with the pistol, wasn't familiar with weapons, and it went off. Number three,' he used his middle finger, making Lydia itch to do the same but in Klumpski's face, 'her fingerprints are on the gun handle. Numbers four and five.' He slammed down his hand on the table with so much force that Lydia's jaw clenched. 'Her husband's statement, her son's statement, and medical records all match about her worrying mental state. And there's more, but I can't talk about it.' He shrugged, shoved the entire slice of pumpernickel into his mouth. 'Case closed.'

Lydia wasn't sure if Klumpski's use of a comic book adjective was what bothered her most, or the fact that the detective had come up with a story he clearly wasn't going to open to discussion.

'But how can you be certain that the gun with her prints on it was the same one used to kill her? Did you find the bullet or its casing?' Lydia was grateful she'd discussed the weapon and ammunition issue with Harry earlier.

His brows drew together. 'It's not information you need to know, and I'm not required to tell you. But if it'll keep your yapper shut for once, rest assured, we never found a bullet in her body or anywhere near it. The lake took it away, I'm certain. Sometimes the case is black and white, Miss Wienewski. Often, in fact.'

'You seem upset, Detective. And you haven't mentioned the

ugly handwritten message the victim received.' Lydia couldn't help pushing back.

'That note was random. For all I know it was never seen by Mrs Chenault. And it had been handled by too many people to hope for prints.' The latter was a dig at her, no doubt, but judging from the sweat beads that appeared on his forehead, Lydia believed he was lying about the significance of the note. But why? What couldn't he talk about?

'I'm not upset by anything, for the record, except your annoying habit of making something out of nothing.'

But Klumpski's face was reddening by the second, and it was still quite chilly inside the café. Lydia had donned an old cardigan she kept in the storage room for cool mornings like this, and had given Grandma her jogging suit jacket back, which the elder wore half-zipped, her camisole's lace trim visible.

'You want to know something?' He pointed his finger at them. 'It's never a good idea to go poking into something that's none of your business. That's how you find yourself slapped with a fine, or worse.'

'Worse?' Lydia wanted him to be specific if he was going issue threats.

'Cuffs, Miss Wienewski. Handcuffs.'

'Here's the thing, Leo.' Grandma purred his name. 'This is Lydia's café and bakery. Her property. So anything that happens to anyone on the premises is her business, de facto.'

De facto? Had Grandma been talking to Stanley, or was this another line from *Police Woman*?

Klumpski issued a tight smile. Lydia detested contempt of any kind and had to bite her cheek to keep quiet. 'The body was on the beach, located exactly in the spot that's between the low and high tide water marks, which technically isn't your property, now, is it?'

'You just said you believe Delphine was on the deck before she fell. That's my property.'

Gotcha.

Klumpski slammed both hands on the table as he stood. 'This conversation is over. You're lucky I'm going to allow you to reopen your business, but don't be surprised if you have no customers.'

Lydia didn't bother pointing out that his grammar sucked.

*   *   *

As soon as Klumpski left the building for the second time that morning, Lydia and Grandma didn't waste a second worrying about the detective's ire. Lydia called Teri and Freddy, to let them know they could come in to work as usual again, and she called Stanley to simply hear his voice.

Grandma had spent a good half-hour on the telephone with Harry but didn't comment on the conversation after she hung up, so Lydia figured he hadn't heard anything new about the case.

'You're telling me that yous' two ruffled the feathers of the Acorn PD detective?' Teri unwittingly sounded like Klumpski as she washed a large mixing bowl in the deep sink, while Lydia julienned carrots and beets. Grandma was in the dining room setting up with the clean linens Teri had brought in from home.

'Yes.' Lydia couldn't believe it, either. Maybe not so much that she and Grandma stood up to the man, but that he hadn't done much more than bluster. 'I honestly thought he was going to keep us shut down for a minute. But he was all threats and no action.'

'What saved you?'

'Saved us from what?'

'Getting caught under the deck?' Teri knew the whole story as Lydia had filled her in as soon as she'd shown up with the two overflowing laundry baskets of clean linens.

'Oh, we used Pacha as our excuse.' She grinned. 'Told them he practically lives there.'

As if on cue, the marmalade-colored feline made an appearance at the screened café kitchen door, scratching to come in.

'OK, sweetie boy, but just long enough to get something to eat.' Lydia held open the door and Pacha trotted inside, but he didn't make his usual sprint for the water and food bowl she'd put out. Lydia kept water in the barn for him but not food.

Pacha sat in front of Lydia and looked lovingly at her.

'Uh oh, that cat's caught another mouse for you!' Teri was not a fan of the cat's hunting prowess.

But when the cat opened his mouth, the object that dropped from his mouth made a soft *plink* on the floor. It was small and brown.

'Ewww, what is that?'

'Thank you, Pacha,' Lydia murmured as she knelt down to inspect another dead critter. But as she peered more closely, she discovered not a dead frog or grasshopper, but a button. She picked it up.

'Look, sister dear. Not an animal. A random button.' Lydia stood and dropped the button into her apron pocket. 'Good boy, Pacha. Now, go eat before I have to kick you out of here.' She nudged Teri away from the sink as she was drying the huge stainless-steel bowl with a large towel, and began to wash her hands.

'Thank goodness. I'm not in the mood to see a dead anything. We've had enough of that this week.' Teri shook her head as if clearing her mind of the tragedy. She looked out the kitchen door, her profile pensive in the late morning light. 'Freddy just pulled up.'

'Great. Just in time as I'm going to unlock the front door in five.' She hoped that by going through their regular routine, it would somehow magically summon their customers to appear.

Dead body and all.

EIGHTEEN

A snapping sound woke Lydia from a deep sleep, and it took her a heartbeat to remember that she wasn't in her usual bed, in the garage loft apartment with Grandma. She stretched out one leg, then another, surprised at how refreshed she felt after so little sleep. It had to be the Lake Erie air, the rhythmic beat of the waves as they lapped against the retaining wall.

Finally. Her lakeside café and bakery was open again and serving breakfast and lunch each day, and her hopes of extending service to dinner might happen this summer. Combined with trying to figure out how Delphine died, the last couple of days had been long and she wasn't simply burning the candle at both ends, she was torching it. But it was all worth it.

Last night she'd worked well into the wee hours, prepping the pumpernickel and rye bread dough for today. She'd also made significant inroads on the breakfast and lunch meal prep, from chopping vegetables to mixing cinnamon and sugar in the perfect portions to sprinkle over both the cinnamon rolls and French toast. To top it off, she'd been able to finish making the fillings for the pierogi and would be able to cook them up fresh hours before the competition.

Bone-weary by the time she finished, she'd opted to forgo the twenty-five-minute drive from the lakefront to Cheektowaga.

Instead of having to keep her Gremlin's windows rolled down so that the cold breeze would keep her awake in the depth of night, she'd curled up atop the bedroll that was supposedly her uncle's from World War II and covered herself with the afghan Grandma crocheted for her over a decade ago.

The café's dining room floor was the perfect impromptu camp-out, nestled between the mirrored wall and former soda counter. The two pallets that had held cases of canned sauerkraut, white beans, and corn served well as a platform to spare her the worst of the damp that invariably crept through the building and especially the floor.

You could crawl back under . . .

As snuggly as she felt curled up in the family heirloom there was no way she'd fall back asleep on the unforgiving pallet mattress. Smudgy gray light eked through a crack from the drapes of one of the dining room windows, was enough to reflect off the mirrored wall behind the once-soda fountain. If she hurried, she might still catch the sun coming up on the lake.

Having slept in jeans and her favorite kitty print sweatshirt it wouldn't take long to dress. She shoved her feet into her white, high-top sneakers and fastened the Velcro ankle straps.

'Lydia!' The familiar lyrical voice with a solid dose of no-nonsense reached her ears from the back of the commercial kitchen and wrapped around her heart. Lydia quickly finished cleaning up her makeshift bed but not before Grandma spotted it when she walked into the dining room.

'Lydia.' Grandma repeated her name but this time her tone was more subdued. 'Please tell me you didn't sleep on the floor. You'll catch pneumonia before you get the café off the ground. And what's with that sweatshirt? You're too young to dress like a frump.' Grandma's eyes rivaled her favorite singer's, Frank Sinatra, and appeared especially bright in the morning sunshine that slanted from the front of the large dining room. It wasn't in Lydia's budget to install more modern blinds yet, so the room was awash with the pale light, as the building faced east and north, offering the best views of the lake on the northern edge. On a clear day the coast of Canada was visible, and not for the first time Lydia marveled at her luck. How had she, the daughter of a butcher, ended up with her own place before the clock had declared she was thirty years old?

'I like this sweatshirt. It's warm. And it's the style.'

'A style for your mother. She gave it to you, didn't she? You're a young woman, at the height of your sexiness. Make the most of it! Show some cleavage, sweetheart.' Grandma's eyes narrowed. 'You slept in that, didn't you?'

'Yes. It was safer for me to stay here, Grandma. Trust me. You don't want me driving that late after working all day, especially after the very early morning we had yesterday. Besides, it was cozy under the Afghan you made me.' She'd told Grandma much of the same last night on the phone, but Grandma Mary was never one to let an argument go, not when it involved someone she loved.

'You didn't leave the butcher shop until after three yesterday afternoon, when you came in for those couple of hours. You mean to tell me you worked all night, too, even after we spoke?' Grandma patted her bottle-blonde hair, teased and tamed into a 'do that Lydia thought of as another facet of her Angie Dickinson style.

'It's OK, really. I won't have to keep helping at shop so much, now that Pop's almost one hundred percent.' This wasn't totally true. Pop might very well always need at least a little bit of help.

'Please tell me you at least got a power nap after we talked.' Lydia had called Grandma when she got back to the café so she wouldn't worry about her.

'I got plenty of sleep, Grandma,' Lydia lied. 'And it was worth it just to have the place to myself this morning. The view is priceless!'

'Hmm.'

'Wait a minute. If you didn't know I slept here, then you didn't stay in the apartment all night, either.' She looked at Grandma, who had averted her gaze for a split second before refocusing on Lydia, sapphire sparks seeming to fly out of her eyes.

'I was at Harry's. Unless you'd rather we'd parked in my wagon again?'

'No, once was enough. I'm so glad you came in early today, truth be told. Thank you.'

'Anytime, sweetie pie.' Grandma hugged her. 'You sure did get a lot done by staying here overnight.' Grandma's gaze swept the large room. The soda counter's chrome trim gleamed, and every one of the twenty-three dining tables was set with a white linen tablecloth and red napkins. Grandma's gaze swung past the expansive windows that framed the lake view to the single window-less wall on which oversized framed prints of wheat fields hung. Lydia had kept them in the barn until she dragged them out last night, determined to put some finishing touches where she'd not had the chance to yet.

Grandma blinked. 'What are those supposed to be?'

'Pictures,' Lydia deadpanned.

'I'm not senile yet, my dear. I understand that, but I guess my question should have been why are they there?'

'I thought they looked like Poland. Maybe.' Lydia had found the pictures, already framed, at a garage sale in East Amherst, a well-to-do suburb of Buffalo. Amidst piles of decorator fabric and vases, the scenes had seemed bucolic.

'Hmm. Have you thought about something more abstract, honey? I respect that you're keeping the place Polish themed, with the red and white and all, and of course your menu.' Grandma didn't mention that she'd tried to persuade Lydia to put at least some Italian cookies on the dessert menu, to offer a little 'variety.'

'What do you mean by "abstract?"' Lydia asked.

'Well, I have some artwork I've kept stored in your parents' attic. Why don't I see what I can find for you?' Grandma's unreadable expression sparked doubt in what Lydia thought was good taste in café decor.

'You don't think the wheat fields look like Poland?' Lydia had never been to Poland, nor had anyone she knew. And there weren't any photos in the library, either, except for a few tiny black and white pictures in the one or two geography textbooks she'd found. The Iron Curtain kept information on her ancestral homeland to a minimum.

Grandma shrugged. 'Who am I to say? No one really knows what it looks like nowadays, do they? I think it's wonderful that you're keeping your Polish heritage alive, but let's face it, your patrons aren't coming here for a history lesson. They're coming for your pierogi and placek.'

'And the morning pastries,' Lydia replied. It was hard to let go of all the ideas she had for the café, but she knew it was important to always please the customer. 'But I don't think Pop will agree with you. He's all about keeping Polish customs going and swears that's the draw.'

'Maybe think about traditions as things that families do, and your menu as a way to preserve culinary history? But I'd stick to more modern décor,' Grandma posed.

'You're a genius, Grandma. And yes, I'm interested in those paintings you're not using.' She knew Grandma was right, but it tugged at her loyalty to Pop to let go of the faux-Poland landscapes.

Pop had insisted that all three of his children pay attention to their American and World History lessons. Heritage was important to him. The truth was that other than whatever each individual family had brought with them through Ellis Island, little was known about what was really Polish and what had been watered down into American culture. Except for the food, which came from recipes passed down through generations. Very little information got in or out from the other side of the Iron Curtain, and Lydia knew of no one who had actually ever been to Poland. Yet the common heritage provided a visceral link to the nation that she shared so much with.

The recent news of labor strikes had only pictured groups of men in factory settings. Father Krohl said prayer at Mass every week in Cheektowaga for the Polish people and the workers that Lech Walesa was trying to free.

'You haven't eaten yet, have you, honey?' Grandma patted her clear plastic tote bag, the one with the orange butterflies embossed across the front. 'I brought some bacon from the shop.' Grandma didn't wait for an answer but headed back toward the kitchen. 'C'mon, I'll make you some eggs and toast. You may as well get used to eating in your café kitchen.'

'I have been eating here, since we opened. And you don't have to bring food here, unless there's something you know for sure I don't have. I'm fully stocked, trust me.' Lydia followed Grandma until she arrived in front of the commercial refrigerator, from which she pulled a flat of eggs, a gallon of milk, a quart of half and half, and a pound of butter. Seeing that Grandma was looking around the clean space for something, she pointed at the spice rack that was out of the shorter woman's vision. 'The salt and pepper are up here, next to the cinnamon sugar.' She lifted the large spice containers down, and added the dried dill, one of her favorite herbs.

'I know where the spices are. I work here, remember?' Grandma smiled and reached for the oregano. 'Keep the dill to your eggs, honey child. I'll take some of that oregano you've got for mine.' As much as Grandma had embraced the Polish customs of half of her deceased husband's family, she drew the line at cabbage of any kind, and dill.

They fell into a comfortable routine of frying up bacon, whisking eggs, and putting on a pot of coffee with the old stovetop percolator that the previous owners left behind. 'Here, let's use this frying pan instead of heating up the whole griddle yet.' Lydia was conscious of saving energy and not because it had been ingrained into all of them when cardigan-wearing Jimmy Carter was the President. She was keeping her overhead expenses as low as possible and the natural gas bill was included in that.

'Sure thing.' Grandma nodded at the butter. 'Put some of that in the skillet, will you?'

'We already have bacon grease.' Lydia spoke as she whipped up two eggs for Grandma's share, added a dollop of milk, and sprinkled salt, pepper and a dash of oregano over the buttercup yellow liquid. At home she had adopted the post-stroke recovery diet that the rehabilitation center prescribed for Pop. Butter and bacon grease were both off limits for Pop and now that her palate had adjusted, she didn't miss it, most days. Being able to enjoy the heavier fare on occasion like today was a nice treat.

'We need a little more butter.' Grandma drew on her fraternal Italian family's tastes.

'OK.' Lydia dropped another pat into the hot skillet. They'd have plenty of butter with the toast but she wasn't about to argue with Grandma. Not after all they'd been through these past days.

The coffee's rich aroma cut across the competing scents of bacon and butter as Lydia used her best bread knife to slice through the round of pumpernickel she'd baked yesterday. It was the only day-old loaf that remained, a fact she took pride in. The bakery part of the business was doing as well if not better than the café.

As large, molasses brown crumbs scattered across the oak-topped work island, she remembered that there were several more loaves she'd left out overnight, ready to go into the commercial oven.

'Can you do me a favor, Grandma, and finish up these eggs? I've got to get the oven preheated. The bread's ready to go in, along with today's lunch rolls.' She made it a practice to keep partially risen rolls in the freezer, ready to bake up with little to no notice. Her breadmaking skills had been improved by what she'd learned from Madame Delphine, no matter how hard it had been to withstand the woman's constant, irascible scrutiny.

The reminder that Delphine was dead tugged at more than her heart. Regret that she and Grandma had run into an impasse with Klumpski's suicide determination stung her pride, but worse, her sense of loyalty toward the woman who'd been humble enough to make amends with her.

Lydia trusted her instincts, and Grandma's, and of course Harry's. There was more to Delphine's death than Klumpski had decided – or he just wasn't telling them.

But who had killed her?

'What do you know about Teri and Johnny?' Grandma tossed back a swig of hot black coffee, the way she always drank it. 'She tell you anything?' They sat on tall stools at the kitchen workbench. They loved to dissect the family problems over coffee or tea, and Lydia had to admit, it already felt as if this had been her place for years, not months.

'Teri's always doing her own thing, you know. She doesn't tell me everything,' Lydia said. Since Teri had dumped her long-term boyfriend at Easter for the butcher shop's star – and only – employee, Johnny Bello, Teri had been keeping to herself. Lydia was happy for Teri. But, being nineteen and in party mode, Teri was prone to very late nights out and often nursed hang-overs during her morning shifts at the butcher shop. She'd been working more and more for Lydia at the café, too, which seemed to make her all the crankier. None of it made for great sisterly conversation.

'I want to make sure she's still keeping her eye on the prize. Sure, she needs to live her life at her age. But she also has to get her degree. It's not good to let a man take away your autonomy.' Grandma was a feminist and had marched in the Equal Rights Amendment, ERA, protests several years back. The ERA had never been ratified, but Grandma always kept the women's rights flame burning bright.

'As far as I know she finished her semester without a problem, and she's taking a summer course,' Lydia hedged. 'Why? Are you worried about something she's done?'

'Oh, honey, you know I don't really worry about any of my grandchildren. Take your brother, Ted.' She referred to the twenty-seven-year-old sibling in between Lydia and Teri. 'Your mother went 'round the bend when he used to play with the butcher shop animals, especially the larger ones. She thought he was missing some marbles.'

'I remember, trust me. Like the time he put the beef skeleton back together.' Lydia recalled that when eleven-year-old Ted had proudly shown Pop his creation, she remembered Pop's cheek twitching. He'd been trying to either not laugh or not cry, she still didn't know which. Mom hadn't bothered holding back her emotions – Mom never did – and had screamed and insisted that Ted was 'just like your great-uncle Stashu' to Pop. Family lore was that Uncle Stashu had suffered from 'bouts of nerves' his entire life, and had been known to do some 'squirrelly' things with an axe. Supposedly he chopped down an elm tree so that he could investigate a raccoon nest. Said nest ended up in the neighbor's bedroom when the elm tree crashed through their roof. Uncle Stashu had served in World War I and been most likely exposed to mustard gas, which is what Lydia blamed the tales of his mental suffering on.

Lydia hadn't put Uncle Stashu together with her parents' terrier-mix dog Stashu until now. The tiny dog's ferocious attitude definitely put him in the 'squirrelly' category.

'Exactly! Do you remember that, Lydia? Your parents were worried about Ted but I saw his intelligence. Now it makes sense that he put those bones back together – look at what he's doing!' Grandma clanged her cup down as they sat at the end of the workbench.

'True.' Ted was an orthopedic surgical resident at Erie County Medical Center, and the pride of her parents.

'And they worried about you when you went off to Ottawa. Not me! I wanted you to get out of that house sooner, spread your wings. And maybe more, if you get my drift.' Grandma winked and Lydia blushed. Grandma was all about a woman's right to explore her sexuality. So was Lydia, she just didn't like talking about the particulars with her family members, no matter how cherished they were. And she much preferred discussing a murder case with Grandma.

'We all know how that turned out, Grandma.'

'Nonsense. You have more here than you'll ever need.'

'Now you sound like Mom.'

'God forbid!' Grandma winked and they both laughed. 'But tell me, honey, I notice Stanley didn't stay here last night. You two still doing all right?'

'Of course we are.' She heard the defensiveness in her voice as her hands fisted. 'He's been busy with his exams and intern-ship, and I'm swamped here, not to mention our new murder case.' Stanley was in law school, financing it with money earned working for his father, and now with the paltry salary at a firm in downtown Buffalo. 'Both of us are stretched thin. It's hard to find time together lately, is all.'

Grandma put her hand over Lydia's. 'Are you absolutely sure he's the one for you, honey?' Did Grandma realize she was echoing Pop's earlier question?

'Absolutely, no question.' The words rushed out. 'We've been through so much, and look at how he saved us both two months ago.' She referred to when, after she and Grandma had figured out who killed Louie McDaniel, Stanley's quick thinking had kept bad from going to worse, which would have involved both of their final curtain calls.

'Nonsense. You saved both of our lives. With a little help from me, I'll give you that.' Grandma's chin jutted. Lydia smiled. Grandma should be proud at how she'd handled being pushed around by a person with a pistol.

'We make a good team, Grandma.'

'And we're great roommates, too,' Grandma agreed. 'But it is time for us to move on. Promise I can help you fix up the cottage?'

'I'm counting on it.' Lydia smiled.

It wasn't lost on her that neither she nor Grandma had so much as whispered Delphine's name this morning. Or Klumpski's. In fact, they hadn't spoken of the case much since Klumpski had cleared her to come back to work. They'd needed a break from it.

Lydia looked out the kitchen window. 'It's going to be a beau-tiful day. I've got to get ready to open for breakfast.' It was already half past seven. 'Here's hoping we get a good crowd today.'

'Other than the sign out front, have you run anymore ads in the paper?' Grandma asked.

'No, just the weekly ad with the coupon for ten percent off on Fish Fry Friday. Word of mouth is my best advertising, though.' And in truth she couldn't afford much of anything else. Her adver-tising budget had been spent on the lighted custom pink neon sign that she'd had installed out on the main road.

'Maybe you're right.'

'Don't get discouraged about Delphine, Lydia. Karma's on our side. You'll get a breakthrough when you least expect it. You just focus on the pierogi competition this weekend.' Grandma had sensed her uneasiness the entire time she'd asked about Teri and Stanley.

'I can't hide anything from you, can I?'

'No.' Grandma burst out laughing.

NINETEEN

Butterflies woke Lydia up on Saturday morning. The last two days had flown by, but not because Lydia had a rush of customers. The workload at the bakery and café was sadly all too manageable, but it did give her more time and energy for her final preparations for the pierogi competition. It meant so much more to her now, to be competing in the international food festival where Delphine would have been one of the judges of honor. Lydia poured her thoughts and musings into every batch of potato, sauerkraut, and farmer's cheese pierogi. She sliced the onions extra thin with a mandoline slicer she'd found in the regional restaurant supply store. It felt a little bit like she was cheating by not using the kitchen knife, but she'd never be able to cut such perfectly even slices – at least not as quickly as she needed them.

All the while something continued to tug at her conscience. She couldn't shake the worry that she'd missed some important clue about Delphine's death. But for the life of her, she couldn't grasp at what her mind was trying to tell her, and chalked it all up to the stress of Delphine's murder and hoping she'd do well enough in the pierogi contest that Pop was hinging his hopes for both of their businesses on.

By the time Saturday arrived all she wanted was to get the pierogi competition over with. Lydia originally thought she was driven to do her best because she didn't want to disappoint Pop, but as the week played out she realized she had to do this for Delphine. For her and Delphine, for the relationship that had barely budded, never given the chance to fully blossom.

Her first task, after a strong cup of coffee, was to take the boiled pierogi she'd refrigerated last night and sauté it with finely chopped onions and butter in her mother's large cast iron skillet. Mom had walked in and shooed her out of the kitchen as soon as she'd finished with the last batch. 'Go get ready for your big day. We've got it from here. Pop and I have the setup ready to go, too. All you have to do is show up.'

Lydia started to argue, wanting to control every detail of the day, but thought twice. This needed to be a family effort, the first time she and both Mom and Pop had been able to work together at something fun since Pop's stroke.

Since Mom and Pop had insisted on bringing the pierogi to St Stanislaus for her, Lydia left Cheektowaga hours before the competition. She pulled into the makeshift parking lot for the contest only minutes after its official opening. St Stanislaus had managed to create a festival vibe with fancy food and drink tents on the church grounds, and Buffalo International Food Festival branding. A former farmer's field had been cordoned off in anticipation of the throngs of attendees expected to gather to cheer the winner and sample some good food.

The weather was Lydia's favorite, after crisp autumn air. Today's breeze was tropical, the warmth soothing to her bare shoulders and legs.

The pierogi judging was taking place in the church hall, which she was familiar with as she'd attended bingo here with Grandma, Mom, and her aunts on more than one occasion. She walked through the makeshift lot, hoping her new sandals wouldn't get covered in dust, nor her feet. She'd painted her toes a bright red to contrast with the white strappy shoes, and to match her sleeveless white sundress. She carried a short-sleeved blue cardigan to appear a bit more professional for the contest. While her storebought outfit had none of the tailored touches that Delphine's classic dress had, it was small way Lydia could privately honor her deceased mentor.

Competing in the pierogi contest was another. But the biggest honor to Delphine remained out of reach, to Lydia's vexation. Justice.

Professional appearance was important to her, as it had been to Delphine. As one of the only female café owners in the Buffalo area, she wasn't only representing the Wienewskis, but any woman who wanted to do a job traditionally linked solely to men.

Thank the Blessed Mother that Pop's ingenuity, along with the brand-new addition of the Buffalo International Food Festival, had given her this opportunity to shore up her public reputation.

Lydia stepped onto the paved parking lot and kept walking, planning to reach the church hall well before the judging began.

'Lydia!' A female voice stopped her and she recognized one of her best friends, Jenny Macki. Becky, her other close friend from since high school, stood next to Jenny. The two were complete opposites in every way. Jenny was the picture of femininity and had always been a girly-girl. Also tall, nearly six feet, she'd been a star basketball and volleyball player on their high school teams. Becky was barely five-foot tall and had the muscular build of an athlete. She'd been the county's premier vaulter and uneven parallel bars competitor on the gymnastics team, and had scored a scholarship to more than one small college with gymnastics. High school was where the three of them had formed an inseparable bond, and their love for each other had deepened as they'd each either gone on to work full time right after high school or, as in Becky's case, did four years in college and returned to Western New York to figure out the rest of their life.

'Hey!' She walked up to them. Fittingly enough, they were both holding steaming hot containers filled with pierogi from one of the food stalls. 'I see you're having a nice, nutritionally balanced lunch?'

'It's delicious,' Becky replied as she gave her a tight hug. 'But not as good as yours at the café. The misfits miss you, girl.'

'I know, and I'm sorry.' She turned to Jenny for a second hug greeting.

They'd referred to themselves as many things over their fifteen years of friendship, including 'the three musketeers' and 'the darned cats.' Both were inspired by their too-frequent TV watching, she remembered. But for reasons not entirely scientific, they'd settled on calling themselves 'the misfits.'

'What are you up to? Every time I need to talk to you, I can't get a hold of you!' Jenny placed her hand on her burgeoning belly and gave Lydia pause.

'Wow, you're really . . . uh . . . starting to show?' Was that OK to say to her pregnant friend?

Jenny thwacked her on the upper arm the same as she did when they thought they ran their high school, parading through the corridors in between classes as if they didn't give a hoot what anyone else thought of them. In fact, all three of them had been belittled and gossiped about, for being alternatively too goodie two-shoes or too studious. They'd supported each other through the nasty bullying, and come out stronger for it. Which was why Lydia had in turn been so concerned about Teri during her high school years, much more recent as Teri graduated last year and had just finished up her freshman year of university at the local community college.

'It's fine, you can say "large," or "big." I don't care what you call it, it's my little muffin growing away.' The smile on Jenny's face was wistful. 'The doctor says all's well, and that the due date is still in the fall.'

'I didn't realize there was a question about when the baby's due,' Lydia observed, acutely aware of the fact that she had zero, none, zilch experience with either being pregnant or having a baby. The getting pregnant part she understood, as in, she and Stanley certainly engaged in a lot of fun that could indeed lead to her belly getting big. Except they were always religiously faithful to practice birth control.

'Well, it's not an exact science, unless you know the exact time you conceived. Which, while we had a good idea, we didn't really know as well, we're doing it a lot.' Jenny giggled. 'You know Patrick.'

'Yeah, he's a real horn dog,' Becky interjected.

'What are you getting at?' Jenny asked, suddenly perturbed by her friend's reply.

'Nothing. I'm tired and I needed my pierogi, like, yesterday.' Becky's no-nonsense profile reflected her personality. She was a woman with a stubborn streak as wide as the frosted highlights in her spiked hair. Becky turned her attention to Lydia. Her gaze took in Lydia's full ensemble, lingering over her sundress and polished toes.

'Have you come to check out the festival?'

'I'm competing in the cook-off,' Lydia replied. 'I got here super early to distract myself. I'm so nervous!'

'That's great, Lydia! What a great idea to promote your new café and bakery. You have no reason to be nervous. You're the best cook I know,' Jenny interjected, her eyes sparkling.

'Yeah, way to go, Lyd.' Becky nodded. The shorter woman was dressed in nondescript khaki shorts, boat deck shoes, and a pale pink polo with the collar turned up. The tiny animal logo on her chest was the penultimate symbol of prep. Jenny, in contrast, was wearing a very loose pale yellow dress that flowed over her pregnant belly, her feet in practical sandals.

'Why don't you join us and get some custard?' Jenny reached her hand out to Lydia, who took it and allowed herself to relax.

She looked at her watch. It was less than two hours until the judges arrived.

She shook her head. 'I can't. It's tempting, believe me, but I've got to head on over to the tasting room soon. Plus, you know me. If I eat anything here I'll be wearing it on my outfit like a baby's bib.'

'I understand. We've missed you, Lyd. You're so busy all the time,' Jenny said.

'We all are busy. It's called "life."' Lydia smiled. 'Have you given any more thought to coming to work for me?' She'd offered Jenny a job as assistant baker, since she had so much experience running the commercial bakery at their local grocery store.

'I really, really would love to, you know I would, but it's too far of a commute for me right now. My morning sickness was brutal, and now I've got to get ready to welcome this one.' Jenny patted her baby bump. 'Ask me when I have to go back to work? You would be a lot more flexible with my hours than the grocery is.'

'You know I will. I'd love a chance to work together, Jenny.'

'I'll work for you, Lyd. But you'd have to train me. My baking skills are limited to a cake box.' Becky grinned. 'But I can fix anything that breaks around the place.' Her father was an electrician and Becky had learned from him, even though she currently worked as an office manager at a car dealership.

'I'd love that, but I probably can't afford to pay you what the car company does. Plus there aren't any benefits, not yet.' Lydia hoped that in the future she could offer her employees more, but for now, an hourly wage was it. 'To be honest, I'm worried that my café and bakery is going to shut down before I have a chance to make it work.'

At their puzzled expressions, she continued, 'Since the body was found on my beach.'

'What?'

'No kidding!'

The women exclaimed in unison and it took Lydia a second or

two to realize what she'd only dared hope. 'Are you telling me that you haven't heard about it? On the news, or in the paper? Jenny, Patrick didn't tell you?' Jenny's husband was a police officer on the Cheektowaga PD.

'Nope.' She shook her head, making her glossy hair swing around her pretty features. 'Not one peep.'

'Let's step away and I'll fill you in.' Lydia pointed to an area behind one of the stalls, away from the growing crowd, where she told her friends what had transpired at Lydia's Lakeside Café and Bakery over the past few days.

'It's just like when you found Louie,' Becky said, biting into another butter-browned pierogi.

'Well, not really. They've determined that Madame – I still can't stop thinking of her as that, even though she told me to call her Delphine – died from a self-inflicted gunshot.'

'Suicide?' Jenny gasped.

'Yes.'

'You don't buy it, Lydia Wienewski, I see it in your eyes.' Jenny sounded like she'd been talking to Pop.

'Are you investigating, like you did with Louie?' Becky wiped her mouth with a sad excuse for a napkin. 'Do you need backup?'

Lydia laughed. 'Becky, you're always ready to go after something.' Her friend had gone after gymnastic and softball victories all through high school and college, and had been a big help to Lydia, as had Jenny, when she'd solved Louie's murder. 'Thank you, but no, I'm good. I mean, yes, you're right. I know without a doubt it was murder. But I can't prove it, not yet anyway. If you'd met Delphine, you'd agree with me.'

'Say no more!' Jenny held up a palm. 'You told us enough about your teacher, and that woman sounded like she'd be the one killing other people, not herself.'

'Although, maybe she led a double life. You know, put a brave face on things to others but inside she was a head case.' Becky spoke quietly, and not for the first time Lydia wondered what was going on in her friend's life that she wasn't telling her, or Jenny.

'Are you doing OK, Becky?' She had to ask.

The lines between Becky's brows immediately disappeared and she visibly brightened. 'I'm good! It's something I saw on a TV show once, is all.'

'Uh huh,' Lydia replied.

Jenny didn't say anything but watched them both, her gaze thoughtful.

Lydia glanced at her watch. She'd been chatting to her friends for ages and had lost track of time. 'Oh crap! I'm going to be late. I've got to go!'

'Go win that prize, Lydia!' Becky cried.

'Call us!' Jenny's words wrapped around her like a hug.

'I will, promise!' Lydia turned and ran toward the school building. She could always count on the misfits to boost her confidence. They believed she'd figure Delphine's murder out.

So why didn't she?

TWENTY

Lydia blinked back tears as she read the professionally designed sign posted on a wrought-iron easel at the entrance to the contest.

This one's for you, Delphine.

She entered the church hall, and stopped.

The space had been completely transformed.

Three long rows of tables stretched from the stage to the far side of the room where she stood. Each table was covered in alternating white and red linen, not unlike her café's theme. Bright blue flames glowed from under chafing dishes placed at regular intervals atop the tables.

Sheer drapes hung from the high ceilings, giving the impression of walking into a palace instead of an auditorium. St Stanislaus, and the City of Buffalo, had gone all out for the prestigious event.

Lydia's stomach roiled as she searched for her parents. She shoved her anxiety down.

You can do this.

'Over here!' Mom's voice struck her inner turmoil and actually calmed it, a bit. Lydia strode to row three, where her parents had set up at the last spot, next to the stage. 'I have six of each kind, with all the extras under the table in my slow cooker.'

Mom lifted the lid of their assigned chafing dish and beamed. Perfectly placed pierogi, browned by Lydia in diced onion and butter this morning, glistened in the chafing dish, ready to be sampled. Relief banished her worry. If her pierogi had been good enough for Delphine, it was good enough for the competition, whether the remaining judges agreed or not.

'What do you think, Lydia?' Pop asked. Mom busied herself

with a notebook, where Lydia saw she'd written down a numbered column, with notes next to each.

'I think there's no stopping the Wienewskis when we put our minds together.' She gave them each a quick peck on the cheek. 'I love you both so much. Thank you for your help.'

'Now listen, girl, when the judges come around, stay quiet. Except for judge number seventeen.' Pop was all business.

'Yes, if judge number seventeen asks you any questions, answer directly and to the point,' Mom added, not looking up from her notes. 'I'll let you know if there's any other judge who matters.'

'Who is judge number seventeen?' Lydia had been concerned only about the quality of the pierogi, and never gave much thought to the actual judges or judging process. Not after Delphine's murder.

'Let's just say that you know them, but don't act like you do,' Pop said.

Lydia stared at her parents. 'Why can't I know—'

'Welcome one and all to the Buffalo International Food Festival. Our parish is honored to host the pierogi cook-off!' The male announcer's voice boomed through the high-ceilinged space, hushing the burgeoning crowd that gathered. 'First, we'll have Father Lewandowski lead us in prayer.'

'In the name of the Father, the Son, and the Holy Spirit . . .' Lydia mechanically blessed herself alongside Mom and Pop, but sent up her own prayer. *St Michael the Archangel, defend us in battle* . . . The memorized prayer from third grade school religion class never failed to calm her down. Probably because she'd been obsessed with anything angelic back then. And maybe a little bit now.

Because, too late, she finally understood what Pop had known all along, what he'd tried to instill in her since she was knee-high and learning alongside him at his chopping block. Why Delphine had been intent on getting her pierogi recipe.

Being a baker and a cook, a café and bakery owner, wasn't just a way to make a living or feed the family. It was a legacy passed from one generation to the next, with all its top business secrets as well as foibles. Lydia carried the mantle of Pop, Dziadzia, and all the Wienewski men before her. And more importantly, as far as she was concerned, the women who'd not been properly recognized or acknowledged for often being the brains and not a little of the brawn behind the family business. Polish food, mostly kielbasa before now, had put her family on the Western New York map ever since they'd emigrated from the old country. This was Lydia's chance to add to the tradition, but with pierogi.

Thank you, Delphine.

Yet even Lydia's enthusiasm languished as the noon hour passed and not a single judge who'd sampled her pierogi had so much as commented on their taste.

'Is it usually like this? I mean, shouldn't they at least say "yum" or "yuck?"' Lydia was perplexed. 'What are the other cook-offs like?'

'This is our first time, too, honey,' Mom said. 'And this isn't a regular cook-off, Lydia. It's an international event!'

'Amelia.' Pop's gruff warning tone rose the hairs on Lydia's nape.

'Hold on a sec. You mean to tell me you never entered our kielbasa in a cook-off before?'

Pop shrugged. 'No. Why would I waste my time on something like this when everyone already knows we make the best?'

'But you said—'

'I said it was a great way for you to get your name out there. Your pierogi are the best, hands down.'

'We believe in you, honey.'

'Thanks, you guys. You're the best. I'll admit I didn't really realize how big a deal this festival would be. Only after I learned that Delphine was a guest judge for the éclair contest did I understand. And of course, she's not here.' Lydia couldn't keep the sorrow from her tone.

'No, but you're here. Just like she wanted you to be. That's what matters most. I knew that you were going to see something big happen with your café, let me tell you.' Mom's proclamation made Lydia start.

'What do you mean?'

'I had a dream two weeks ago that a dark storm cloud was over your bakery and café, and it was raining stale cookies. You came outside on the deck and waved your slotted spoon around, you know, the one you take the pierogi out of the water with, and the cloud disappeared.' Mom detailed her dream as if it were a fact and not the conjuring of her eternally overactive imagination. While Lydia and Grandma read mystery clues and criminal intent into otherwise benign circumstances, Mom saw messages from heavenly powers.

'You never mentioned that to me. Did you tell Grandma?'

'No, I suppose that after I said my morning rosary that day I forgot about it. I didn't think about it again until just now.' Amelia Wienewski was ever practical in her faith when it came to turning things over. She said a prayer about something and let it go. Over the years Lydia had thought her mother was naive or even ignorant, but the last year of her life had proved her mother more of a wise sage than superstitious.

'Hi, Lydia.' The greeting came from Miriam, who stood next to her twin, Marie. Two people she never thought she'd see again.

'Hello! What are you two doing here? I thought you'd be halfway to Ottawa by now.'

Marie nodded. 'We planned to get home right after the awful news, but our parents convinced us that we should use the money we'd saved for this trip and see more of Buffalo and Western New York.'

'Plus, we wanted to check out as many of the international food festival's venues as we could. Your city is quite cosmopolitan, you know.' Marie added to her twin's sentiments.

'And you wanted to see the pierogi competition?'

'Yes, and the éclair contest. We felt we had to do something to honor Madame Delphine. We barely knew her, but still . . .' Marie trailed off and turned to her sister for comfort. Miriam put her arm around her shoulders. 'It's all been very upsetting.'

'I understand.' Lydia respected their decision to stay and make the most of their time here. Unlike her former roommates. 'You don't happen to know if Elodie and Chloe made it back to Canada, do you?'

'Yes, they did. They had a fantastic row in the hotel parking lot before their taxi came, though, didn't they, Miriam?'

Miriam nodded. 'Yes. And you'll never guess what they were fighting over!'

Lydia looked at them, wondering what was coming next. 'I've no earthly idea. They told me they were going to start a business together.'

'Well, they'd planned to. Until a man got between them.'

Lydia knew her mouth dropped open and didn't care. 'Are you kidding me?' Was there any student of his mother's that Pierre hadn't dallied with?

'It was Pierre!' Miriam's eyes glittered with satisfaction.

'He's always getting into trouble.' Marie's deadpan delivery made all three of them laugh.

'Why do you say that, Marie?' Lydia's pulse picked up. Could the two she'd dismissed as suspects know a vital clue?

'Well, not to gossip, but I suppose since Madame is dead it's not really gossip.' Marie's gaze was intent. 'I overheard Elodie telling Pierre that he'd better get Madame to give her certificate to her without her having to repeat part of the course or she'd tell everyone what she knew and ruin it all for Madame. That it'd be his fault if she did.'

'OK, but did you hear what she meant by any of that?'

'She meant that she'd inform the CBC about Madame's terrible antics at her school, and how abusive an environment it is, of course!' Miriam answered for Marie.

'You heard Elodie say that, Marie?' Lydia needed to know how Miriam had made such a leap of logic.

'Well, no, what I heard is what I told you. But it all makes sense now! We found out from Elodie and Chloe, who said they found out from Cecile, that Madame lost everything, and what else could it be from?'

Marie nodded in agreement.

'He tried to flirt with us too, of course, but men don't realize that you can't mess around with twins. We know how to take care of one another.' Marie put her arm around Miriam's shoulder.

'Well, I'm glad that you outwitted the likes of Pierre, but most happy that you decided to stay for the festival. Delphine would be so pleased.' Lydia had heard what she needed.

'We hope you win, Lydia. Your sauerkraut pierogi is sublime. I had three of them at your café.' Miriam's praise was earnest.

'Thank you. Enjoy the rest of your time here, and thank you for sharing what you know with me.' Lydia wiggled her fingers in a small wave goodbye before turning back to her parents, who patiently waited for more judges to approach their table. Her mind raced with possibilities. From what the twins had said, Lydia didn't think that Elodie was just upset about Delphine's teaching style; she also knew something that Delphine didn't want anyone else to find out about. Had her initial explanation been right? Had Elodie somehow found out about Delphine's secret and written the note? She could believe that, even accept that Elodie had called the CBC TV channel about Delphine's struggles in a fit of anger and linked her mental state to her strict teaching style, knowing that would give the show pause about putting Delphine on their broadcast. But why would the CBC believe an individual student from a still modestly-sized school?

It did, however, make sense that if Chloe had known anything about Elodie's transgression, she would have ended their friendship. Chloe wasn't perfect, but she would never have behaved in such a horrible way to Delphine.

Frustratingly, though, it didn't help to answer the most important question. Was Elodie angry enough over being forced to repeat part of the course to murder Delphine?

'Smile, Lydia. You'll scare away the judges with that frown.' Mom gave her shoulders a quick squeeze.

'What do you suppose is taking so long?' Lydia shifted on her feet, the strappy sandals not as comfortable as she'd hoped.

'There are fifty-three contestants, and sixteen judges. It's going to take some time, is all.'

'You said there were seventeen judges?'

'Ah, I said there's a judge number seventeen, who has a special role.'

'Hello. May I sample your cheese pierogi?' A woman dressed in authentic Polish dress stood before her. The woman wore a long-sleeved puffy white blouse under a red-trimmed and embroidered black bodice above a bright, festive, multicolored skirt. Twinkling eyes met hers and all of Lydia's worries seemed suddenly trivial, of no import.

'*Dzien dobry*, Lydia Wienewski.'

'Mrs Wozniak.' Lydia addressed the tenth-grade home economics teacher who'd been her nemesis before she'd ever heard of Delphine Chenault. Mrs Wozniak had referred Lydia to the principal's office for her role in nearly burning down the classroom kitchen because she'd refused to follow the safety protocol about using the gas burning stovetops. The fifteen-year-old students had been instructed to remain at their assigned stove, watching their pot of melting butter that they would whisk flour into, to make the perfect white sauce for tuna over toast. Lydia had goofed off with Jenny, whispering about her recent date with Stanley, and instead her butter had burned to deep black, the smoke setting off the school fire alarm and mandating the evacuation of twelve hundred students into a snowstorm. When Mrs Wozniak had confronted her in front of the entire class, she'd erupted into a fit of giggles. The rest of the semester had been excruciating for Lydia.

'Judge number seventeen, yes, please help yourself,' Mom interrupted. Lydia turned her gaze to her mother and was greeted with Amelia's insistent stare. She followed Mom's gaze to land on the sticker affixed to Mrs Wozniak's decorative bodice.

Yvonne Wozniak, Judge #17, Tie Breaker.

No way was she going to win the competition. Not now, not ever. She tried to stifle a groan.

'Shhh.' Pop patted her back, his way of reassuring her.

'Showtime, honey,' Mom whispered in her other ear as she pressed a platter of cut pierogi samplings into Lydia's hands. The faux silver dish was flimsy at best. Caught off guard and expecting a heavier serving dish, Lydia's hands involuntarily overreached. Pierogi flew through the air with remarkable grace, making perfect arcs before landing on the three judges standing in front of their table. Including Mrs Wozniak, who looked down at the two huge spots – one on her white blouse sleeve, and one on the black bodice – Mrs Wozniak's bust was pushing the fabric past credible limits – and screwed up her face as if she'd taken a mouthful of Grandma's fresh horseradish instead of the tamer cheese pierogi.

'Lydia! Help her!' Her mother's whispered admonition grated but before Lydia could defend her accident, Mom transitioned into fix-it mode. 'Here, let me get some soda water on that right away, Yvonne. And we have more samples ready to go, don't worry.'

'Here.' Pop shoved a paper plate of pierogi in front of the judges with his good hand.

Mom and Pop took over and the judges attempted to regain their composure, but Lydia wasn't thinking about the competition.

For when the platter had flipped and sent her pierogi to high heaven, a shaft of bright sunlight had pierced through the aged, wired glass hall windows, through the fancy shear curtains hanging over them, and reflected off the cheap silver serving dish.

Bright. Shiny.

A perfectly formed pierogi had bounced off the belly of another one of the judges, leaving a huge grease stain next to his shirt button.

Missing button.

Like the cogs on the industrial grist mill at the Quaker Mills factory in downtown Buffalo, Lydia's puzzle-solving brain parts clicked into place. Why hadn't she thought of it sooner?

'I've got to go.'

TWENTY-ONE

'Lydia! What the heck is going on?' Teri straightened from the half-dozen plated meals she'd been placing parsley on, her brows knit together in obvious annoyance.

'I don't have time to talk, sis.' Lydia made a beeline for the small ceramic bowl she'd hewn with her nine-year-old hands in Mrs Applebottom's fourth grade art class. She snatched the piece of her childhood from the window ledge and plucked out the button Pacha had presented earlier.

'Just as I thought.'

'As you thought what?' Teri was beside her, and they both stared at the tortoiseshell four-hole button in her palm.

'Table three says their crepes were soggy. They can kiss my dupa. I saw Freddy plate them myself and they were perfect. Thank heavens they're the last customers until dinner.' Grandma issued the edict as she walked into the kitchen. 'Lydia! Did we win?'

'Win what? Oh, the pierogi competition. I don't know.'

'What do you mean you don't know? Mercy, Lydia, don't tell me you forgot about it. I agree with your father on this one. Being a winner at Buffalo's International Food Festival could change your life overnight. All of our lives. Better than winning the lottery!' Grandma stood in front of her.

'I didn't forget. I was there, and to be honest there's little chance we won. I left before the end, and our presentation was interrupted. I threw pierogi on the judges. I didn't do it on purpose . . .' She shook her head as if it would clear her mind. 'That's not what's important right now. This is why I had to come back here.' She held up the button Pacha had brought in between two fingers as if it were sacred. As far as justice for Delphine was concerned, it was the holy grail. 'This isn't just any button!'

'Spit it out!' Grandma had her hands on her hips. Teri and Freddy stared, mouths open, waiting for the next Wienewski shoe to drop. Or button.

'This button is the exact match for the buttons on Jean

Chenault's dress shirt. It was open at the neck and missing a button when we saw him in the hotel the morning I found Delphine!' She looked at her impromptu audience, awaited their gasps of comprehension.

'So Pacha found the missing button. Probably from when the group came for lunch, Lydia.' Freddy, the last one to ever add his thoughts to anything unrelated to what was sizzling on the griddle in front of him, spoke as though she was a toddler.

'Or when Klumpski brought the Chenaults to the deck that night.' Grandma sounded discouraged.

Lydia shook her head. 'No. None of the group from Delphine's class were on the back deck, they weren't allowed. We were all on duty and would have caught anyone trying to sneak onto it. Jean Chenault wasn't wearing his vest when he came here with Klumpski. And Pacha has been camped out either on or under the deck since Kishka and Dolly set up their nest. I'm betting he found this button under the deck, or near it.'

'I don't see how a smart cat waiting for seagull chicks has anything to do with this.' Teri blew out an exasperated sigh. 'You're losing it, sis. I mean, I get it. All you think about is this café and bakery, and sure, you found a dead body of someone you know. Again. But you've got to snap out of it. Not every little thing is an eff—'

'That's enough!' Grandma sliced off Teri's epithet. 'Lydia's right. There's no such thing as coincidence.' She turned back to Lydia. 'Trust your instinct. I'll call Harry and let him know you think you found a clue.'

'There's no time for that now! Follow me, Grandma! Teri, you and Freddy finish up the lunch service and start the clean-up. I'll fill you in the rest of this later.'

The kitchen door banged behind them as Lydia and Grandma went outside.

'What's the rest of it, Lydia?' Grandma didn't sound stressed or worried like Teri. She might not understand exactly what, but she intuited that Lydia had figured out something critical.

Maybe.

'I've overlooked an obvious clue.' Lydia grew more excited as they neared the barn, where once inside she went to an old exten-sion ladder left behind by the previous owner. Lydia had figured she'd use the ladder for when she had to repaint the café, or even the barn when she had extra funds to blow. But it turned out that this was exactly what she needed to do what she knew in her gut was her most important detective work to date.

'Umph.' The ladder was heavier than she'd anticipated and waved wildly in the air for a scary second. Lydia held tight, knowing that if she dropped it, it would delay her proving her hunch.

'That's too heavy for you!' Grandma protested.

'I've. Got. It.' She spoke through clenched teeth as she leaned the top low against the barn wall and walked under it, pushing her arms overhead. When she reached the wall she turned and lowered the ladder to the ground.

'I'll lift it here, and I need you to take that end. Give me a sec.' She walked over to the barn wall where a wide variety of hand tools and sports gear hung. Several battered baseball bats, no less than three worn mitts, five hockey sticks that had seen better days, and an assortment of hats speckled the aging drywall. But she wasn't looking for a baseball cap or painter's hat. Lydia took a worn white, blue and red helmet from its hook and blew out the dust. She sent up a tiny prayer to Saint Anthony that she wouldn't find any spiders in the tattered lining. Without another word, she returned to the front end of the ladder, nearest the wide door.

'OK, ready?'

Grandma nodded. 'I go wherever you do.'

They carefully navigated across the graveled parking lot, each woman at one end of the double ladder and Lydia also holding a helmet by its front piece. Once they reached the set of stairs to the café's deck, Lydia looked at Grandma. 'We're going up the steps to the deck. Let me get to the top then we'll lower the ladder and slide it up the stairs one at a time.'

'Got it.' Grandma was mission-focused.

When Lydia's feet hit the deck landing, she walked backwards until the ladder began to rest on the top stair.

'OK, push!'

Grandma pushed as she pulled the ladder up until it lay flat. Lydia waited for her to come up the stairs. They stood looking out at the lake, catching their breath.

'The gulls' nest is up on the roof, just out of sight. It won't take but a minute to find what I'm looking for.'

'Are you certain there isn't any way to get up on the roof from inside?' Grandma didn't bother to ask her what she was hoping to find, and Lydia wondered if she'd already guessed. Lydia hadn't said what her target was, afraid that she'd jinx the proverbial scent trail she sensed she was on.

Since the dining room blinds were shut tight to discourage diners from attempting to come out here, they were hidden from view, as was the gulls' nest. Lydia wanted to get up there, find the corroborating clue, and get back down the ladder before any lingering customer or someone using her parking lot as a turna-round saw her. A dead body was enough to ward off customers; she didn't need word to get out that she was harboring wildlife that could spread disease on her property, too.

'There's no way to get up there, not even an attic.' She'd already thought of that.

'I think we need to call in the fire department, Lydia.' Grandma was no-nonsense. 'Or better yet, call your cousin Jeannie. She married one of the Becker boys. You know, of Becker Trees and Shrubs. They probably have a cherry-picker.'

'We don't have time, Grandma.' Although the thought of being able to ride up in a bucket via a crane was more appealing than climbing onto her lakeside roof with such a strong breeze. 'I have to get a look into that nest now.'

Lydia craned her neck but no matter which way she stretched she could only make out a few scrawny twigs of the nest jutting past the roof's peak.

Grandma shook her head. 'This is too much, Lydia. Wait for someone to help us. Please let me at least call Harry.'

'Hold the bottom while I climb up.' Lydia ignored Grandma's request and shoved the helmet on. She had to squeeze it past her ears, as always. She'd inherited the Wienewski batwing ears. Once her ears snapped back into shape she gently shook her head, and adjusted the helmet's chin strap. It wasn't a perfect fit but it would do.

'Please, Lydia. Why don't you let Freddy climb up there?' Grandma was a liberated feminist except when it came for heights and letting a man do anything she considered dangerous.

'It's not that high. It's just awkward to get to. I won't be up there long. Believe me, Grandma, I know what I'm doing.' She started to climb.

'What's hard to get to? What do you—' Grandma's eyes widened as she spotted Kishka swooping overhead, followed by a distinctive *plunk* as he landed on the roof. 'No, Lydia. You can't go near their nest now or they'll attack! You'll fall off for sure.' But even as she admonished Lydia, Grandma stepped up, grasped the sides of the ladder and leaned all of her weight onto the bottom rung.

'I'm fine. I won't fall, and they can't hurt me with this on my head.' Lydia had already considered her options. 'It's actually perfect for the job, isn't it?'

'I thought that was for when you fall and crack your head open on the deck,' Grandma snapped.

The image of Delphine's broken noggin flashed in her memory and Lydia shuddered, pausing on the third rung.

'Are you getting vertigo? Just get right back down here before we have two dead bodies in one week.' Grandma's voice was at its panic pitch, not usual for her intrepid grandmother.

'I'm. Fine.' Lydia spoke through clenched teeth and kept climbing before Grandma's fear metamorphosed into reality. Grandma retreated into silence and Lydia had no doubt the elder was doing a mental lap around the rosary beads, or invoking Saint Anthony to find sanity for her granddaughter, or most probably both.

She refused to look down, around, or up at her target: Kishka's and Dolly's nest. Instead, she focused on the weather-worn wooden siding that covered the café's back wall. The once-bright, or maybe pine, green was faded to a soft lime, with traces of rust red beneath. The café building was more than fifty years old, and showed it.

Just two more steps.

The top of the ladder reached to approximately one foot below the peak, but Lydia would have a good view of Kishka and Dolly's abode from the second-to-last top rung. She'd never admit it to Grandma but she really didn't want to climb to the top rung. Clinging to the roof edge for dear life wasn't her idea of a good time.

One more.

She reached for the top rung with her left hand, then her right, and pulled herself up one more, her head and shoulders fully above the roof line and with a perfect view into the nest. Which was much larger than she'd anticipated.

And had two downy soft heads peeping above the layers of twigs, paper, and feathers. Lydia's heart constricted. Baby gulls! *'Caw!'*

A hard knock to her helmet made her lower her head and hang on for dear life. And for Delphine's justice.

Lydia waited out the assault by a very pissed-off seagull. Kishka or Dolly, she couldn't tell. She didn't dare lift her head to see as she kept her chin pressed against her chest, her body as snug against the ladder as she could.

'Caw caw caw!' An angrier seagull screech than the first. Lydia braced for the second bird to strike.

But instead, the attack abruptly ended. Silence broken only by the whisper of the waves far below surrounded her, competing with her racing heartbeats. Slowly, with a pause between each movement, she raised her head. Sweat poured down her temples, into her eyes, and she blinked, not daring the risk of wiping her eyes.

A sense of otherworldliness greeted her when she finally focused her gaze on the nest, the chicks, and their two very proud parents. Kishka and Dolly stood side-by-side on the apex of the roof, protecting their nest while allowing her to see the results of their bonding.

'Thank you.' Lydia could feel more dampness on her cheeks but it was tears of gratitude, relief, instead of sweat. 'Thank you both.' The pair regarded her with sharp eyes. They knew Lydia, recognized her as safe, but still not one of them.

Before the proud parents changed their minds, she did a quick sweep of her gaze over the nest. Lifted herself onto her tiptoes, the rung hard under her sneaker soles. Several shiny objects reflected the sunlight streaming through cotton ball clouds that raced across the sky. Aluminum scraps, a length of what might have once been a bicycle chain, several candy wrappers. But not what she was looking for.

'Honey, you OK up there?'

'I'm . . . I'm good.' Disappointment deflated the high she'd been on since what she'd taken as inspiration had struck her at the festival. Not only was she wrong, she'd failed her family by going after a nonexistent clue instead of staying put and shoring up the family business coffers.

Lydia slowly began to climb back down. At least she'd put two and two together with the button. But it wasn't as strong a clue as it would be with what she sought.

As she climbed down she allowed herself to check out the rest of the roof as it sloped down to either side of the building, to the gutters that lined it. The gutters were full of pine needles and leaves, and she'd have to get back on this same ladder to clean them at some point.

A glint flashed amidst the left gutter's detritus, the gutter closest to the deck. Lydia halted her descent.

'Lydia, please come down. Now.'

'I will, but . . .' She didn't hesitate this time as she climbed back up until she was able to swing, lean over and get her belly flat albeit tilted at a forty-five-degree angle, on the roof. The roof shingles made her shirt ride up and she knew she'd have a decent road rash but none of that mattered right now.

All that mattered was that she got what she thought she saw in the gutter.

Please don't let this be my imagination playing tricks on me.

She belly-crawled to the gutter until her left hand could reach into it, while her right hand clutched at the roof. As long as she stayed flat, she'd be OK. It was going to have to be blind trust that she relied on, unable to lift her head, helmet or no, to look at where she was reaching. Placing her hand in the gutter, she swirled the dried mess with her finger until a short, warm cylindrical object hit her fingertips. Not unlike the shaft of Lydia's crochet hooks, in fact, which were measured in millimeters.

The shiny, modern-looking bullet casing bore no resemblance in appearance or length to an older bullet, the type Pop had deep in the basement. Which meant it didn't match the Chenault family's World War I Webley pistol, the weapon Klumpski had determined Delphine used to kill herself.

Had one of the seagulls found the casing from the actual bullet that killed Delphine?

TWENTY-TWO

'I still think we should have called Leo, too. This is his jurisdiction, after all. We need to make sure we keep our side of the street clean if we want to stay in this business.' Grandma sat in the passenger seat of the Gremlin while Lydia gunned it to the Acorn Bay Hotel. By her calculations they had two minutes before checkout time.

'Harry will tell him. And who says we'll ever do this again? I never want to find another dead body.' Lydia's exasperation made her teeth hurt. She'd given Grandma thirty seconds to run back in the kitchen and make what she'd insisted was a lifesaving call.

'If Harry gets the message, that is. I had to leave it with a deputy. So I called Ned, as a backup. He was a big help with Louie's case.' She referred to her nephew by marriage and Lydia's first cousin, Cheektowaga Police Officer Ned Bukowski.

'I wondered why it was taking so long.' Lydia shifted into second, then first gear as she neared a red light. Her foot itched to floor it through the empty intersection but at least the hotel was in sight.

'Do you really think they'll still be there? You said Jean was anxious to get back to Canada.'

'But Pierre wasn't going to leave without Delphine. And when I called the coroner's office the body was still there.'

'How did you get them to tell you?' Grandma displayed rare shock in her tone.

'I used a French Canadian accent and said I was her sister.'

'Good girl! Delphine would be proud.'

Lydia's anger at the injustice of Delphine's murder rushed adrenaline through her body, making her finger and toe tips tingle. She revved her engine and burst out at the green light.

'Enough with the Mario Andretti, Lydia.' Grandma was smiling, though. She loved the thrill of the chase for justice as much as Lydia.

They were less than a five hundred yards from the parking lot entrance when Lydia spied Madame's car. It was backing out of its spot, and turned toward the exit. Lydia pulled up and parked perpendicular to its anticipated route, blocking all access to the lot. She set the parking break and opened her door.

'Hang on, honey bunny.' Grandma's words were sweet but her tone and expression were stern as her hand gripped Lydia's forearm. 'If you believe Jean fired the shot that killed Delphine, he's dangerous. He has the gun that killed her.'

'OK. Maybe you should stay in the car, then. Duck if he fires.' Lydia wouldn't be deterred from her objective.

'Like hell I will!' Grandma let go of her arm and opened her door.

Grandma waited while Lydia walked around the front of her car. Both women stood together and stared down the Chenault men, still inside their car. Pierre was in the passenger seat, and she saw his eyes bug out before he broke into a wide grin of recognition. Jean's face, however, screwed up into a snarl before he smoothed it back into a modicum of neutral detachment.

Pierre sprung out of the car and ran up to Lydia. It was only then that she realized he thought she'd had a change of heart . . . about him.

'Use your womanly wiles,' Grandma stage-whispered out the side of her mouth and Lydia fought back a groan.

'Lydia!' Pierre stopped a foot in front of her, already encroaching on her personal space without even knowing why she'd shown up at the last minute.

'Pierre.' She sucked in a deep breath, kept Jean in her peripheral vision. 'I'm so glad I caught you. Before you head out.'

'Yes, well, we're going to stay in a hotel downtown, while we wait for my mother's body.' Grief broke through his momentary elation and compassion swamped Lydia's best intentions to remain detached and cool.

'I'm so sorry, Pierre. This is very hard.' She closed the short distance between them and gave him an awkward hug, using the vantage point to observe Jean, who'd stepped out of the car and slowly walked toward them. There was no sign of a weapon, and as he wore a short-sleeved collared shirt and Bermuda shorts, both tight fitting, she didn't think he had a holster on underneath.

She stepped out of the hug and faced Jean, searching his form for a handgun, anything that looked like a weapon, and found none.
Hold your ground.

'Jean.'

She'd never addressed him as anything other than 'Mr Chenault,' and he clearly recognized the change in her demeanor toward him as he threw his shoulders back and tilted his chin up.

'Lydia, what's this about? As you can see, Pierre and I have an important meeting to get to. Maybe you and he can talk on the phone, arrange a time to meet up over the next month or so?'

'A meeting? That's funny, because Pierre tells me you're on your way to a hotel in Buffalo. What meeting do you have?'

Jean clenched his jaw and his eyebrow began to twitch. 'That's none of your concern. Will you please move your vehicle, Lydia.' It wasn't a request but a demand.

'I sure will, Jean, as soon as you answer some questions for me.'

'What's this about, Lydia?' Pierre echoed his father's query as he looked from Jean to her and back again, disappointment etched in the circles under his eyes. He must have figured out she wasn't here for amorous reasons.

Jean puffed out a sigh. 'I don't have time for this. Pierre, get back in the car.' The elder Chenault turned his back on her.

'Where were you the night Delphine died, Jean? Be very careful how you answer.'

'I owe you no answers. Anyone ever tell you you're nosy?' Jean flung the retort over his shoulder.

At the same descriptor Klumpski had used, Lydia saw red. She made a straight line for the driver's door and placed herself between Jean and his escape. The metal body of the car was hot under her back.

'Not so fast, buster.' She spread her arms across the door, planted her feet.

'Buster?' What, is that some kind of American slang? Look, this has been a hard time on all of us—'

'Stop with the lies. Where were you when Delphine came to get her cigarette case?'

'Dad, what's going on?' Pierre spoke to his father in French.

'Stay out of this and get back in the car, son.' Jean's response was nothing short of menacing. But instead of cowering as Lydia had witnessed Pierre do in the past, Jean straightened, his facial muscles strained. But his eyes . . . his eyes spewed venom at her.

'Maybe you need to answer the question, Dad.' Pierre sounded resigned. Did he know his father was capable of something so heinous?

'Yes, Jean. Answer the question.' Lydia stood her ground.

'I was here, at the hotel. Where else would I have been that night?'

'You're certain you didn't go with her? Because I have evidence that you were on my café deck with Delphine the night she died.'

'Evidence? Like what?' Jean's confidence wavered.

'You. Were. There.' Lydia kept pressing without giving up the evidence she had on him, what she *hoped* she had on him. It was after all a fairly generic button, which could match other buttons, which might in all truth not even be his button.

But it matched his vest's buttons, and he had a missing one the morning Delphine was found.

'I, I . . . OK. I admit it. Yes, I went with Delphine to the café. I had to talk to her. She'd been saying crazy things.' Jean was scrambling for more lies.

Let him. Harry taught her to wait, to listen. Let the bad guy confess on his own.

'Dad!' The agonized cry ripped from Pierre's throat. 'What are you saying?'

Jean was saying that he'd lied to his son, to the police, to her. But Lydia wanted, no, needed, to hear it from him.

'It's no secret that Delphine and I had our differences. The last several years have been . . . difficult. We grew apart. But I've never stopped loving her. When she told me, out of the blue two weeks ago, that she wanted a divorce, I had to act. I had to do anything to save my family.'

'Go on.' Lydia struggled to maintain a modicum of control, which wasn't easy as her back remained pressed up against the hot car, and Jean was definitely in her personal space. She tried to find Grandma in her side vision with no luck. Where was she?

'Yes, Father, go on.' Pierre's ardor had fled his tone.

'I begged to come here with her and Pierre, so that I could talk some sense into her. I wanted to make her see that I was sorry, that we could still make a go of it.'

'Sorry for what?'

His expression darkened. 'That's none of your business.'

'I think it is, considering I found her body on my property.' It was technically the county's property but she hoped he'd forgotten the tiny detail.

'We had problems. I . . . I've not made the best decisions with my career, for sure. I lost some money and was trying to get it back. Our last quarrel was a complete misunderstanding. She wouldn't talk to me the entire time here, at the café or at the hotel. Did you know your mother was so angry with me that I had to get my own room for this trip?' Jean posed the question to Pierre.

'You didn't do it to give her space to prepare for her presentation at the Chautauqua Institute?' Pierre's confusion appeared sincere.

'*Non*. But I was in her room trying to get her to see reason about us when she got the call about her contracts being cancelled.' He pinned his angry gaze back on her. Lydia's skin crawled from the malignant attention. 'I convinced her that I should drive to get her cigarette purse; she'd had a glass of wine at dinner and again in her room.'

'She never mentioned you were with her when I called.'

'Why would she? You and she, you weren't close. You were her worst student. She hated you.'

Lydia's stomach clenched in unison with her jaw at his last. Because she knew it was a lie. She and Delphine had made their peace in the café kitchen, over a loganberry stain on her beautiful dress. And in that moment had cemented a bond that reached beyond death. Delphine may have struggled with depression, but she wouldn't have thrown it all away when she got the news about her book or her contracts being cancelled. The bad luck would have only spurred the woman Lydia knew on to try again. And again.

Jean thought he had Lydia in his web, that his tale would satisfy her, and also Pierre's, curiosity.

Let him think that.

'I went with her back to your café, so what? She took the call from you to come get her purse.'

'Cigarette case.' Lydia immediately bit the inside of her cheek. Nowicki had taught her to let the suspect talk. They gave up more when they thought you were listening, that you believed their words.

'Whatever.'

'And did you, get the case?' Lydia already knew the answer.

'Well, yes, it was on the deck, where you left it for her.'

'I didn't leave it on the deck. And you never got it because you never gave her a chance to look in the milk box where I told her it would be, did you?'

'What the hell are you getting at?' Spittle flew from his mouth. 'My wife was impetuous. She ran up there, and before I knew what she was thinking she'd taken the pistol out of her purse and shot herself.' He covered his face with his hands. 'It was terrible.'

At least he wasn't trying to fake cry, Lydia thought.

'But she didn't die by a bullet from your family's World War I pistol with her prints on it, did she?' Lydia said the words loudly, as she wanted Pierre and Grandma and whoever else was nearby to hear. She didn't dare take her eyes off Jean Chenault to see if anyone else was in the vicinity. Not if she didn't want to end up like Delphine had. Dead.

His fingers parted a sliver and she knew he was looking at her, determining his next words.

'Jean? What was the weapon that killed Delphine?'

'Father.' Pierre's tone vibrated with hurt, anger, and the worst, betrayal. 'Answer her.'

Jean lowered his hands. 'It wasn't me, you have to believe me! Listen to me, we were followed to the café by a thug, and he mugged us, held us up. He waved his gun around like it was a water toy, but then, it fired, and it hit Delphine.'

'But her prints were on your family's World War I pistol left at the scene. How did that happen?'

Jean scowled, fury rising. 'It was easier for everyone if it looked like she'd killed herself.'

'Why did you bring the gun over the border?' Lydia persisted. She wanted him to spill it all.

'I did it for my . . . my family's safety, of course!'

'You protecting us? Really? You're the one who brought danger to our door in the first place, in over your head from gambling

again.' He didn't address his father with 'Dad' or 'Father.'
Resignation and disgust was etched in his deep frown.

Gambling. That was the shadow that must have hung over
Delphine, the reason for her anxiety and depression. Debts from
Jean's poor life choices, and worse, the stain on her reputation,
the family's legacy if people found out. People like Elodie.

'It was the last time, Pierre, I swear. But they were threatening
my life. They followed me to the border, and I thought I got rid
of them. But then their local thugs here in Buffalo showed up. It
was a good thing I brought the gun with me! Except I never had
a chance to fire it.'

'Wait a minute – the note in Delphine's room, it said, "You're
finished." Was that a threat to you from these thugs if you didn't
pay your debts?'

'If you must know, yes! I found it left on my car when I left
the business meeting the day before you found Delphine . . . I
took her room key from the car when I got back to the hotel,
and I put the note in her room thinking it would preoccupy the
police. But it was completely separate to the TV show being
cancelled. The CBC must have somehow found out about
Delphine's anxiety and depression. Then, when the TV show was
cancelled, someone at the network knew her editor at the
publishing house and let them know. But don't you see? It's not
my gambling that's the problem or culprit here, it's the creditors
who want their money back.' Jean was in classic addict denial
mode. But Lydia was past any compassion she'd ever felt toward
him and had to get to the bottom of Delphine's death.

'What happened to the killer after Delphine fell?' Lydia's gut
churned. 'Don't tell me he ran off.'

Jean looked at Pierre, ignoring Lydia. 'It was for the best,
Pierre. She was already gone, and what you stood to inherit from
her side of the family would pay for all of my debts, give us
enough to start over, somewhere else. She never gave me access
to her trust fund, but you have it all now. Don't you see? I did
it for you, son.'

'Don't ever call me "son" again.' Pierre spat the words.

As Lydia watched the already fractured bond between them
dissolve, she tried to make her mental cogs fall into place. Jean
had used Delphine to defend himself from the killer, a man who'd

wanted payback for a gambling debt. Then he made it look like suicide, using the antique pistol.

He might not be the murderer, but he was definitely complicit. And Pierre . . .

'Pierre, did you agree to give Elodie her course certificate so that she wouldn't spread rumors about your mother's depression? How did she find out?'

Pierre's mouth gaped open. 'What? No. It's not as awful as you're making it sound. I was only trying to protect my mother, the school, from his . . .' He stared venomously at Jean. 'Elodie had found out about your gambling when she overheard you pleading with someone you owe money to on the phone in the lobby. The CBC believed her – Elodie said they have contacts in the police and sensed a huge story was brewing about our family and organized crime. The publisher wasn't going to risk the book once they found out. If I hadn't had to worry about Elodie going to the papers, I'd never have promised her that certificate, either! All of this, it's all your fault.' He condemned his father.

Lydia had heard what she needed from him. He was as self-involved as she remembered but he wasn't a killer.

Was the gambling ring part of the 'bigger case' Klumpski had mentioned? Was this what Harry had been so tight-lipped about, his secret?

'Did you tell Detective Klumpski anything about your gambling debt?' She faced Jean.

'No, he didn't. We already knew after we spoke to the thugs he owes money to.' The deep voice behind the hood of the car made Lydia jump with surprise. She turned to face Leo Klumpski. She'd been so focused on getting Jean's confession she hadn't heard him walk up. A glance past his shoulder revealed two cruisers and no less than three officers poised in triangle fashion, weapons drawn.

'I couldn't tell you!' Jean shouted at Klumpski, his facial expression at war with itself; his eyes were wide with desperation while his upper lip curled in a snarl. Lydia looked to Klumpski to continue the interrogation, but only saw the detective's gaze briefly widen before she was hit sideways by Jean. He grabbed her shoulders with both hands, his strength surprising after she'd pegged him for a grieving widower. Lydia tried to kick and claw

at him but before she gained any ground Jean twisted her around
to his front, his arm tight around her neck.

'Stand back or I'll snap her neck!' The way his arm tightened
against her trachea gave Lydia no reason to doubt he'd do it. She
dug her fingers into his forearm, tried to pull it away but it was
like Pop's workbench vice grip.

'I have three officers who are expert shots, and each of their
weapons are trained on you. Let her go or I'll issue the order.
You'll drop in a second.' Klumpski displayed the sensible demeanor
she'd observed in Nowicki. His countenance gave zero indication
of his feathers being ruffled or even touched by the life-threatening
scene before him.

'Give me a chance to explain.' Jean shifted his weight which
brought Lydia more tightly up against him, his arm digging
deeper. She fought from grimacing as she wanted Jean to confess
here and now.

'Let her go, then we'll talk.' Klumpski was not in a bargaining
mode.

'I didn't know what to do when he pulled his gun! He was
going to kill me right there, in front of Delphine—'

'Let. Lydia. Go.' Klumpski lifted his hand as if signaling his
officer. Lydia squeezed her eyes shut.

'So I pulled her in front of me, thinking he'd see reason. How
was I supposed to know he'd shoot right then?' Jean's voice
cracked and he let go of Lydia but made sure to shove her down,
hard, as he turned and pulled on the car's driver seat handle.

Lydia landed on all fours and flattened, expecting bullets to fly
at any moment. When they didn't, she risked turning her head to
see what was going on.

Pierre sat behind the steering wheel, window rolled up, staring
at his father. He must have run around, and slid into, the car when
Jean took her hostage.

'Let me in, son! Right now!' Jean pounded his fists against the
door. Footsteps pounded on the parking lot as the Acorn Bay PD
officers rushed Jean and quickly subdued him.

'You can get up now.' Klumpski reached down his hand and
helped Lydia stand. She was still out of breath as she dusted off her
knees and elbows, the front of her dress. Her blue cardigan was
ruined, but she didn't care. Maybe she'd crochet herself a lacy one.

'You OK?' The concern in Klumpski's low voice gave her a new appreciation for the detective. Maybe he wasn't such a bad guy after all. 'Good job, by the way. Getting him to confess. I heard everything. Although . . .'

'What?' Exhaustion washed over Lydia and all she wanted was to call Stanley, or better, meet up with him. Whether here in Acorn Bay or in Cheektowaga, or Timbuktu, she didn't care. She wanted her man.

'Nowicki said you found the bullet casing. I think it'll probably prove a match for the shooter's weapon, but it doesn't prove Chenault was on the deck with Delphine. How did you get him to confess, exactly? I heard him, but not everything you said first.' Klumpski might have truly been concerned about her welfare, but he wasn't ready to give her credit for solving the case until he knew every detail.

Scratch her previous nice thought.

'I was able to get him to confess because he thought that I absolutely had proof he was on the deck that night from the way I spoke, although he never asked how I knew. But I do.' She reached into the dress pocket and pulled out the small, round button. 'Here you go.'

'A button?'

'It's a match for Chenault's suit vest, which was missing a button the morning I found Madame.' She watched Klumpski take in her explanation. When he nodded, she continued, 'So now you tell me something, if you can. What was the bigger case going on? Does it have something to do with Jean's gambling?'

Klumpski didn't hesitate, didn't show any sign of trying to throw her off the scent. He grunted. 'You're a smart cookie. So you must read in the papers that we have big gambling rings operating in Western New York, and across the border. But I can't confirm or deny.'

But he had. Which meant Lydia had earned the detective's trust. And as the truth dawned on her, she saw Leo Klumpski in a different light.

'You didn't give the note any credence because you already knew it was meant for Jean from the gambling thugs. You stuck to the suicide determination to protect all of us, didn't you? To keep us safe from the organized crime ring.'

The detective never made a sound, but the steady gaze he shared with her told her the truth.

'We never had this conversation. Leo.' Before he could respond, sirens sounded. Seconds later a Cheektowaga PD cruiser turned into the parking lot. The cruiser pulled up next to the two Acorn Bay PD vehicles and Nowicki stepped out of the passenger side, while Stanley got out of the back. Relief lifted her heart, still aching for Delphine. Leave it to Harry to get here to support her, bringing her true love with him.

Harry had missed the drama but must have called Klumpski right after Grandma called him, or Klumpski wouldn't have been able to save her from Jean Chenault. Who knew what the man would have been capable of if he'd exploded in rage without Acorn Bay PD here?

Klumpski stared at the button in his palm. 'I'll have my team take a look at Chenault's clothes. This may not be admissible . . .'

Lydia heard no more, because she was running toward Stanley.

TWENTY-THREE

'Why can't they use the bullet casing that Lydia found?' Grandma poured herself an iced tea and added a thick slice of lemon. She, Lydia, Harry and Stanley were seated at the worktable in the café kitchen.

'Who says they can't?' Harry looked up from the cinnamon roll Lydia had rustled up for him, leftover from this morning's breakfast.

'Leo told me he can't.' Lydia stroked Pacha, curled up on her lap, as Stanley's arm draped around her shoulders. She was literally surrounded by love and soaked it up. 'It doesn't matter because Jean Chenault confessed and Leo heard him.'

'He'll have to run ballistics on it, see if it matches the gun used by the organized crime henchman. I suspect it does. That was brilliant thinking on your part, by the way.'

'What a way to connect the dots, honey bunny.' Grandma beamed.

Stanley stayed silent but his hand massaged her shoulder before sliding to the nape of her neck and gently kneading. Lydia let out a sigh of sheer bliss.

'Kishka's always stealing anything shiny that he finds around here. When I first moved in, I dropped my change purse in the parking lot because my hands were so full of supplies. I went into the kitchen to dump them and when I went back, not two minutes later, all of the nickels were gone.' She paused. 'But if Pacha hadn't found that button, I don't think I would have ever put it together that Jean killed her, even if it was indirectly.'

'Coward. Can you imagine, pulling your wife, the mother of your son, in front of you to avoid being shot.' Grandma slammed her half empty glass of tea down and Lydia double checked to make sure she hadn't shattered it. 'Well, he's done. Locked up for good, if the DA does his job right.'

'Was the big case Leo spoke about related to the gambling ring, then?' Lydia knew the answer but wanted to hear Harry's side of it.

She leaned forward and took one of the raspberry jam sandwich cookies that were her personal favorite. She bit into the confection and relished how the butter crumb texture contrasted with the sweet tang of the raspberry jam.

Harry nodded. 'Yes. He gave me an inkling as to what was really going on when I handed over the photos. Leo knew it was a suspicious death from the start, and when you found the note, he knew it was from one of the gangs as he'd already seen similar notes sent to other victims from the same gang. It didn't take long to discover Jean's gambling debts. But there wasn't any evidence to tie the note and Jean's debts to Delphine's death, and Leo wasn't going to publicly reverse his decision until he had conclusive proof the two were linked. Leo asked me to keep an eye on you both due to the ruthless nature of the gangs, which I was happy to do, while hoping you might just find a clue that led us to the killer. I'm sorry I had to keep some of this back from you. As with any sort of organized crime, it's an ongoing investigation and when it involves international connections, the FBI gets involved, too. In this case, so does the Canadian Mounties.'

'So we'll never know where that particular investigation goes? With the gambling ring?' Stanley kept his arm around Lydia as he asked the question.

'Maybe, maybe not. But I can say that the man who shot Delphine instead of who he was aiming at – Jean Chenault – is in custody, as are two of his buddies. Leo and the federal agents have leverage, as they can offer a lesser charge if he's willing to turn on his organization.'

'Jean Chenault won't have a problem ratting anyone out.' Grandma stated the obvious. 'He's spineless.'

'Well, I'm done with crime solving. I've got a business to run.' Lydia paused and looked at Stanley. 'How did you get here with Harry? Weren't you at the festival?'

'I was, until Ned ran in and grabbed me. He tugged on a strand of her hair. 'I should have gone with you when you ran out.' His last came out on a growl. She always welcomed Stanley's protectiveness. He believed in her ability to take care of herself but she never doubted he'd take a bullet for her.

Unlike Jean Chenault.

'Who won the pierogi cook-off?'

The contest! Grandma asked the question Lydia had completely forgotten about.

'I need to call Pop and Mom. They have to be so worried!' She stood to go to the phone. Pacha jumped off Lydia's lap and made a beeline for the garbage can.

'Oh no, not again!' Grandma pointed at the broom, in the corner. 'Get ready, Lydia!'

'I have no problem with four-legged rodents.' She put the phone back on the hook. 'It's the two-legged variety I hope I never meet again.'

'*Meow.*'

Pacha curved his supple albeit chunky body around the covered refuse container, flashing his bright gaze at Lydia.

'What, sweet pea?'

Knowing he caught her attention, he trotted over to the storage pantry's closed door. Lydia's stomach sank. Had someone left the sugar or flour open?

She opened the door and Pacha bolted, his second meow drowned out by a chorus of far more insistent mewls.

There, in the far corner under a small window that's screen was missing, was a black cat and several kittens.

'Pacha! These can't be yours . . .' She'd had Pacha and all of Luna's brood, including Luna, neutered last winter. She turned around and faced the others. 'I don't know how it happened, but there's a momma cat in my pantry with a litter of new kittens. I know for certain Pacha's not the father.'

'What, you've never heard of adoption?' Grandma's observation boomeranged around the small space, as did her ensuing laughter. Harry let out a guffaw and Stanley grinned.

And they still didn't know if she was the new Pierogi Princess. *You mean the Pierogi Queen.*

Lydia supposed it was too much to ask to solve two mysteries in one day, but she wanted to know if her instincts about Yvonne Wozniak were correct. Had her tenth-grade teacher sealed her fate as a winner, or loser?

She reached for the phone receiver to call her parents just as the phone rang, making her jump.

'Answer it, Lydia!' Teri screeched.

Lydia lifted the receiver, held it to her ear, and smiled.

RECIPES FROM LYDIA'S
CAFÉ AND BAKERY

Old Fashioned Cheese Pierogi

For the pierogi dough:

> 6 cups flour
> ¼ pound butter
> ½ tsp salt

Work like a pie crust, until mixed well, in a bowl or on your counter. Add in:

> 2 beaten eggs
> ¾ cup warm milk
> ½ pint sour cream

Knead until smooth, then flour your rolling pin and roll out on a flour surface until thin. Using a glass or jar the size of your choosing, dip the open edge in flour and cut out circles.

For the filling:

> 1 pound of farmer's cheese (use cottage cheese if you can't find farmer's but make sure to drain it well)
> 1 egg
> 4 tbsp butter
> ½ tsp salt

Place one to two tablespoons of filling in the middle of each round, then fold over and seal closed with pinching motions or a fork. Dip your fingertips or fork in cold water as needed.

Place in large pot of boiling water and cook until the pierogi float. Then sauté in butter and sliced onion, if desired. Serve alongside fresh sour cream and your favorite kielbasa.

AUNT DOT'S RASPBERRY JAM BITES

1 pound butter
1 cup sugar
8 egg yolks
1 tablespoon vanilla
4 cups flour
Raspberry jam – use the best quality you can afford

Cream butter and sugar together. Add egg yolks, one at a time, on lower speed. Add in vanilla. On low speed or by hand, mix in flour.

Refrigerate for 2 hours or overnight.

Shape dough into 1-inch balls. Place on parchment lined cookie pan at least 1 inch apart. Bake at 375 degrees Fahrenheit for 10–12 minutes – do not overcook.

Cool on rack.

Spread a thin layer of jam on the bottom (flat) portion of each cookie, then press together. Store in a tin or in the refrigerator depending upon your climate, but don't worry, these bites of heaven won't last very long!